The Adventures of Miss Becky McCoy

Sherrie J. Lyons

ISBN Paperback: 978-1-64873-395-6

Media Contact: Writers Publishing House
info@writerspublishinghouse.com

Printed in the United States of America
Published by Writers Publishing House
Prescott, AZ 86301

Cover and Interior Design by
Creative Artistic Excellence

Also by

Sherrie J. Lyons

The Tragedy at Cambria,
   a 3-act medieval-era play written in rhyming iambic pentameter

To

James A. Lyons

This book is dedicated to my husband because without his support, it would never have been written.

Acknowledgments

I would like to thank the following people for their help with the content and publication of this book:

James A. Lyons for traveling with me to Southeastern Arizona for research and for sharing his vast reservoir of general knowledge about Arizona's history and geography, firearms, and farming. Who else would have known that balers had not been invented at the time the story took place?

Scott Lyons for providing me with resources for finding potential Apache consultants.

Ann Skidmore and Nicole Cosen for their comments regarding Apache perspective, customs, and culture.

Lizzy McNett of Writer's Publishing House for getting this book into publication.

The errors in this book are solely mine.

The Adventures of Miss Becky McCoy

Late August, mid-1880s,

Southeastern Arizona Territory

Thursday

Chapter 1

Cody slid the wooden slat aside and peeked through the door's peephole at the sounds of Shep barking and the light rapping on the door. He hadn't heard anyone ride up. The Apaches could be as quiet as snowfall, but they didn't knock. He swung the door open at the sight of a slight figure standing on the ranch house porch holding a bulging, tattered carpetbag. The blue overalls and plaid work shirt suggested a boy, but the bright pink cowboy hat sporting a pair of long, fluffy, black-and-white ostrich feathers through its band established that the visitor was a girl. Cody guessed from her size that she was a year or two younger than his own fourteen years. He stifled a laugh into a broad smile. He and Pa didn't get many uninvited visitors, and this one was decidedly unusual.

"Howdy!"

"Howdy, back! My name is Miss Becky McCoy. Are yer folks at home?"

He was amused that she had introduced herself with a title, but being mannerly, he played along with her pretensions. "I'm Cody Campbell of the Camp Bell Ranch. It's just me and Pa, and he's out on the range. What can we do for ya, Miss Becky?"

"Well, Master Cody, I was wond'rin' if'n you'd have some work I could do in swap fer supper an' a barn bed fer the night. I can cook an' clean an' launder. I can also curry an' feed an' muck out stalls. An' I'm real good with horses. I'm small, but I'm stronger than I look. I don't eat much, an', truly, I'm happy to sleep in the barn. Yer pa leave ya a list o' chores?"

Cody nodded in reply as he pondered Becky's request. Pa *had* left a long list of chores that needed completing before he returned, many of them women's work, which they both detested doing. He and Pa were expecting company for supper, and Cody figured that two could complete the chores much faster than one, besides which, having his own company would make for a more interesting afternoon and evening. He knew Pa had never turned away a hungry stranger, so that just left the sleeping arrangements.

Their adobe house contained only one bedroom, which the two of them shared. Male guests typically slept on a cot in the combined living/dining area. They had never sheltered an unmarried female guest, but he recalled one of Pa's lectures regarding the impropriety of allowing a guest of the female persuasion to spend the night in the house with them. Cody could hardly relinquish the house to the girl and volunteer Pa to sleep with him in the barn, so Becky's sleeping out there made sense. One thing still didn't sit right with him, however. "I didn't hear ya ride up. Where's yer horse?"

"Haven't got one. Rode a bicycle." Becky pointed to the side of the house.

Cody walked out onto the porch and turned the corner, his boot heels clicking on the wood as he went. "Well, I'll be!" He strode over to the machine and gave it good measure. "I've never seen one like this before, what with the wheels bein' the same size. How'd ya come by it?"

"It were a gift."

Cody let out a long whistle. "Ya must've done somethin' real special to get a fine gift like this." He looked to her for an explanation.

"I reckon I did." Her face brightened with a mysterious Mona Lisa smile when she said it, and Cody liked the mischievous twinkle he saw in her green-gray eyes.

"Think I can ride it?"

"Shorely. I reckon there'll be time to play with it in the mornin' afore I move on."

"Then, Miss Becky, you've got yerself a deal."

Becky spit in her hand and thrust it forward. Cody hesitated but for a moment before doing the same and vigorously pumping her arm twice to seal their agreement.

*   *   *

Mid-afternoon, tall, sinewy Mason Campbell loped Raven through the west pasture toward home. As he rode, he thought of all the housework that needed to be completed prior to supper. The house he and Cody had built five years prior, after transplanting from Missouri when Emma's soul had gone to see the Lord, was small but comfortable. He took pride in his house and the improvements he and Cody had made: the well; the buildings, including the barn, shed, tack room, and outhouse; the corral; the garden; and literally miles of fencing. Ranching was hard. The Arizona Territory land was hard. Raising a boy alone, seeing to his education, teaching him skills, responsibility, ethics, and values was hard—and never ending—but Cody was his top priority. His boy took after Emma, with his dark hair and deep brown moon eyes, eyes that took the shape of half-moons when he smiled, and Mason delighted in seeing Emma in him. Though he rarely said the words, he loved his son deeply, and he was pleased with the young man Cody was becoming. Now that they were established in the community, at forty, Mason felt satisfied with his life. If Emma could look down at them from heaven, he felt sure she would be smiling.

Mason hoped Cody had completed his chores, and his first sight of home was encouraging. As he rode through the tall grass in the pasture, he saw clothes hanging limply on the line. With no breeze, some items might not be dry until tomorrow, but at least they were clean. He saw their union suits, work trousers and shirts, socks, towels, and some rags. And what was that? He was at the side yard now, where the clotheslines were strung. He removed the glove from his left hand and pinched the item—yes, it was indeed a pair of frilly, white pantalettes. The pantalettes were dry to his touch. They appeared to be brand spanking new and made of silk. They were craftfully sewn and decorated with multiple rows of lace on the legs. He'd never seen the likes of them sold at Sam Hill's, Leaning Rock's general store, and the only clothing store for fifty miles around. He couldn't imagine where Cody had gotten them or why he had laundered them. Still pondering, he passed the clothesline and dismounted at the corral, where he reflexively wrapped one of Raven's reins around the top rail. Raising his voice, he called for his son: "Cody?" Upon hearing no response, he strode across the yard to the porch, where a mop stood leaning against the wall near the door. He felt the mop head's strips of rag—dry. Not happy, he called more forcefully: "Cody!"

Cody hated mopping. He often complained about having to wring the rag strips with his hands. When he was younger, just the thought of touching the cold, wet, dirty strips could cause him to shudder involuntarily. Apparently, the thought had been enough to discourage him from mopping this afternoon, and Mason had wanted a clean floor, if not to impress his guests, at least to show that two bachelors could keep house reasonably well. Still hearing no answer from the boy, Mason rang the cowbell hanging from the porch eaves. Cody should hear the summons and return pronto.

There was little sense in waiting outdoors, so Mason entered the house. He was greeted by an enticing aroma. The beef roast and potatoes were coming along. The table was set for five with Emma's good china, and a salad sat in its center. Neither Mason nor Cody particularly liked greens, but they ate them anyway, mainly because the garden produced a steady supply through the summer. He saw the bread pan covered with a towel on the sideboard in the kitchen. Lifting the towel revealed that the dough had risen and was ready for baking. He had planned on biscuits, but bread was a nice upgrade. And then Mason noticed that the floor was, in fact, clean— it looked even better than usual, especially in the corners. Cody must have swabbed early for the mop's strands to have dried already. Pleased with all he saw, Mason left through the kitchen door and headed up the slight hill to the barn.

The stalls in the barn were clean, and the horses had fresh water in their buckets. Two stalls were conspicuously vacant: the ones for Star, Cody's twelve-year-old, lame, bay gelding, and Star's replacement, a palomino mare named Athena. Mason continued down the aisle and came upon their cot, set up with a blanket, pillow, and carpetbag sitting on it. Next to it, leaning against the side of the barn was a bicycle, the likes of which he had never seen before.

Things were adding up: someone had dropped by and helped with the chores. Cody had invited him to stay for supper and the night. After finishing the chores, they had gone for a ride. Sure enough, when Mason exited the barn's far door and strode up to the gate leading to the south pasture, he saw two figures coming toward him. Cody was atop Athena, and what appeared to be a younger boy wearing an atrocious hat was straddling Star. Cody sat tall in his saddle, whereas what Mason determined was most likely a girl was riding bareback, hunched low to Star's neck as the gelding trotted toward him.

Mason observed Star's gait carefully. He had warned Cody not to put any weight on the gelding until his leg injury healed, and the leg was still swollen when they checked it yesterday. It wasn't like Cody to put an animal at risk. If Star were injured further, it would be a hard lesson for him. Fortunately, the girl was slight, and Star did not look like he was limping.

Presently, the girl slowed Star to a walk and slid gracefully off him. Cody offered her a hand up to ride behind him, but she shook her head no and began leading Star by the reins through the tall grass toward the barn. Cody nudged Athena forward, leaving the girl behind. When Cody arrived at the gate, Mason lifted the latch and swung the door wide to let him out. As he passed through, they exchanged greetings.

"Hello, son."

"Hello, Pa. I didn't expect ya this early."

"I imagine you didn't. And I didn't expect to find Star out of his stall. Didn't Doc Prescott tell you exercise would aggravate his injury?"

"Sure, Pa, it's just—" But his explanation was cut short by the arrival of the girl.

"Howdy, Mr. Campbell. My name is Miss Becky McCoy." The girl, still on the field side of the gate, removed her hat and wiped the sweat from her forehead onto her shirt sleeve. With the motion, her red, tumbleweed hair fell to her shoulders, and though Mason kept a straight face, he smiled inwardly at the comical sight of this little girl with the outrageous hair and even more outrageous hat trying to sound like she was all grown up.

He tipped his hat to her. "A pleasure to meet you, Miss Becky." Out of the corner of his eye, he saw Cody nod in what he assumed was approval, as if in appreciation for his playing along.

Before Mason could further admonish his son, Cody addressed Becky. "What do ya think about Star?"

Becky stood in front of Star and rubbed the soft spot between his nostrils with the knuckle of her index finger. Then she massaged both of his cheeks near his jaw bones and up to his ears, bypassing the star on his forehead. She had begun tickling his neck when the animal responded by shoving his muzzle into her shoulder. At that, she reached around and gave him a neck hug. Both she and Star appeared to be totally relaxed in reverie.

Cody repeated his question.

When Becky replied, she was still hugging the horse, and she did not turn to face either person. "Well, I wouldn't shoot 'im yet."

"Shoot him? Even if I could never ride him again, I wouldn't *shoot* him!"

The distress in Cody's voice must have brought her back to the present since Becky abruptly released the horse and turned toward the Campbells. "Sorry, Master Cody! I was jus' meanin' I think he'll be okay. I know how to help 'im heal."

Mason piped up at that: "Are you a veterinarian?" His voice sounded sharper than he had intended, but he was annoyed. First this girl was pretending to be a lady, and now she was pretending to know more than a vet.

"No, sir!"

"Well, our vet, Doc Prescott, said it's a sprain and Star would be fine after six to eight weeks of rest."

"How long's it been?"

Cody had the number at the front of his mind. "Nine."

Mason thought Becky looked smug, as if saying, "So there. Your vet was wrong," but her next words carried only concern:

"Well, he's still hurtin'. Even though he didn't limp, I could feel 'im favorin' his right front leg."

Mason was incredulous. "You could feel that, huh?"

"Yes, sir. First thing ya need to do is undress 'im."

"*Undress him?*" Cody looked to his father, but Mason shrugged that he didn't understand either. "Ya mean to take the bandage off?"

"Shore, it hasta come off, but my meanin' was to remove his shoes."

Cody smiled. "Oh."

"Next thing is to re-bandage 'im usin' a tongue depressor to reposition the tendon that's pressin' on the nerve."

Mason wasn't convinced. He didn't want to argue with Becky, but he did want Cody to use some common sense. He knew from personal experience that even young girls had feminine wiles that could keep a man from thinking straight—not that Becky was trying to trick his son—she just seemed to have an unwarranted influence on him. He attempted some middle ground: "Doc Prescott is coming out first thing in the morning, Cody, to check on Bella Dama's pregnancy. We'll have him reevaluate Star then."

Cody kept his voice even when he answered. "Pa, you're always sayin' how I'm old enough to make my own decisions, and Star is *my* horse. I believe Miss Becky can help him. I want her to try. We can still see what the doc says tomorrow."

Cody's taking a stand surprised Mason, but not unpleasantly. Cody had been respectful, plus Mason knew his son was right. He *was* always saying that, and the horse did belong to Cody. He wavered fleetingly before agreeing. "Okay, son, but we don't have a tongue depressor. We'll have to make one."

During the discussion, Becky had occupied herself by whispering in Star's ear and caressing him, generally giving more attention to him than to the conversation, but now that a decision had been made, she spoke up. "No need to trouble yerself, Mr. Campbell. I have what I need in my bag. An' Master Cody, ya should know that Star is tired o' bein' cooped up in his stall. Corral 'im fer a few hours every day. Keep his spirits up. Star has heart, Master Cody. If'n a band of Apaches was on yer tail, he'd run—not 'til his leg gave out, but 'til his *heart* did."

Mason saw Cody nod his head in agreement, but he kept his own opinion to himself.

"I'll take Athena to 'er stall an' fetch those supplies." Becky extracted Athena's reins from Cody and made a beeline for the barn.

As soon as she was out of earshot, Mason poked for information. "Son, who is she?"

"She told ya, Pa. Her name's—"

"Miss Becky McCoy. Yes, I got that. What's she doing out here all by her lonesome?"

"Pa, ya always told me to keep my nose clean of others' business."

He's quoting me again. It looks like Cody has *been listening to my fatherly advice,* Mason thought. *I kind of brought this on myself.*

"She needed a meal and a bed, and I thought I was doin' right. Besides, she's real good with horses."

"We'll see about that, but don't get your hopes up. I'm sure Doc Prescott knows more about horses than that girl. And another thing, it's not proper for her to sleep in the barn."

"Yes, sir, but it's not proper to let her sleep in the house with us either."

"Son, she's a young lady at most, not a woman. It would be more improper for her to sleep in the barn than in the house."

"All right, Pa, but you'll have to convince her yerself. Here she comes. I'll go rustle up yer farrier tools from the tool shed."

Not much later, Becky finished wrapping Star's leg. Cody moved the horse to his stall, and Mason put the tools away. The three of them reconnected at the corral, where the Campbells found Becky holding Raven's rear left hoof.

"What are you doing with my horse, Miss Becky?"

"He has a touch o' thrush."

"What? Let me see."

"His stall's the middle one on the left?"

"Yes, it is." Mason moved closer to take a look. He pulled a jackknife out of his Levi's front right pocket and carefully scraped around the frog on the underside of the hoof.

"Well, when I was muckin' it out, I noticed that the drainage isn't as good in that stall."

"His foot looks okay to me."

"It's jus' startin' to take hold. Put yer nose right down close an' take in a big whiff."

Mason complied. "Hard to tell." He wasn't sure he smelled anything unusual, but he did give her some credit. "You're right about that stall. I just haven't gotten around to fixing it yet."

"I could whip up an iodine solution fer the thrush."

"Thanks, anyway, Miss Becky, but I'll wait to see what Doc Prescott says tomorrow. Meantime, I'll move him next to the pregnant mare."

"Shorely. Um, ya know that foal is backwards in 'er?"

Mason knew it, but he was surprised that Becky did. "Doc thinks it will turn in the next few days and she'll foal at the end of the week."

From the look on Becky's face, he thought she was about to laugh, but she apparently changed her mind, and her lips transformed into a beguiling smile. Then she looked away and said, "Could be."

Chapter 2

By late afternoon, the chickens and hogs had been fed. It was early for the animals to eat, but the Campbells could hardly excuse themselves to do time-consuming chores after their own supper, leaving their guests to entertain themselves. The day had begun sunny enough, but by now some large, fluffy clouds could be seen lying on the horizon like a giant's pillows on a distant bed. Soon the daily afternoon storms would return, but not today.

Mason and Cody had washed and changed into clean clothes. They sat on the front porch with Shep at their feet, awaiting their guests, while Becky cleaned up and changed clothes in the barn. A rocker and one chair were usually stationed on the porch, but the hosts had brought three additional chairs from their dining set outside in preparation. Being narrow, the porch could not accommodate that many chairs arranged in a circle, so they were lined up pretty much in a straight row.

The Campbells were awaiting Mason's lady friend, Miss Elizabeth Hill, and his best friend, the town's sheriff, Tom Claiborne. Elizabeth was a proper and relatively wealthy woman of thirty-five. She typically wore fashionable, conservative clothing and jewelry. Of the latter, she most often wore a cameo pin at her throat. She usually kept her long, light brown hair piled in knots at the back of her head, but on occasion Mason had seen it in its full glory, falling in waves down to the middle of her back. Elizabeth's parents owned Leaning Rock's general store, and Elizabeth had worked there since childhood. She was an excellent seamstress and an accomplished pianist.

Tom Claiborne was also about thirty-five. He was average height with an athletic build and sported thick black hair, sideburns, and a well-groomed, medium mustache. Mason had joined one of Tom's posses when he had first bought his ranch, and the experience had taught him that Tom was a man of good moral character with a cool head and unparalleled bravery. Mason trusted him implicitly, even with his life, because Tom had once saved his life.

As they waited, Cody explained that the mop had been dry when Mason arrived because Miss Becky preferred to clean the floor on her hands and knees with rags. She had used one in each hand, a scrubber and a rinser, while he followed behind with another rag to dry the floor. *That accounted for both the dry mop and the rags on the line*, Mason thought. *On the line.*

Just then Shep gave a warning bark as Elizabeth's horse and buggy turned from the main road onto the long trail leading to the Campbells' house. At that intersection stood two large upright posts at the sides of the trail with a wide cross-board attached at the top, serving as a gateless entry. On the board was engraved "Camp Bell" in a fancy, rope-like cursive, and on each post, horse high, hung a heavy cowbell. After passing through the entry, a few mature trees lined the trail, but the land was mostly covered by dried grass and yuccas.

Cody shushed the dog but echoed his sentiment: "Here they come, Pa!" He was not prepared for his father's response.

"Shoot! I knew we forgot something!"

"What, Pa? Everything is clean, includin' us; the animals are set; the bread goes in the oven after they arrive. We're ready for company."

"Look around, son, what do you see on the clothesline?"

"Oh, no!"

"Well, it's too late now. Miss Elizabeth and Tom are waving and will see us if we jump into action to remove them." Mason waved back to his guests. "We'll have to pray they don't notice the pantalettes."

Cody, however, had his own idea. Trying to distract the visitors, he ran to the porch's cowbell and rang it long and loud, waving wildly all the while. It was soon apparent that his tactic had failed. The Campbells saw Miss Elizabeth nudge Tom and point toward the clothesline, and then they saw Tom veer the buggy off the trail and over to the pantalettes. Cody groaned as Miss Elizabeth reached out to touch the undergarment, but at the exact moment when she unpinned the pantalettes from the line, they were whisked away in a blur. Miss Becky, who was dressed in an oversized shift and her pink hat, had biked around the perimeter of the house at full speed and snatched her prey.

Mason anticipated Elizabeth's skittish horse rearing in fright and bobbling the buggy, but the mare stood stolid, perhaps too stunned to react. Once the pantalettes were in her hands, Becky was off again, leaving Elizabeth and Tom to wonder *what-in-the-world?* Cody cheered aloud at Becky's successful exploit. Although Mason found the encounter opportune and even humorous, he didn't think Elizabeth would be laughing, and he knew he was in for some explaining. The feeling recalled his childhood and having to report to authority figures. Why did he sometimes feel like a little boy around Elizabeth, like she was mothering him or judging him?

With Tom's maneuvering, the buggy returned to the trail and soon came to a standstill in front of the porch. Everyone hollered their greetings, and Mason jumped up to help Elizabeth down. He first took the pie she was holding and handed it to Cody, who carried it into the house. While inside, Cody took the meat out of the oven to rest and replaced it with the bread. The aroma of the food made his stomach gurgle impatiently.

Meanwhile, Mason lifted Elizabeth gently by the waist and set her securely on the ground before giving her a friendly hug. His nose detected a fragrant scent from around her neck or hair, and he was pleased that she had gone to extra effort for her evening out. He thought she might be wearing a new dress, too.

Tom hopped down from the opposite side of the buggy, came over and shook Mason's hand. Mason noticed that Tom was wearing his Sunday best with a fancy, carved-stone, eagle-shaped bola tie. Though he wasn't wearing his sheriff's vest and badge, he was packing, as always, his pair of Colt Peacemaker 6-shooters. Mason wished that he had spruced up with fancier clothes. He hadn't expected his guests to dress up.

Once Cody returned, he led the horse and buggy away to unharness, water, and corral the beast. In his absence, the others sat, with Elizabeth choosing the rocker and immediately activating it with her feet. Before Elizabeth or Tom could inquire about the pantalettes incident, Mason mentioned they had another guest, and it was she whom they had encountered. He would have explained more, but he saw Cody returning with Becky trailing behind him.

Becky was wearing a simple floor-length dress, rather drab in color, with a rounded collar and three-quarter length sleeves. It had a tie at the waist and ruffles at the hem and elbows. She had captured her unruly curls and wrapped the longest strands into a bun at the base of her neck. The rest of her hair hung like coiled springs around her face. Her earlobes were decorated with a pair of sparkly diamond and ruby earrings. Like her pink, feathered hat, they looked inappropriate with the rest of her outfit. She chose the only vacant chair, one that was next to Cody, and sat.

Cody introduced the other guests to her before speaking his mind. "Ya clean up real nice, Miss Becky."

"Thank ya kindly, Master Cody."

"How are ya likin' them fancy pantalettes?"

Elizabeth's jaw dropped. "My stars, Cody! Hasn't your father taught you any manners?"

Becky's fair face had turned sunburnt red, and Mason was rather embarrassed himself: first, that Cody had asked such an inappropriate personal question, but also because he had never heard Elizabeth criticize Cody before. She was always so proper with her thoughts and speech, and this insult hit hard, like a punch in a bar brawl, because it reflected on his parenting abilities. Mason wasn't sure how to make things right. Should he ask Cody to apologize, or would his mentioning the unmentionables again make things worse? Should he pull Cody aside and give him a lecture? Which action would Elizabeth be more likely to approve? "Son, uh, son . . ."

Fortunately, Becky took the reins. "Ya got it all wrong. I took what Master Cody asked the same as if'n he asked how my new boots were fittin'. I told 'im those awful pantalettes have been causin' me no end o' grief, an' he jus' wanted to know if'n washin' 'em had helped. It was jus' a faux pas. What made me blush was not what anybody said but the hard truth that I'm not wearin' 'em. I tried. I really tried, but I can't do it, not even fer Godmother."

She sounded forlorn, but Mason felt relieved, not only because Becky hadn't been embarrassed by Cody's question, but also to hear that the girl had relatives. He intended to ascertain more about her family and history at supper. Prying may be wrong, but maybe he could coax her into volunteering some information.

While Mason was thinking, Cody backtracked. "What was that fancy word again, Miss Becky?"

"Ya mean *faux pas*? It's French. Means 'social mistake.' I learnt it from my social graces tutor. Did ya know, Master Cody, that besides undergarments, ya mustn't mention how much or how little a guest eats?"

"No foolin'!"

"Ya can't ask a lady 'er age neither."

"That one, Pa taught me." He nodded toward Mason, who felt gratified he'd done something right.

"I 'spect that's common knowledge." Becky's comment was a bit of a blow, but Mason didn't think she was trying to belittle his parenting efforts.

"Ever heard of *faux pas* before, Mace?"

"Not that I recall, Tom. Have you, Miss Elizabeth?"

"Of course, Mason. All proper young ladies learn such things."

Now Mason did feel a bit belittled, but he had no time to ponder her intent. Elizabeth had returned the conversation to the previous subject, and this time everyone knew full well that she was committing a faux pas.

"Miss Becky, I glimpsed your pantalettes on the line, and they're the loveliest I've ever seen. I'd like to procure some to sell in my family's store."

She lied, Mason instantly realized, cognizant that no locals could afford them. He had never known Miss Elizabeth to be deceitful, and he saw no purpose for it in this situation. He believed honesty was the best way to deal with children. Then he wondered if she had ever lied to *him*. His thoughts were interrupted by Elizabeth asking where Becky had bought the item.

"Oh, I would never buy somethin' like that. They were a gift."

"Ya mentioned earlier that yer bicycle was a gift. Did ya just have a birthday?"

"Naw, Master Cody, that was fer services rendered. I get lotsa great gifts, like this fashionable hat." She reached up and adjusted the feathers slightly.

At that, the sheriff sat a little straighter in his chair. He was typically quiet and thoughtful, preferring to listen than to speak.

"'bout them pantalettes, my godmother sent 'em all the way from Paris, but I jus' can't tolerate 'em. The silk is soft, but the lace or threads or somethin' are scratchy. I wish she'd sent somethin' everyday-practical to wear. I tend to burn through clothes right fast."

Mason understood what she meant. He himself sometimes had trouble keeping Cody covered in properly sized, respectable garments, and he appreciated hand-me-down gifts from compassionate townsfolk. The pantalettes, however, were definitely not secondhand.

"Maybe the pantalettes were stitched with fine wool thread. Some folks are allergic to it. If you'd like, I'll take them home with me tonight, and I'll see what I can do about it. You can fetch them in town at Sam Hill's, my family's store, tomorrow." Elizabeth continued to rock in a gentle motion, back and forth, back and forth, never changing rhythm or missing a beat.

"Thank ya, Miss Elizabeth. That's right kind of ya."

The sun was low in the sky, turning the distant clouds orange and red with the help of the dust in the air. Soon the air would cool and night critters would emerge. Sunset and dawn were the best parts of the day as far as Mason was concerned. He kept his eyes on the landscape, but his ears were still attending the conversation.

"Your earrings are stunning, dear. Are they a gift from your godmother, too?"

"No, ma'am, though they *were* a gift—they're glass fer sure."

"Even so, they're quite fine." The scent of fresh-baked bread reached Elizabeth "Oh! We don't want that to burn!" She excused herself to go inside and finalize supper, and Mason volunteered Cody to help her and to take some chairs in with him. As she entered, Elizabeth hung her bonnet and shawl on the hat rack inside the door and primped her hair with her fingers.

Now the sheriff took an interest in the jewelry. He arose and approached Becky. Then he held his hand behind her right ear so the dangly earring hung positioned in his palm. "Miss Becky, they are right pretty. Who gave 'em to you?"

"Jus' a man on the road."

"What for?"

"Services rendered."

Tom and Mason looked at each other with the same question in mind. Those were words that implied prostitution, but surely Becky was far too young for that. Since Mason remained silent, the sheriff asked the question. "What kind of services, Miss Becky?"

Before Becky could reply, "Supper's on," came from the house, and Becky dodged between the men and scurried inside.

*　　*　　*

Mason entered the house last and hung his gun belt and tan hat on a peg below Tom's black hat. Then he took his place at the head of the rectangular table. He offered Elizabeth the seat to his left; the sheriff, the seat at the foot; and Cody, the seat to his right. That left a space for Becky at Cody's right and the sheriff's left. The roast sat in front of Mason, and he expertly began carving. "Miss Elizabeth, medium rare?"

"Yes, thanks, Mace."

Mason set a generous portion of meat on her plate. "Miss Becky?"

"Well done, please, an' jus' a shave. I, uh, I'm savin' room fer Miss Elizabeth's pie."

Elizabeth's eyes twinkled at that revelation. "The store has an overstock of apples at the moment, so I hope you like apple pie."

Cody raved about her apple pie, having tasted it several times in the past, and Becky agreed that she loved apples. While they spoke, Mason continued serving the others, and lastly, he took a slab of bloody, rare meat for himself. The other foods were passed around, and after everyone had partaken, Mason lifted his fork to begin eating.

"Mr. Campbell, mind if'n I say a blessin'?"

Mason returned his fork to the table. He didn't figure Becky for the religious type, but with the surname McCoy, she was probably Catholic. He and the others were good Protestants, well, sort of good Protestants, and he had heard miseries about long, Catholic prayers. He and Cody generally prayed only on Sundays and only if they made it to town for church. It's not that Mason didn't believe in God, just that organized religion took time and effort, and he focused most of his time and effort on work.

Elizabeth filled the silence for him by expressing her approval. "That sounds lovely, dear."

"Join hands an' bow yer heads." Becky reached toward Cody and the sheriff.

Elizabeth offered her hands to the men, and Mason noticed that Cody showed no reluctance in taking Becky's hand. In fact, he seemed enthusiastic to do so. As far as Mason knew, Cody had never taken notice of girls before, and he certainly had not held one's hand. "Is that what you do in your family, Miss Becky?"

"Doesn't ever'one, Miss Elizabeth?" Her reply sounded sincere to Mason, not like a rhetorical question but as though she really wanted to know. But no one answered her, and when their hands were connected and heads were bowed, Becky recited her prayer: "Oh God in heaven, giver o' gifts, we thank ya fer this food an' fer all yer blessin's. Amen." In unison, the others amen-ed, and in short order the eating commenced. The metal utensils clinked on the china as the diners cut their food and set down their knives.

Between bites, Mason probed Becky. "I was expecting a longer, Catholic prayer."

"Well, my mama's not Catholic, so's I'm, uh, experimentin' with options. I don't figure God cares too much 'bout length, as long as yer thankful, an' Papa says there's no sense lettin' good food get cold."

The mention of family gave Elizabeth an opportune opening: "Oh, do tell us what suppertime is like in your family."

Becky looked around and sighed. "Well, my big brothers are Matthew, Mark, Luke, an' John. Then comes me. Then comes the twins, Timothy an' Thomas, an' Anabelle is three. She's feebleminded but has offsettin' qualities. Most usual, we all eat at the big table on Sundays, but other days, if'n I'm lucky, I get to eat in the kitchen with the littler ones."

Elizabeth swallowed a bite before continuing: "Why is that lucky? Don't you like to eat with the adults, dear?" She took another mouthful while awaiting Becky's answer.

"Well, Miss Elizabeth, we have lotsa old-men visitors, an' if'n I eat with 'em, I hafta entertain 'em."

Now the sheriff had a reason to speak. "Your papa makes you entertain men after supper? What does your mama say to that?"

"She tells me to go down to the barn with the men for a while an' then come back to the house an' sing or dance, or worse of all, to play piano." Becky scrunched up her face in a look of disgust.

Elizabeth smiled. She loved the piano, but she had tried to teach many students who were less than enthusiastic.

Cody swallowed hard to down a bite he should have chewed a bit longer. He jumped in before the sheriff could follow up: "You can play piano? I've got a guitar. Taught myself."

With a look of relief, Becky sat quietly and finished her greens, while Cody talked about the songs he could play and sing. During the process, he corralled her into sitting with him on the porch after supper and making some music with him. It occurred to Mason that Cody was developing his first crush, and he found the idea both amusing and disconcerting. He wanted his son to experience falling in love and getting married just as he had, but what was wrong with the local girls? Thankfully, this red-haired maverick would move on to different pastures in the morning.

When Cody was done speaking, Elizabeth kept the conversation alive. "You must live in a mansion to house that big of a family, Miss Becky. How many bedrooms are there?"

"One." She paused, then churned out an afterthought. "Well, two, if'n ya count the bunkroom, Miss Elizabeth. Mama an' Papa share the one room, an' the rest of us sleep in the other. Fact is, boys clomp in an' out all times o' the night an' snore an' stay up talkin'. I prefer to sleep in the calm of the barn."

Mason found her answer to be the perfect segue into sleeping arrangements. He drained his coffee cup, set it down, and addressed her. "I was going to talk to you about that, Miss Becky. I know Cody prepared a cot in the barn for you, but I'd feel better if you slept in the ranch house. We'll move the furniture around and make room for the cot in here."

Becky frowned. Mason thought she was going to argue the point, but it was Cody who made the argument.

"Pa, the deal I made with her is that she sleeps in the barn. We spit and shook on it."

Mason was doubly surprised; first, that his son who balked at touching a wet mop would willingly touch a girl's spit, and second, that he would put up an argument in front of guests. "Well, son, deals can be amended when all parties agree. Miss Becky?"

"If'n ya don't 'low me to sleep in the barn, I'd rather sleep in town. Sheriff Claiborne, would ya drive me there when ya leave with Miss Elizabeth?"

"It would be a pleasure, but do you have money for the boarding house?"

At that, the color rose in Becky's face for a second time that evening.

Miss Elizabeth came to her rescue. "That's okay. You could stay with me, dear."

Mason wasn't surprised at Elizabeth's offer. She had taken Cody in several times when he was too young to be left alone and Mason couldn't pack him along on business, such as when he was on posse duty helping Tom. She seemed to like children, though she wasn't as motherly as Emma had been. Perhaps she would be more nurturing with her own children.

"Pa! We're not amendin' our bargain, are we Miss Becky? She promised to teach me to ride her bicycle in the mornin'!"

So that was his interest. Mason felt relieved.

"I'd rather not be beholden to the sheriff an' Miss Elizabeth, an' I've already worked fer my lodgin'."

"All right then, but I have to know two things. First, are you a run-away?"

"Why, no, sir!"

Her eager response and emphatic tone were pretty convincing, but Mason half stood and leaned across the table toward her to look her in the eyes, trying to discern any deceit. Apparently, she had been through this type of scrutiny before.

"Cross my heart an' hope to die. Stick a thousand needles in my eye!" She drew an x over her heart as she spoke and aimed her fingers toward her face, as though they were needles.

The sheriff turned to Elizabeth. "That's plenty good enough for me."

"And for me for the first question." Mason continued his interrogation with his second question: "Can I expect your father or any of those brothers of yours to show up and give me trouble in the night?"

"No, sir! If'n I was 'lowed to swear, I'd swear it."

"Okay, then, it's settled. You can sleep in the barn."

Cody and Becky looked exceedingly pleased. Tom took advantage of the mention of Becky's bicycle and remarked that he and Elizabeth were astounded when she rode by and snatched the unmentionables. That livened up the party with laughter. When the chatter died down and all were finished with the main course, Mason and Cody cleared the table and reseated themselves, after which Elizabeth rose, cut the pie, and distributed it. Then she picked up the coffee pot. "More to drink, anyone?" The kids still had some milk in their glasses, but the adults nodded their assent. Elizabeth began to refill Tom's coffee cup.

"I'd like coffee. I'll fetch a cup. I know where ya keep 'em." As Becky popped up to retrieve a cup, Elizabeth looked questioningly at Mason, who passed the look to Tom. Cody, meanwhile, sported a wide grin and moon eyes. Clearly, he was amused by the adults' uneasiness.

Mason said what they were all thinking: "You're pretty young to be drinking coffee, Miss Becky. It will keep you awake."

"I'm nearly thirteen—my birthday's tomorrow—an' that's a faux pas on ya, mentionin' what a guest eats or drinks."

Mason recalled his own coffee experience before settling on a solution. Although he didn't think she was old enough to be drinking coffee at twelve, she was a guest, and since this was her preferred drink, he would try to accommodate her. "Faux pas or not, you can have half-and-half. Elizabeth, pour her a half cup, and Miss Becky, use your unfinished glass to add milk." All eyes were on Becky as she poured a scant swallow of milk into her dark, steaming half-cup of joe. Mason guessed that would have to do.

"Pa, could I—"

"No son, you cannot have any." Mason was certain that Cody had no interest in drinking coffee and was just testing him.

As Cody finished his second piece of pie, Becky began clearing the dessert plates. "Is it okay if'n Master Cody an' I start on the dishes now? If'n we hurry, there'll be time to go outside an' play."

Play? The only games Cody had played recently were checkers and marbles. Mason couldn't imagine his son would take pleasure in playing with her.

"Papa says I must play at somethin' every day, lest work without play will ruin me."

"We wouldn't want that, would we? You both are excused. I'll take care of the dishes myself since you did most of the cooking."

"And they did an outstanding job, don't you think, Tom?"

"By all means, Elizabeth. It tasted better than anything Mace has served me before. And you?"

"Most certainly."

It was just like them to tease him about his cooking. He had learned the basics over the years without Emma, and most folks complimented him on his meals. These two, however, made him wonder if the others were just being polite. No matter. His cooking was certainly good enough for Cody and him. Becky's voice brought his thoughts back to the present.

"Thank ya anyways, but that wasn't the deal." Becky began pumping water for the dishes into a large pot. Cody joined her in the kitchen and scraped the food remnants into a slop pail to save for the hogs; the adults remained seated at the table.

"What's that, Miss Becky?" It was hard to hear over the running water.

"I hafta wash tonight, an' Master Cody dries; an' in the mornin' I cook, Mr. Campbell, you wash, an' Master Cody dries."

"You struck a hard bargain, Cody, making a guest clean house and launder clothes and cook two meals just to be able to sleep in the barn."

"Sorry, Pa. I didn't mean to ask too much. We helped each other, and the work went fast." Cody stoked the stove's fire box, and Becky placed the pot on top to heat.

"Well, I think you got the better deal, especially since you wangled yourself out of washing both times, but to Miss Becky's credit, when she makes a deal, she's not one to back out of it."

"Papa says stickin' to a bargain is a sign o' maturity, but I do have a betterment to offer. Are ya a bettin' man, Mr. Campbell?"

"I've been known to play some poker. But I won't wager for money against a youngster, uh, young lady, if that's what you had in mind. Plus, I think we established that you don't have any."

If Becky was offended by his words, she didn't let on. "I'm not 'lowed to take money from men, an' I'm not askin' ya to risk any. Here's the wager: Ya said yer vet thinks yer mare will foal at the end o' the week. I'm willin' to bet that she foals tonight. If'n I win, ya hafta cook breakfast in my stead an' still do the dishwashin'. If'n I lose, I'll still cook, an' I'll take over yer dish-wash chore."

Mason was new to horse breeding. His expertise was cattle. He had bought two broodmares to diversify his assets and increase his income. He had bred the "proven" mare twice, and she had not settled either time. He bought the pregnant mare not knowing that she was. Most foals came in the spring. What was this one doing coming in August? Doc Prescott had told him the signs to watch for: milk production and going off her feed. Mason hadn't seen any indication of either, so he was confident that he would win. However, he also thought that Becky had already earned her keep, so he felt a bit guilty that she would have extra work to do when she lost. But not guilty enough. She was the one who offered the bet, and it could be a lesson for her. "Okay, Miss Becky, you're on."

"Pa, do ya think I could get some side-bet action?"

Elizabeth and the sheriff had been listening with amusement, but now they both unsuccessfully stifled laughs. Mason also saw humor in his son's request. Cody was full of surprises when it came to this girl. Mason had lectured him on betting and weighing the odds and being able to afford the risk. He knew Cody had made small bets with school pals and had lost some playthings: marbles and arrowheads. If Cody had ever bet money, Mason was unaware of it. "What did you have in mind, son?"

"If Bella Dama foals tonight, you have to do my dish dryin' along with Miss Becky's cookin' and yer washin'. If Bella Dama doesn't foal, I'll do yer dish washin'. And how's this: if she doesn't foal, I'll also pick up the cookin', since I overcharged Miss Becky for her overnight stay."

"That sounds generous of you, but I think you're forgetting that if Bella Dama doesn't foal tonight, Miss Becky will be cooking and washing the dishes, not me, so you're not offering me anything. Are you so sure of your bet that you're willing to mop the floor for a month if you lose?"

Cody hesitated for a moment. "That's a lot of moppin'. How about two weeks' worth?"

"No, it would have to be a month. So, do you want in on the action?"

"Ya saw Miss Becky is real good with horses, Pa. I believe in her, so yes."

"All right, you two. I accept both wagers. Now hurry and finish those dishes so you'll have time to go out and play before it gets too dark."

Becky and Cody didn't have to be told twice. The water was ready, so Becky carefully poured some into the wash and rinse buckets, and Cody handed her the bar of soap and wash rag. Becky lathered the first plate and set it in the rinse bucket. As she started washing another one, Cody swished the first plate around, withdrew it, and wiped it with a towel. The dishwashers established a rhythm, soaping, rinsing, and drying without creating wait times or bumping hands as they reached in and out of tubs.

As the adults rose to relocate to the more comfortable chairs in the sitting room at the front section of the house, Becky called over her shoulder with an addendum: "Mr. Campbell, jus' so's ya know, I like my egg smashed an' my bacon burnt."

"Whoa there, Miss Becky. You mean *scrambled* and *crispy*?"

"No, sir. *Smashed.* First boil an' cool the egg. Then smash it with a spoon an' stir in some mustard, if'n ya have any. That's the only way I eat 'em. An' the bacon should be black."

*   *   *

Tom and Elizabeth moved to the sitting room. There were two stuffed chairs facing the hearth, typically one for each of the members of the household. A fire had been set in the fireplace but had not been lit. There was still plenty of heat in the house from the oven, the meal, and the near full capacity of people in the small house. The guests each chose a chair, and Mason carried a chair from the dining area for himself. Tom and Elizabeth settled in, placing their coffee cups within reach on small tables. Mason set his chair down facing backward and then straddled the seat to face the others.

Elizabeth giggled. "If I were you, Mace, I'd be hoping to lose that bet. If that's how Becky eats eggs and bacon, that's probably how she cooks them. I could tolerate the egg, but burnt bacon?" She shuddered at the thought. "Did you notice how little supper she ate?"

Mason nodded. "Mostly greens and pie."

Tom leaned into the conversation and placed his index finger to his mustache. "Shh. They'll hear you. That's a shameful faux pas!" At that, the adults broke into laughter. After they quieted, the sheriff floated an idea. "Do you think we've been played? Is it possible that Becky broached the subject of the food and drink faux pas this afternoon to set herself up for assured approval for coffee at supper?"

While Mason rubbed his chin, thinking, Elizabeth came quickly to a conclusion. "I don't think so. I think she's too young to be that wily. Mace?"

Mason was still pondering. Tom hadn't said much during the meal. He was quiet by nature and a good judge of character. Mason's experience with little girls was limited, but he knew they could be manipulative. Perhaps Tom was right about Becky and the coffee. Unsure, he hedged his bet: "If she did play us, she is as cunning as a coyote."

Once again, they laughed. This time, however, they were drowned out by a cacophony emanating from the kitchen, the sounds of sloshing water and clanking platters, along with raucous laughter. Becky and Cody had picked up their pace but lost their rhythm, splashing water onto themselves and the floor.

"We're not the only ones in good humor. Those two seem to have taken to each other like pigs to a mud bath."

Elizabeth's comment stung Mason slightly. She was a wonderful woman: kind, pretty, smart, and well respected in town. She came from good stock, and he could always rely on her, whether he wanted an unbiased opinion on some issue or whether he needed a child sitter. He enjoyed her company and had participated in courting activities with her: the church picnic, a barn dance, some afternoon rides. He had even taken to calling her Betsy when Cody wasn't around. But he hadn't taken to her like a pig to a mud bath or a bear to honey. She was a friend and a confidant. Although she possessed many fine qualities and he was attracted to her, for some reason he hadn't been able to picture her as his wife.

The conversation had progressed without him, and when Elizabeth and Tom turned to him for a response, he had no notion as to what they had been discussing. "Sorry, I was lost in thought." Mason smiled weakly at them. "What was the question?"

Tom responded by shaking his head and rolling his eyes, but Elizabeth graciously filled him in. "Tom was just asking if you would be coming into town for the bronco-busting contest."

The Campbells spent most of their time at the ranch, but they rode into town now and again for supplies and church. During the school year, Cody rode in regularly for school, but this time of year they were isolated from the community and welcomed news; thus, the invitation for supper on a weeknight. "I expect to. Is the town bustling?"

"Everything's been quiet so far. I've got no one behind bars, but that will probably change tonight, since Pruitt showed up yesterday with the herd of broncos. The bronco-busting contest is set from 12:30 to 4:30 tomorrow afternoon and Saturday. The boarding house is starting to fill with contenders. I saw an interesting name in the registry."

"Hold up a minute." The volume of youngsters' laughter had begun to interfere with the conversation. Mason stood, as he intended to go shush them, but they came running past and stopped abruptly at the door. He noticed that tear streaks lined Becky's face.

"We left the last pan to soak, okay, Pa?"

"Okay, son. But is everything all right, Miss Becky? You look like you've been crying."

"Laugh attack is all. Sometimes I laugh 'til I cry. And sometimes I cry 'til I laugh." And then she laughed again, this time apparently at his confounded look.

Girls! Mason thanked the Lord he had a son. He didn't understand females and their emotions and feelings at all.

"Well, what in tarnation was so gall-darn funny?"

"Horse tales, Sheriff Claiborne. Miss Becky has been tellin' me horse tales."

"Anything akin to fish tales?"

"Why, no; cross her heart, Becky says they're all true."

"I'd like to hear a knee-slapper, Cody."

"Sure, Miss Elizabeth, but we're tryin' to beat the dark, so I'll just give ya a short account: This last one was about seven old broodmares tied in a line at a long hitchin' post in the early evenin'. Miss Becky's brother was strummin' his guitar, and she was singin' soft-like. Well, the mares began to relax and sway with the music, so the line was goin' like this." He stood next to his father and motioned Becky over to stand on the other side of Mason. "Sway, Pa, left then right." Mason felt uncomfortable, but he played along. The three of them swayed to imaginary music, when Cody suddenly pushed his weight into his Pa, who bumped the petite Becky to the floor, as though she were a domino.

Mason was flustered and immediately lifted Becky to her feet, apologizing profusely. His discomfort made the situation all the funnier, and when he saw and heard the others in stitches, he couldn't help but join in.

"Okay, you two, out! Go play!"

And they ran, giggling, outside.

*   *   *

After Cody and Becky left the house, Mason, Elizabeth, and Tom continued their conversation in peace. The name Tom had seen in the boarding house registry was John McCoy. He remembered seeing the kid ride into town, his dark, wavy hair visible from around the edges of his hat. Tom estimated the young man to be in his late teens. He sat his splendid chestnut gelding well, wasn't packing a pistol, and appeared to be affluent by the looks of his fancy black boots and hat and his ornate silver belt buckle. After he had checked in at the boarding house, he visited the bank. Tom expected he'd head straight to the saloon, like so many cowhands did, but instead, he had moseyed over to the telegraph office. After a few minutes, he strutted out, mounted up, and rode off in the opposite direction from whence he came. Coincidentally, the direction he rode in from would have taken him right past Mason's spread.

"What do you make of that?"

"Tom, why didn't you mention him when Cody introduced Miss Becky to you?"

Tom shrugged. "Sometimes I unearth more information by observation than by interrogation. You could learn from me."

"Hah!"

Within the group, speculation and theories abounded. Clearly, John McCoy was Miss Becky's fourth brother, if they believed her story. Elizabeth proposed that the two of them were traveling together and had a falling out. John abandoned her and would come back when he'd cooled off. Mason reminded her that Becky planned to ride her bicycle the five miles into Leaning Rock the next day. Undeterred, Elizabeth modified her theory to allow Becky to meet up with John when *she'd* cooled off.

"Could be, Miss Elizabeth, or maybe they're con artists."

Tom's theory was that John habitually dropped Becky near farms or ranches, where she befriended folks and either robbed or entertained them. Her brother sold most of the "gifts" she obtained and was living easy off the proceeds. He went on to suggest that they had misinterpreted Becky's second blush. She turned red because she *did* have money, not because she *didn't*. She hadn't outright lied to them about it; she simply let them draw their own incorrect conclusion.

"Well, I expect the truth will come out tomorrow. Meanwhile, I'll go search them out. First, they're louder than a lost calf; now, they're quiet as death."

"You don't suppose they're canoodling in the barn?"

"Heavens, Betsy, your imagination is running full bore tonight!" He laughed as he said it, but a thought wormed into Mason's mind. Maybe canoodling was on Elizabeth's mind. He really ought to talk about his feelings with her, but he didn't want to lose her friendship. On the other hand, he didn't want to hobble her. If she wanted a husband, he should let her loose to find one. He stepped outside and rang the cowbell. "Cody, Miss Becky!" After allowing some time, he repeated his call with no better results than before, so he headed up the hill to the barn with Shep trotting nearby. Mason had his hand on the door latch when the silence was broken.

"Move, Pa! Move!"

"Outta the way, Mr. Campbell!"

Cody and Becky were running directly at him from opposite directions. Becky held her skirt hitched up as she ran, but she didn't seem hampered. She ran like a boy because she was built like a boy. Cody was coming faster but from farther away. "What is it? What's wrong!"

"Move!" came their simultaneous reply.

Mason took the only escape, entering the barn and slamming the door behind him. From inside, he heard, "A tie! We tied." He carefully opened the door and saw the children facing each other, holding onto each other's shoulders, jumping up and down.

"What in tarnation!"

Cody caught his breath first. "Sorry, Pa. We were playing a game, and the latch was home base."

"Well, thanks for warning me. I've had my fill of being bumped tonight," and he winked to let Cody know that he wasn't in any trouble for having fun. "I'm glad the game ended well."

Maybe playing had some merits, though there certainly wasn't time for it every day, and without siblings, playmates were a scarcity for Cody. "I saw that you fed the horses, and they're settled for the night. Good work. Miss Elizabeth and Sheriff Claiborne will be leaving soon. They want to hear your music first. Are you willing to oblige them?"

"Sure, Pa!"

Becky didn't sound as thrilled: "Entertainin'. Jus' like at home," but then her face brightened. "I wrote a song, Master Cody. I can teach it to ya right quick."

With their audience still socializing by the fireplace and the front door open, Becky and Cody sat on the porch step facing out into the evening. A few stars had twinkled into being, and the air had begun to cool. Out of sight, crickets chirped, divulging their existence. While Cody picked and strummed, he and Becky crooned some folksongs. Her voice was honest and soulful; his, clear and passionate. Mainly, they sang the melody together, but sometimes they were able to harmonize. Their final number was "Serenity," the song Becky had written. She sang the verses, and Cody strummed the chords:

> There's this place I know
> Where I often go
> When I wanna be alone
> I can laugh or cry
> While the stream flows by
> It's the privatest place I've known
>
> But sittin' there
> In the brisk fall air
> I came to realize
> I'm not alone
> I've a chaperone
> God sees me with His eyes
>
> God loves me the way I am
> He's my shepherd; I'm His lamb
> He is everywhere with me
> He's what gives me serenity.

"That was real fine, Miss Becky." Cody patted her hand. "I know why folks ask ya to entertain 'em."

"Thank ya kindly. It was more fun with a friend. Yer good."

Mason and Miss Elizabeth clapped their appreciation while the sheriff whistled enthusiastically. Then it was time for the adult guests to leave. They gathered their belongings, and Tom placed Miss Elizabeth's wrap over her shoulders while Mason went out to wrangle her mare from the corral. As Mason was hitching the buggy, Becky fetched her pantalettes from the barn and gave them to Miss Elizabeth. The group stood around the porch saying thanks and goodbyes until Mason appeared with the buggy, at which point Tom shook Mason's hand before climbing up and waiting for Mason and Elizabeth to say their goodbyes. Meanwhile, Becky took the edges of the mare's bit in her hands and gently huffed her breath into the horse's nostrils, after which she whispered something. The horse's ears rotated forward, and she nickered softly.

"Thanks for an interesting evening, Mace. Will I see you tomorrow?"

"I expect so, Betsy, at the bronco-busting contest."

"Shall I plan on having supper with you and Cody?"

"Sure, you do that. Goodnight, Betsy."

He helped her climb onto the seat next to Tom. Tom indicated for Becky to move out of his path, and the buggy started for Leaning Rock, leaving a trail of dust behind.

Shortly after, Cody walked Becky to the barn door. He presented her with a lantern and some matches, and per his father's instructions, he told her they wouldn't bolt the door to the house—

she should come right in and wake them if she needed anything. Cody also advised her that Shep slept outside on the porch and was a born watchdog. Becky assured Cody that she'd be fine, and from his vantage point on the porch, Mason saw them hug. He wondered if Elizabeth had been expecting a hug from him.

Friday

Chapter 3

Mason sprang up in bed. *A shot!* "Wake up, Cody!" He grabbed his trousers and slipped them on. Cody was not as instantly awake, but the second shot roused him to action. He stuffed his legs into his britches and followed his father to the front door, hopping on one leg as he pulled a boot over his foot. Shep was barking wildly from the porch. Mason's first thought was of Becky's brother.

Cody's thoughts were elsewhere. "Bandits? Apaches?"

"Unlikely."

Mason cracked the door. "A light's on up at the barn, and the barn door is open." Mason ordered Shep to quiet, and the dog instantly obeyed. He reached down to pat Shep's head and noticed a paper hanging from his neck. Upon further inspection, he saw a red hair ribbon tied around Shep's neck, holding the paper in place. "Light the lantern, son." Mason snatched the paper and read: "HURRY. Mare in truBBl. Bring 2 carrets, Wisky, cake pan, sopy Water, rins Water, 1 of Master CoDy's old rag shirts, vassoleen, hunting nife, lots of cleen rags, biggest neeDul you got, cat gut or thik threb. Miss Becky McCoy."

Mason was annoyed at being awakened by gunfire and was angry at himself for unwittingly allowing a girl with a pistol to sleep in his barn. Her crude spelling was a reflection of her lack of effort and poor parenting. What kind of parents allowed a twelve-year-old girl to carry a gun and skip spelling lessons for a "social graces" class? And Miss Becky McCoy had the nerve of a Gila monster if she thought he would allow her to birth a foal.

"It's an odd list, Pa, but I'll fetch the water, shirt, and knife, if you gather the carrots, whiskey, cake pan, and sewing stuff. There's Vaseline and rags in the barn. Meet ya out there." Cody shot to the kitchen, grabbed their stew pot, and started pumping water into it.

"Hang it all! This is crazy!" Despite his vexation, Mason darted past to fetch their needles and thread from the bedroom. From there, he heard Cody's reply.

"But Pa, Miss Becky is *real* good with horses. And if Bella Dama needs help—"

"Then we need a vet."

When Mason and Cody entered the barn a few minutes later, their arms burdened with supplies, the pregnant mare, Bella Dama, was lying on her side in her stall. They could see that two of the foal's front legs had been born up to the cannon. Becky was tying colorful hair ribbons around Bella Dama's tail, wrapping it like a mummy. Before Mason or Cody could speak, Becky started giving orders.

"Mr. Campbell, soak the carrots in whiskey in the cake pan. Master Cody, I need another ribbon from my bag an' grab my rope twitch while yer at it, an' toss it to yer pa, an' mind ya, take care reachin' in, my pistol's still loaded. Next, cut the sleeves offa the shirt."

As they began obeying, Mason took a deep breath. "Miss Becky, what's the trouble? Front legs born is good."

"*Was* good, but there's been no progress the last several minutes, even though 'er contractions are strong. I 'spect the foal is sittin' like a dog, hind legs squattin'. We don't have much time to stretch 'im out an' get 'im out." She nodded her thanks to Cody for the ribbon and told him to wash and rinse the knife blade in the water. Then she finished wrapping the tail. Ready with that shirt?" Cody handed the now sleeveless shirt to her.

She was wearing a white, knee-length nightgown with sleeves tied at the elbows and a pretty pink rose decoration in the center of the neckline. Jeans and boots were visible below her knees. She turned away from the Campbells, pulled the gown over her head, and slipped the shirt on. When she had fastened most of the buttons, she turned around. "Okay, let's get 'er up. Gravity will help position the foal. Mr. Campbell, move to 'er head, an' put the supplies within yer reach. Once Bella Dama's standin', hold 'er by 'er halter an' feed 'er the carrots if'n she'll have 'em."

At Becky's nod, Mason clicked to the horse and pulled up on the lead to encourage her to rise. Bella Dama raised her head, and he repeated his actions, this time with Becky's added encouragement of a slap on the rump. The mare struggled to her feet.

"Can ya grab an' hold 'er tongue?"

Mason nodded yes, but he wasn't actually sure he could do it. He pushed at the back of her lips, and Bella Dama opened her mouth. He caught hold, but she jerked her head, and he lost his grip on the slippery tongue.

As he tried again, Becky explained the purpose. "Stops contractions. Don't want 'er pushin' the opposite direction as me."

"I've got her tongue."

"Good. Now, Cody, I need a crate or somethin' to stand on."

The boy leapt into action and returned shortly with a wooden box, which he placed behind the horse.

"Okay. Goop me up."

Cody dipped his fingers into the Vaseline and began spreading it over Becky's arms.

"Be gen'rous."

After her arms were glistening with lubricant, she eased them around the foal's legs and into the mare. "Yep, he's sittin'." She grasped the foal's front legs just above the knees and pushed them back inside his mother. Then she explained that she was cycling the legs, hoping he would kick his hind legs in response, straightening them. "He's gonna need more room. Cody, knife."

"You want me to do it?"

"No, I got it."

"You've done this before?"

"Once."

Mason nodded his go ahead. That was once more than he had done.

Becky removed her arms from the mare and wiped her hands on the shirt she was wearing. "Let go 'er tongue, Mr. Campbell, an' put the twitch on 'er nose. Take care not to catch yer pinky in it. She's not goin' to like what I do, so hold 'er head tight." Becky turned to Cody. "If'n yer blood shy, now's a good time to turn away, but be ready with a rag. And stand clear—she may kick." When the twitch was secure and Mason had stabilized Bella Dama's head, Becky made a quick incision. Cody pressed a rag to it to absorb some of the blood. Becky reinserted her arms and when she felt a contraction, she cycled the foal's legs until he kicked good and hard. With the extra space secured by the episiotomy, the front legs reappeared, quickly followed by the foal's head. Becky again removed her arms, and she let nature take its course. Within a few minutes, the shoulders were born. "Master Cody, ease the foal down to the ground to a soft landin'. Then clean the mucous from his nostrils an' from in his mouth. I'm gonna need that needle threaded."

They were still awaiting the final push. "I'll do it, Miss Becky." Cody rushed the needle to her, stabbing it through her shirt for safekeeping until she was ready. "Here he comes." Cody helped the foal to the floor.

Miss Becky washed the mare's hindquarters with the soapy water and began to quickly sew the incision she had made, while Mason kept the mare as still as possible. "How's the baby, Master Cody?"

"Not movin'!"

"Rub 'im vig'rously with a rag."

"Still not movin'!"

"Slap 'im on the rump."

"Nothing."

"Keep trying, son. You're doing fine."

"Master Cody, blow into his nostrils, then put yer hands on his heart an' push hard to the beats o' my singin'." She began singing a song, emphasizing the downbeats with a nod of her head.

"Okay, release the twitch." Becky sank down next to Cody and the foal, and Mason eased his way past the mare and stood beside them. "Come on, baby." Becky placed her hands over Cody's and helped him push. "Keep goin' a little longer, Cody."

"It's no use, he's dead." Cody rose and walked out of the stall, making more room for Becky to examine the foal. She placed her ear to his heart.

"You did it, Cody! He's alive! I can feel his heart beatin'. He jus' needs time to rest a bit."

"Well done, son! Well done, Miss Becky! I can hardly believe we did it."

"Whiskey!"

Mason handed the bottle to Becky. He didn't know why she wanted it, but she obviously knew what she was doing. "Tradition is one swig fer a live mom an' baby; two swigs if'n only one makes it; an' three if'n they both die." She raised the bottle. "To a one-swig success!" Then to Mason's horror, she took a mouthful of whiskey, swallowed it, and proceeded to pass the bottle to Cody.

"Pa?"

"Uh . . . This is a *very* special occasion. If you want, just this once, you can have a *nip*."

So Cody did.

Mason stifled a laugh when he saw Cody scrunch his face from the burn. Cody's reaction to the alcohol assured him that his son hadn't been sneaking drinks. After taking his nip, Cody passed the bottle to his father, who took a big swig. Meanwhile, Becky had wormed her way to Bella Dama's head and was lavishing affection on her, petting her and telling her what a good girl she had been and what a beautiful boy she had produced. She kissed the horse on her forehead before slipping past Mason and out of the stall. She looked a mess.

"You'll wanna burn this shirt when I'm outta it. Papa says I tend to burn through clothes right fast." She seemed surprised when the Campbells laughed. "Well, I'm gonna wash up. You'll find me sleepin' in the house when yer done cleanin' up out here. I've been up all night walkin' an' talkin' to Bella Dama so the foal would turn, an' I'm plumb tuckered out. If'n the colt isn't on his feet in an hour, wake me, an' the same if'n Bella Dama doesn't pass the afterbirth. An' jus' so's ya know, the other time I did this procedure was a three-swigger. Near 'bout broke my heart. I still cry when I think on it. Well, cowboys, it's been a real pleasure." And as Becky walked through the barn, Mason noticed that all his other horses trotted over to their stall gates and whinnied at their apparent pleasure of seeing her.

"She's sure somethin', Pa."

"Sure is."

*   *   *

Becky was scrunched up on one of the chairs by the fireplace, completely buried under a blanket.

"Good mornin', Miss Becky, and happy birthday!"

"Ugh. Is it really mornin'?"

~ 56 ~

Cody chuckled, which appeared to prompt Becky to come alive. She stuck her head out from under the covers. "Somethin' smells good."

"Burnt bacon?" came Mason's voice from the kitchen where he was cooking.

"Coffee!"

"It's ready when you are." He poured her a full cup. He hadn't properly thanked her for saving his horses, and he decided she could have pretty much anything she wanted for last night's services. *Services*. More of the puzzle pieces were fitting together. Boy, would he have a story to tell Tom. He placed the cup on the small table closest to her. "Happy birthday, Miss Becky!" If she heard him, she ignored him, just as she had ignored Cody's greeting, but Mason wasn't surprised that her mind was focused elsewhere.

"Mare an' foal doin' okay?"

"Yep."

"Then it *is* a good mornin'. Master Cody, think ya could find some clothes fer me?"

"Got 'em right here." He set them on her chair and turned around to give her some privacy. "Hurry and dress. Yer smashed egg is on the table." Then he added, "I'm tryin' a smashed egg, too."

When they were seated and eating, Mason mentioned that Doc Prescott had come by. The vet had been impressed with her knowledge and skill, not only regarding Bella Dama but also Star's sprain and Raven's thrush. He had said he couldn't have done better himself.

"I heard 'im ride up an' out. Wasn't here long."

"He has calls to make at outlying ranches this morning and wanted to be back in town by noon." Mason took a swallow of coffee before showing his hand: "He knew of you, Miss Becky. He said you've been written up in *American Veterinary Review.* Your folks own the finest horse breeding farm east of the Mississippi. Your papa and older brothers have all manner of horse knowledge, but you're known as the family 'horse whisperer.' The article said you aren't much for the three Rs or social graces, but you have extraordinary other abilities."

Becky blushed a deep red, her skin almost matching the color of her disheveled hair. "That so?"

Mason was confused and disappointed. Why was she blushing this time? Embarrassment about her family's wealth? Embarrassment about the ridiculous "horse whisperer" label? He was hoping Becky would use this opportunity to acknowledge the information that the veterinarian had revealed about her family. Then it occurred to him that she might not have been aware of the article, and even if she had been, her inadequate reading skills might have prevented her from deciphering its contents. He agreed with

Doc Prescott that no one could converse with horses, but like the doc, he was curious just the same.

"That's not all, Miss Becky." Cody finished eating his last bite of egg and set his fork down on his plate. "He's offerin' ya work as his assistant if you're goin' to be stayin' in Leanin' Rock!"

The excitement in his voice told Mason that Cody clearly hoped she would be staying.

"Even if you're not stayin', you're invited to work with him tomorrow mornin'."

Becky responded impassively with another "That so?" Then she changed the subject. "I heard John ride up, too."

"Did ya get *any* sleep, Miss Becky?"

She shrugged toward Cody and then extended her cup toward Mason for a refill. He complied with her request without hesitation. Becky crunched off a bite of burnt bacon and appeared to relish it, but rather than finish the rasher, she dipped it into her brew. A brittle piece of the strip broke off and fell into her cup. She fished it out with her spoon and swallowed it like she was eating soup. "Bacon's perfect, Mr. Campbell." After a brief pause, she spoke again. "Well, what did John want?"

She was looking less sunburnt by then and seemed to Mason to be waking up. He was pleased by her compliment, though it didn't take any skill to burn bacon. Her simple praise reminded him that she wasn't completely lacking social graces. Best he answer quickly or be accused of having poor social graces himself. "Ah, well, John looked over your work from last night and said he was proud of you. Then he said in honor of your birthday, your folks would be arriving tomorrow on the afternoon stage. Your mama isn't coming because she's 'preggers' again, but your godmother has come all the way from Paris and expects to see you all gussied up and wearing that . . . uh . . . faux pas item. Your papa sent birthday money to you so you could buy some clothes." Mason reached into his shirt pocket and pulled out fifty dollars in bills and coins.

Cody's eyes popped open like a great horned owl's. "Great bonfires! That's enough money to buy a horse and a saddle."

"Son! That's a faux pas for sure."

"Sorry, Pa." Cody stuffed a biscuit into his mouth as if to plug it.

"You're to buy yourself a party dress and some travel clothes. The party is tomorrow night, and the whole town is invited. And expect to do some entertaining." As he handed the money over to her, he noticed that she looked distressed. "And save some of this money. John invited us to supper at the Leaning Rock Café tonight at five o'clock and said you're buying. But I'd like to include Miss Elizabeth and Sheriff Claiborne if you cotton to the idea. I'll cover them. And one last thing, you're to meet with your brother at the boarding house today at 12:15."

"You all right, Miss Becky?"

She looked terrified, as though a momma grizzly had appeared out of nowhere and was running straight toward her. Tears had welled up in her eyes. She used her right hand to pinch her tear ducts closed, but some water leaked around the dam and down her cheeks. "Not Godmother! He was funnin', right? Tell me John was jus' funnin'." She picked up her napkin from her plate and covered her face.

"Don't cry, Miss Becky! Please don't cry!" Cody reached out and patted her left hand.

Mason didn't know what to say. As far as he knew, all the news and instructions John had dealt out were from the top of the deck. If her brother was dirty-dealing Becky, Mason had missed his sleight of hand. John had seemed to be a handsome, well dressed, articulate young man who had come by to escort his sister to town. When he learned that Becky was asleep after a long night, he had agreed that Mason could drive her and the bicycle into town, so long as she was there by noon. There was nothing to indicate duplicity, nor could Mason understand what about her godmother would bring Becky to tears. Her emotions were a mystery to Mason, and because it didn't take much to prime Becky's pump, maybe her brother liked to push her until her pipes burst. "I don't know, Miss Becky. I just don't know—but I mean to find out."

Becky lowered the napkin and sniffled. "Sorry. I . . . I . . . jus' sorry." She wiped her nose on the napkin and let out a big sigh.

"You don't have to explain, Miss Becky. Pa always says when you fall off yer horse, just get right back up. It's nothin' to be ashamed of." He patted her hand again.

Cody's words had the desired effect. Becky sat up straight, blew her nose, and moved on. She slid some bills across the table toward Mason. "I'd be obliged if'n you'd pocket this fer supper."

Mason took the money and agreed to mind it for her.

"Miss Becky, we owe you a debt of gratitude and some money for birthing the foal last night. I know you just received a nice birthday gift, but here's ten dollars more from us. You earned it." He placed two coins in front of her.

"Thank ya kindly, but Papa doesn't 'low me to accept money." She pushed the coins back to Mason.

"Miss Becky, could ya accept a gift?"

She looked at Cody, and for the first time that day she smiled. "Shorely."

Mason also smiled. He was proud of his son for finding a satisfactory solution.

"What would ya like?"

"New hair ribbons would be welcome . . ."

Her hair looked like a fluff ball around her face, and Mason silently agreed that ribbons were a good choice, but he also recalled last night's use for them and wondered if new ones would ever grace her hair. He had burned the old ones along with Cody's shirt, and Mason smiled again as he recalled her comment about burning through clothes.

Her voice had trailed off, as though she were trying to think of more ideas, and then she did. "I'm plumb outta cat gut, an' I broke my last needle a couple days back."

"Anything a bit more personal?"

"Well, in actual fact . . ."

"What is it, Miss Becky? What would ya like?"

"A good soak. Do ya'll mind? I saw yer tub out back."

"That we can do. Cody, I'll bring the tub into the house. You start hauling water."

"Yes, sir."

"I don't suppose ya have any bath oils?"

Cody looked questioningly at his pa. Mason doubted that his son even knew what they were. He shook his head no. "Sorry." Even when Emma was alive, they had not owned such things. So the Campbells paid their bill with the simple gift of a bath.

*   *   *

After Mason finished washing and drying the dishes and Becky finished her bath, the group strode up to the barn to feed the stock and to fetch the bicycle for Cody's lesson. The horses were extraordinarily vocal when the people walked in: neighing, whinnying, and snorting. They trotted over to their stall gates and fussed.

"Ever seen anything like it, Pa? Eerie, isn't it? Like wolves howlin' on a moonless night. Every time Miss Becky enters, all seven horses come a runnin' like girls to the school bell—and just as chatter-y."

While Mason and Cody loaded hay into the troughs and doled out grain, Becky greeted each horse. She snuggled their necks, rubbed their jaws, and blew breath into their nostrils, all the while speaking softly to them in a whisper. When they arrived at Bella Dama's stall, the foal nickered and rose on wobbly legs to meet his visitors. Becky entered the stall. She spoke with him and gave him a quick once-over. Bella Dama stood facing away from Becky. Becky approached her from behind and examined her wound, speaking to her as she did. Then she walked around to the front of the mare and gripped Bella Dama's jaws between her hands while she whispered something to her face. Mason caught "beautiful lady," but the rest was too muffled for him to understand. Bella Dama nickered, as if in reply. Then Becky made her way around the stall, poking at soiled straw, until she circled round back to the gate, which she exited.

"She's looking good, thanks to you." Mason expected Becky would acknowledge the compliment, but she acted distracted, as though she hadn't heard it.

"When's the last time ya cleaned the stall, Master Cody?"

"Well, uh . . ."

"It looks fine, Miss Becky. Cody can't be out here cleaning it every hour."

"Middle o' the night?"

Cody nodded yes.

"An' 'er water?"

Mason was becoming annoyed that Becky was nitpicking about the conditions of the stall. "No need to change it now. It's still full and clean."

"She's developin' a bladder infection. It's a common complication."

"What? Doc Prescott didn't say anything about that. Neither did your brother. They said she was fine."

"She could o' been, but she isn't now. Here's what ya gotta do: I'll give ya a powder from in my bag. Mix a spoonful into 'er grain fer seven days. An' bring the stallion over from his quarters. Put 'im in the stall next to 'ers fer two hours, no longer, both mornin' an' afternoon. We should start now." She headed toward her carpetbag, and Cody headed toward the barn door.

Mason wasn't at all comfortable with this new diagnosis or treatment, but Doc Prescott had given her high praise. What harm was there in humoring her? "Hold up, there, son. I'll fetch Don Juan. You know how spirited he is."

"Pa, you should see. He calms right down for Miss Becky. He's as mellow as an old milk cow."

"I'd like to see that. Let's all go."

When Becky returned to the stall with a canister of powder, Cody was speaking. "I don't doubt Miss Becky, Pa. All I'm sayin' is what she learns from whisperin' to horses is downright spooky." He turned to her. "Come on, Spooky, we're all goin' to fetch Don Juan." Cody reached for Miss Becky's hand.

As quick as the words were out of Cody's mouth, Becky slugged him in the upper left arm and ran down the barn aisle. As she whizzed by, the horses reacted as if there were a fire in the barn and they were desperate to escape: stomping, throwing themselves on the gates and walls, screaming in fear. Mason could scarcely believe his eyes. His initial reaction was to grab Cody's upraised right arm, but he quickly released it.

"Ye-ow, that smarted! Bet it bruises." Cody rubbed his fingers back and forth over the spot.

"I thought you were going to punch her back. Never, *ever*, hit a girl, Cody."

"I know. I *know*, Pa. I just reacted without thinkin'."

The cacophony from the horses was still raging. "I'll settle the horses. You go after Miss Becky."

"What should I say, Pa?"

Females were such a mystery, and this one was more so than most. "I don't know. Try apologizing."

"She's the one that sneak-punched *me*."

"Just do it!" It wasn't like Mason to yell at his son, and he immediately regretted it, but it did push Cody to action. Cody ran down the path between the stalls and out of the barn into the daylight.

*   *   *

Cody found Becky rocking wildly in the rocking chair on the porch, Shep at her side. Her face was red hot, and tears were pouring down it as she sobbed. He chose the chair next to her and sat down. "I'm sorry, Miss Becky. I'm real, real sorry."

After a while, she stopped pushing off with her feet and rocked the chair with her weight and momentum. When her tears subsided and she began to sniffle, Cody untied the bandana from around his neck and placed it in her lap. She picked it up, wiped her face, and blew her nose, and then she kept her eyes glued to it as she fingered it in her lap.

"Horses okay?"

"I think so."

"Good. I'll check on 'em in a bit. Listen, Master Cody, only one person is 'lowed to call me Spooky, an' *yer* not *it!*"

"Sure. I didn't mean nothin' by it. John said it was yer nickname—everybody back home calls ya Spook or Spooky."

"Grrr. He was funnin' with ya, hopin' you'd say it, an' ya did. He just wanted to rile me, an' it worked."

"Sorry, Miss Becky. I didn't know. I didn't suspect he's mean."

Becky began another sentence, but her first word was interrupted by an unrestrained, loud hiccup. Cody found it funny and broke into laughter. Becky looked appalled at first, but she quickly joined in. "Dang it. This always—hic—happens after a—hic—hard cry—hic."

"Hold yer breath while I fetch some water from the well." Before she could answer, Cody ran off. When he returned a minute or two later with a bucket and ladle, Becky was still holding her breath. He assumed she hadn't held it all that time, but she was full of surprises, and he wasn't sure.

"Ya can let it out now. Here, drink this."

She blew out her mouthful of stale air with a whoosh, sucked in some replacement air, and then gulped a few swallows of the cool liquid from the ladle.

"I gotta warn ya—hic—after I'm over 'em, I always belch. I don't mean to be rude, but I can't control it."

"Want to have a belchin' contest?"

"Naw, no point. I always—hic—lose to my brothers."

Her crying jag had passed, and Becky seemed better. She used the rest of the water to rinse her face.

"Ready to go check on the horses?"

"Not yet. I wanna splain somethin' to ya first."

"Sure." She was looking down again, fiddling with his bandana. "Uh, Miss Becky, when Pa wants to explain somethin', he likes me to look him in the eyes. By seein' my face, he can tell if I understand or not."

"Sorry. I ferget, 'cause I don't hafta look at horses in the eyes to know if'n they understand me, an' I talk to horses more than people."

"Hm. That's real interestin'."

Becky adjusted her position and lifted her chin to look him square in the face before continuing: "Yer real good at social graces, Master Cody, so's I think you'll understand what I wanna tell ya. Have ya got a boy at school all the kids make fun o', call 'im a nickname like Fatso or Dim Tim or such?"

"As a matter of fact, a bully named *Gordo*. It means *fat* in Spanish. He's my age but much bigger, and he's already sproutin' a few lip hairs. Why?"

"Well, if'n ya call a person by a name long enough, ever'body sees 'em fer that one thing."

Cody scrunched his eyebrows and pursed his lips, trying to follow her meaning.

"Maybe he's fat, but maybe he's also the clev'rest kid in the class or the best artist or musician. Maybe if'n ya called him by his real name he'd be nicer to ya, an' ya could find out if'n he has any good qualities.

"Folks have been callin' me Spooky my whole life. Maybe I seem spooky, but there's more to me. Ya saw that all the horses 'ceptin' Bella Dama greeted me with joy in their hearts. Either she was feelin' poorly or she was riled with me fer the pain I caused 'er. Her foal wet the straw in a few places; there were no puddles big enough or smelly enough to be from Bella Dama. That means she's not passin' water. When an animal gets a bladder infection, it hurts to pass water, so's they try to avoid it. That means they stop drinkin'. Bella Dama had stopped drinkin' water. To get rid o' the infection, ya hafta wash it outta the bladder. Since ya can't make a horse drink, ya gotta make it *wanna* drink, make it thirsty. Puttin' the stallion next to 'er will make 'er nervous, but it could make 'er too nervous, so's he can only stay a couple hours. Bein' nervous will make 'er thirsty. After Don Juan is back in his stall, she'll drink. I guarantee it. The powder has some salt, which will also make 'er thirsty, but mostly it has dried cranberries. Vets aren't sure why they work, but the theory is that what makes 'em tart also keeps the infection from stickin' to the linin' of the bladder. The powder keeps the infection in the liquid in the bladder 'til it leaves the body. When she passes the liquid, the infection will be washed out." Becky paused to wipe her nose. "See, there's nothin' spooky 'bout it. It's science an' knowledge an' experience."

Just then, she belched a loud forceful *braap*.

"Good golly!"

"Scuse me, but I did warn ya. Leastways, I feel better now."

"That's fine, real fine. But just so ya understand, I wasn't commentin' on yer burp; I was exclaimin' about yer explanation."

"Oh. Do ya have any questions?"

"Only one." Cody rubbed his bruise. "You pack quite a wallop! Where'd ya learn to slug like that?" When he laughed, she joined in.

"I meant respectin' the infection, but since ya asked, my brothers can be bothersome, so's I've learnt some ways to get 'em to leave me alone. Master Cody, I don't go to a reg'lar school. I'm not good at readin' an' writin', an' I'm not good with social graces. When I get riled up, sometimes I hurt people, an' I'm truly sorry I hurt ya. I hafta be careful, 'cause horses react to my emotions. *That*, I've got no science explanation fer—yet."

"All folks have both good qualities and bad, Miss Becky. Ya may not be good at those things ya said, but you're real good with science and horses. I'm bettin' someday, you'll have yer answer."

"Thanks, an' speakin' o' horses, let's go finish with 'em so's we can ride the bicycle an' get to town."

They strode together up to the barn with a new understanding.

*   *   *

Mason looked up from his work. He knew Becky had entered the barn because once again the horses reacted to her presence, calling out to her. He watched as she walked to the cot, sat down cross-legged on it, and closed her eyes. She breathed slowly and deeply, and a calm demeanor came over her face. As it did so, a calm also came over the horses. Shortly thereafter, Becky rose and hurried over to Mason and Cody, who were standing by the stall next to Bella Dama's, now containing Don Juan. Bella Dama was acting skittish, maneuvering around her stall nervously, but taking care to dodge her foal. Mason saw Cody wink at Becky and wondered what that was about, but he didn't ask, and he thought it best to pretend the previous scene had never occurred. He would act normal and wait until he was alone with Cody to ask what had transpired on the porch.

All the horses were now fed, and it was time to start harnessing the team to the buckboard that would take them to town. The big sorrels that comprised the team were housed in neighboring stalls, and the proven broodmare, Stella, occupied the stall at the end of their row. Becky went over to talk to her while Mason and Cody each caught a sorrel and took it outside to be harnessed. When Cody returned, Becky was packing her bag.

"Pa said now is a good time to try out yer bicycle."

Becky's face lit up like lamps at dusk. "Fun!" She snatched the contraption by the handlebars and began rolling it toward the barn door. "Have ya ever been throwed?"

"Sure."

"Well, this could throw ya, too, but you'll be closer to the ground when ya take the fall. There's no reins, so's the only way to stop is to drag yer feet or topple. I'll coast down the hill. Ya won't be wantin' to start on an incline."

When they were both on flat ground, Becky instructed Cody to remove his boots because it was easier to pedal without them. She held the bicycle until he found his balance and ran holding on behind as he learned to use his weight to stay upright. Once he could ride in a straight path without tumbling, he progressed to turns. Within fifteen minutes, the bicycle was an extension of his body and fully under his control. The children's laughter and exhilaration as they took turns riding was interrupted by Mason, who had finished harnessing the team.

"Okay, you two, it's time to load the bicycle. Miss Becky, fetch your bag. Cody, socks don't grow on yuccas. You'll have to darn those yourself or use your allowance to purchase new ones."

"Sure, Pa."

The look of pure joy on Cody's face told Mason that his son thought the ride was worth the price he would have to pay, and he admitted to himself that all work and no fun didn't make for a satisfactory life. If he'd been shorter, he might have tried riding the bicycle himself.

Cody headed toward the house, but instead of going directly to the barn, Miss Becky moved to the front of the buckboard and conversed with the horses while petting them and playing with their bangs. By now Mason reluctantly accepted her uncanny skill and abilities. He felt a bit foolish, but he decided to be prudent.

"Are they okay, Miss Becky?"

She nodded her head. "Shorely."

That was a relief. He gave one of them a pat on the rump as he passed by with Becky on the way to the barn.

"It's jus' that . . ."

Mason cringed inside, hoping she wasn't going to spring bad news on him. "It's just *what*, Miss Becky?"

She looked at him sheepishly. "Well, they want *me* to drive."

Mason gazed at her in disbelief. She seemed serious. She wasn't cracking a smile or holding back a laugh as far as he could tell, but he found her difficult to read, both now and in general. She was certainly old enough at thirteen to drive, but it was hard—

maybe even ridiculous—to believe that a horse could care who drove him. He made his decision. "All right, and that being the case, I believe I'll ride Raven into town. You and Cody can take the buckboard."

He and Becky hustled the rest of the way to the barn: she, to collect her bag and say goodbye to the horses; he, to move the stallion back to his stall and to move Star into the corral for a change of scenery. Cody was in the house changing his socks and counting his money.

When they were ready to leave, Cody climbed on board the rig and offered a hand up to Becky, but she had already begun clambering aboard of her own accord. Rather unexpectedly to Mason, she had chosen to wear boy clothes and her outrageous hat. He had thought she would want to dress up for a visit to town, but when he had suggested she reconsider her outfit, she had replied that she would "dress proper" for their supper that evening. He couldn't help but notice, however, that she was presently wearing the dangly earrings he'd seen the previous night.

Cody passed the reins to Becky. Mason had given him stern instructions to make sure they arrived in town safely. As an added reminder, he reiterated that he would be following a few minutes behind them. Raven was saddled and waiting; Mason wanted to don his gun belt before leaving. Although he wore a single handgun holstered on his left side, he could shoot equally well with either hand, and he was well known for his firing speed and accuracy. The citizens of Leaning Rock respected his skill and temperament. He didn't show off, and he prided himself in using a gun as a last resort to solving a problem. When Tom needed deputies, Mason was the first in line to volunteer. He had killed some outlaws over the years: cattle rustlers, horse thieves, and a bank robber, but he had more often used his pistol for killing rattlers and coyotes and for putting sick or injured animals down. He rarely wore a gun at home, but he always wore one when out.

"Gidd'up, boys!" The sorrels leapt into action as Becky slapped the reins down, and she and Cody were on their way.

Chapter 4

It was midmorning, and the August sun was already beating down on them, but it was of no consequence to the young'uns, as they drove the forty-five minutes from the ranch into Leaning Rock. They passed their time in easy conversation. Becky asked Cody about his ma and learned that she and his younger sister, Caroline, had died in a twister. Cody asked about Becky's godmother, and Becky shared that she had never actually met the woman. She was a rich, old relative from her papa's side. Becky's fear of the woman stemmed from years of falsehood.

"She thinks I'm a prissy, high-societal girl, so's every birthday she sends me unwearable, frilly fashions. She doesn't know I'm deficient at writin', 'cause when I hafta write 'er, I get our cook's girl to scribe it fer me. I tell 'er half-lies, like I play piano an' I go to a special school where I'm learnin' social graces, but she doesn't know the real me. She invited me to visit 'er this summer with brother John as a proper escort, but I begged Papa an' Mama not to make me go to Paris, to lemme learn 'bout my own country afore sendin' me off to a foreign one. My godmother jus' *can't* learn the truth, plus I'm a-scared o' the ocean."

Cody patted Becky's knee. He felt sorry for her. She had a specialness that he felt overrode her shortcomings. If he could see it, why couldn't others, or more importantly, why couldn't she? But he couldn't say that to her, so he responded to the noncontroversial part of her statement.

"I've never seen the ocean, but I'd like to."

"Seein' it is like seein' the Texas prairie, 'ceptin' one's waves o' water, an' t' other's waves o' grass. They both go on as far as yer eyes can see."

While Cody took a moment to absorb the comparison, Becky apparently contemplated her previous analysis.

"Mayhap it's not the ocean I'm a-scared o'. Maybe it's drownin'. I can't swim—another o' my deficiencies."

"Ya can't? Well, I could teach ya right quick tomorrow. There's a spring near here where all the townies come to cool off, and there's a rope swing and everything!"

"I reckon not, but thanks fer the offerin'."

They heard the clip-clop of a horse approaching from behind and looked to see Mason riding up on Raven.

"Everything all right?"

"Sure, Pa."

"Then I'll see you in town. Check in with me at the sheriff's office when you arrive." Raven whinnied a greeting as they passed, drowning out Cody's affirmative reply.

When Mason was out of earshot, Cody followed up on Becky's godmother dilemma. "I don't think yer godmother would make the trip here. She sounds too old and prim to make the crossin'."

"I'm o' the same mind. I've reasoned out that she can't be comin' here. I think John was jus' tryin' to torment me. We've been travelin' together all summer as a growin' up experience fer 'im afore he goes off to business school in California, an' a growin' up experience fer me afore I . . . well, anyways, we can get under each other's skin like chiggers, but I know he'd back me in a brawl. Sometimes he jus' can't help but act brotherly, an' by that, I mean spiteful."

Becky pulled back on the reins to slow the team as they went around a curve. As the road straightened, the team seemingly without instruction moved to the left to position the buckboard to avoid a pair of deep wagon wheel ruts.

"How come he left ya with us last night?"

"Mostly we've been campin' out, but he had some town business to attend to, an' I don't sleep well in towns. I was hopin' fer a quiet sleep in yer barn, but Bella Dama had other plans."

Cody laughed, remembering the events of the previous night. "I think Pa suspects ya gave Bella Dama somethin' to bring on her labor just so ya could win the bet."

Now Miss Becky laughed, but she didn't deny the accusation. Instead, she steered the conversation back to her present day's problems. "Master Cody, I'm a loner type, an' towns full o' folks scare me as much as drownin'. It might help if'n you'd describe Leanin' Rock."

So, Cody told her that the town was aptly named after a monolithic granite rock at its north end that looked like a giant had tried to push it over and gave up, leaving it pointing between one and two o'clock, if the spire were the hand of a pocket watch. He held up one arm with a bent elbow to indicate the amount of slant. Cody went on to say that the Indians had a legend about the rock, saying it was the remnant of a burning arrow shot during a heavenly war. They believed that when the arrow hit the earth, it had turned to stone.

Miss Becky did not seem interested in the history of the town's name. She apparently wanted to know about the town itself, so Cody described the main businesses on Main Street. On one side, there were Doc Prescott's veterinary practice, the bank, the Rustler's Stoop saloon, a gun shop, and Sam Hill's. On the other side were the blacksmith's with the stables behind it, the stagecoach station, the telegraph office, the sheriff's office, the medical doctor office, the boarding house and restaurant, a bakery, and the feedstore. The school was farther down on the far side of town, just past the church, which doubled for the town hall. The train depot was on Front Street, which ran perpendicular to Main Street, and the tracks ran behind it. Beyond the tracks was a barrio where Mexican laborers lived. About fifty families lived in town or at the surrounding ranches.

As they approached town, the road forked, and Cody pointed to the right. He explained that the road to the left led to the railroad depot and barrio. Instead of following his finger, Becky whoa-ed the horses to a full stop.

"Somethin' the matter?"

"I don't go into towns much. All the horses, well, ya know how they react—they all start talkin' to me at once."

"Ah." Cody recalled the horses' whinnying when Becky walked through the barn. "Ya need to greet 'em?"

"They'll likely be fidgety 'til I do."

"Okay, I'll drive, and we'll take it slowly." He took the reins and headed them toward Main Street.

The first structures Cody and Becky encountered were a pair of make-shift corrals that had been erected on the outskirts of town. Cody was familiar with them from previous years. He explained that the larger corral with the attached chute was for the horse being broke, and the second, smaller one was to be used as a holding area for the other horses awaiting their turns. The corrals were empty, but a big sign with red and blue lettering hung on the rails, saying "Contest at 12:30 today." Already, a dozen wagons and buggies surrounded the large corral, positioned like spokes on a wheel, and acting as reserved seats for spectators. Some of the vehicles had one horse rigged to them; others, two; and yet others, none, as the owners had presumably unharnessed them and were sheltering them somewhere nearby.

When Cody brought the buckboard within fifteen feet of the closest wagon, the first horse began to nicker. Within seconds, all dozen had joined in with greetings of their own. He drove the team to the left and into an empty area near the vehicles. Becky hopped down and climbed through the fence into the corral. She sat on the ground in the center of the ring and repeated her cross-legged calming technique from earlier that morning. As the horses began to settle, she arose and made the rounds, patting each one, blowing into their nostrils, and whispering things to them. She moved quickly and with purpose, and before long she had met them all and climbed back aboard. Cody turned the team back onto the road and drove on.

They passed the blacksmith shop on the right. Cody pointed out the large livery stable behind it and said the broncs would be transferred from there to the corrals just before the contest began. A heavyset wrangler was leaning against the building, smoking. His job was to discourage riffraff and looky-loos. Gazing ahead, still to the right, Cody and Becky could see Mason's horse tethered to the hitching post in front of Tom's office. A tightly strung banner hung on ropes between the sheriff's office and the saloon on the opposite side of the street, advertising the bronco-busting contest with a two-hundred-dollar prize for breaking El Diablo. The sign was festooned with swags of bunting, making the town appear festive.

Leaning Rock was abustle with activity. Multiple horses were tied at the hitching posts in front of the establishments, and wagons hogged the narrow street. Bonneted women were carrying packages wrapped in brown paper and string and holding the hands of small children sucking on or holding tightly to peppermint sticks. Cody assumed Miss Elizabeth was doling out the candy at Sam Hill's like she had the previous years. He hoped there was some left. Lively piano music was emanating from the saloon, and as they drove by, a cowboy came flying out through the swinging doors, barely missing the buckboard when he landed in the street with a thud.

Cody hurried the horses forward. "What now, Miss Becky, Sam Hill's for clothing?" The truth be known, he had no interest in shopping with Becky for clothing. He was simply eager to obtain a free peppermint stick.

"Lemme off here, an' I'll start workin' the horses. Try an' find a place to park by Sam Hill's, an' I'd be obliged if'n ya placed my bicycle outside the store so's I can keep an eye on it. Meet up with me at the doc's office. That it by the sheriff's?"

"Yes, that's Doc Ritter's. Are ya feelin' poorly?"

She looked poorly, he thought, like she was trying hard to maintain her composure. He imagined too many voices were talking to her at once. If she heard his question and answered, Cody missed it. She had hopped down from the seat in an instant and walked around to the back of the buckboard where her carpetbag lay. He saw her remove a purse from it before setting off down the street. Cody thought she looked a sight in trousers, a plaid shirt, her pink, ostrich-feathered hat, the sparkly, dangly earrings, and the newest addition on her wrist: an exquisite, framed, pink and purple beaded silk purse with kissing locks.

He clicked his tongue to start the horses moving and easily found a place to park the buckboard down the road in the field between Sam Hill's and the church. He leaned the bicycle against the store's front wall as requested, and then he crossed the road and continued down to the sheriff's, where he stuck his head in the door just long enough to wave to his pa.

The doctor's office was next door, and a high-backed bench stood conveniently in front of it under a window with drawn shades. Cody plunked himself down and waited, all the while watching the townsfolk and especially Becky, as she darted in and out among horses. After some time, she finished meeting all of the horses and arrived at the doc's.

"Okay if I go in with ya?"

"Shorely."

The doctor's wife and assistant, Margaret, a bespectacled, serious-looking, middle-aged woman with a beehive hairdo, opened the door to Becky's knock and invited the youngsters inside to the reception room. All the waiting chairs were empty, and the desk was piled high with stacks of journals and papers. A folded army cot leaned in one corner, presumably for overflow patients.

"Hello, Cody."

"Howdy, Mrs. Ritter. This is my friend Miss Becky McCoy. We'd like to see the doc."

"Hello, Becky." She had seen all manner of patients, but Mrs. Ritter didn't know what to make of this one.

"Nice to meet ya, ma'am."

Peculiar as she looked, at least the girl was polite. Mrs. Ritter addressed them both, inquiring into the nature of their visit.

Cody didn't know the answer, and Becky hesitated a second too long, so he nudged her. "Go on. Tell her."

"It's the inability to become preggers, ma'am."

The lenses in her specs magnified Mrs. Ritter's eyes to dollar size as she registered the words. The nurse turned her face to Cody and said he had some explaining to do. But at that moment, the doctor entered the room from a door that led deeper into the building.

"Howdy, Cody."

"Howdy, Doc Ritter. This is my friend Miss Becky McCoy." He motioned in her direction.

"How do you do, Miss Becky? Doc Prescott stopped in this morning and mentioned you to me. I'm very pleased to meet you." The doctor made no outward sign that he thought her manner of dress was unusual. He simply smiled and held out his hand for her to shake, which she did.

"Likewise, I'm shore."

Doc Ritter was a medium-tall man with a large belly. A fringe of gray hair fell from ear height downward, but his pate was bald and shiny. His cheeks dimpled when he smiled, and laugh lines surrounded his mouth and deep-set, sapphire-blue eyes. "Come through and tell me what I can do for you today."

Curious, Mrs. Ritter began following her husband, but he said he'd call for her if he needed assistance, so just Cody and Becky trailed the doctor down the hall and into an examination room. A wooden exam table topped with a leather cushion was pushed against the back wall. A glass-doored hutch stood on a chest of drawers against another wall. Visible behind its panes sat a collection of medicines. The chest's flat surface held a variety of bandages and instruments, including scissors, tweezers, and more specialized, less familiar, devices. There were two wooden chairs with wicker seats against the third wall. Above them hung a diagram of the innards of a human body.

The doctor offered the chairs to his patients. As Cody settled into his, Miss Becky snapped open the lock on her purse and pulled out a small glass vial. "Do ya have a microscope?"

"Yes, ma'am! I have a lab in the back. What have you here?"

"Vaginal mucus."

Doc Ritter glanced at Cody and saw no signs of uneasiness. Taking time to think, he crossed his arms, cocked his head slightly, squinted his eyes, and looked hard at Miss Becky. After a moment, he spoke. "Equine?"

"O' course."

He laughed, dimpling his face. "Of course." He accepted the vial from her. "And just what am I to look for?"

"It wouldn't be right fer me to tell ya. Jus' lemme know what ya find."

"Very well. Just tell me why you didn't ask Doc Prescott. He has a microscope."

"He's makin' rounds to ranches. Yer here."

"Fair enough. I'll get to it. I have to be at the bronco-busting contest at 12:30, but I should have some results for you afterward."

"Fine. By supper fer shore?"

"For sure." He smiled and nodded with his response. "That will be two bits. You can pay Mrs. Ritter. Now move on out. I have work to do." With that, the doctor shooed them through the threshold.

Mrs. Ritter was busy organizing the mess on the reception room desk, but she looked up from her work as Cody and Becky came through the hall door.

"Doc says we owe a quarter."

Becky unlatched her purse and started burrowing inside.

"I can make change if you need it."

"Never mind. Jus' bill Mr. Campbell." Becky snapped her purse shut with a flourish.

"I'm not sure about that. Cody, does your pa know about this office visit?"

"Uh . . . I reckon not—but go ahead and bill him. I'll vouch for it."

"You're agreeing to pay if he won't?"

"Shorely. Uh, I mean, yes, ma'am." Cody looked to Becky, but she did not seem offended by his slip. In fact, he wondered if she'd even been listening. She had wandered over to the door and had started to turn the knob to leave.

*   *   *

When they exited the doctor's office, Becky turned left, heading them toward the sheriff's.

"Miss Becky, Sam Hill's is the other direction and on the opposite side of the street."

"I know. I jus' wanna look at the wanted posters a minute." On the wall outside the sheriff's office hung a board for placing public announcements. The top section was reserved for criminal activity; the lower part held a few ads for real estate for sale, rooms for rent, and employment. The only job openings at the moment were for cowhands. "I gotta go in."

"Well, all right, but I already checked in with Pa."

"It won't take long." Before entering, Becky stopped to pat Raven and the other horse that was tied to the post in front of the sheriff's office.

The sheriff was seated behind his desk wearing a white shirt with a bola tie and his familiar black hat. The tie's turquoise ornament was an upside-down arrowhead, and the aglets on the cord were a shiny silver. The color of the metal contrasted with that of the brass badge pinned to the breast of his black leather vest. Mason sat in one of two chairs for visitors, his feet resting on the desk. He cradled a cup of coffee on his lap.

"Howdy, Miss Becky." Tom tipped his hat. "Cody." He nodded toward the boy.

They returned his greeting in unison.

"What are you two up to?"

Cody looked to Becky for an answer. She strode forward a few steps and unfastened the earrings from her lobes. "Well, sheriff, I'm thinkin' these aren't glass. The man in yer poster outside gave 'em to me. I reckon the rightful owner's gonna want 'em back." She placed them on his desk and turned to leave.

"Hold up there, miss."

Becky swung back around, and Mason removed his boots from the desk and sat upright.

"Big Bart Bennett gave the earrings to you?"

"Yes, sir."

"Why?"

"He believed in me."

Tom was at a loss. "I don't understand, Miss Becky."

"His horse had buckshot in his behind. I told 'im I could help. Big Bart believed in me. He liked the way I talked to his horse an' kep' 'im calm an' plucked the shot out fast an' painless. He tried to give me money fer my services, but Papa won't 'low it, so he gifted me the earrings."

The sheriff recognized that Becky's being small, female, and a child were to her disadvantage, and her wild hat and manner of dress added to her lack of credibility. Tom knew that he wouldn't have believed in her if he had encountered her in the same situation. The only reason he placed trust in her story now was that Mason had just finished sharing with him the morning events that had transpired at the ranch. In the back of his mind, he had thought Mason had fabricated the incredible tales just for amusement.

Tom ran his right thumb and forefinger down his mustache and around his mouth until they met in the middle of his chin. While he was thinking, Becky had moved toward the door. She seemed eager to leave, but Tom had more questions.

"When and where did you see him?"

Becky sighed. Then she took a deep breath before she answered. "Two days ago, 'bout twenny miles east o' the Campbells' ranch, headin' west toward Leanin' Rock."

"Where was your brother?"

"Oh, ya know 'bout 'im. Well, he was settin' up camp. I was havin' playtime, ridin' my bicycle when Big Bart came ridin' down the path, an' I knew his horse was hurtin'. Could I go now?"

Tom shook his head no, but before the sheriff could ask anything else, Mason joined the conversation. "Tom, didn't you say the Las Cruces stage was robbed by *three* bandits?"

"Yes, that's what the wire said. But Big Bart was the only one the stage driver could identify. The gang could have split up or had a falling out."

"There were two others with 'im."

Tom raised his eyebrows. "Well, why didn't you say so? What did the men look like?"

"Ya didn't ask, an' I can't rightly recollect."

"Try, Miss Becky. Were they tall or short, young or old, clean shaven or bearded?"

"I can't recollect! I'm not good with people!"

She probably meant "with faces," but Tom silently agreed that she was not good with people matters, social situations. He could hear the tension in her voice and didn't want to upset her further.

"All right, Miss Becky, but is there anything else you can tell us?"

"No, sir. Can I puleeze go now? I have business to attend to." Once again, she started toward the door.

The sheriff couldn't imagine what business she could possibly need to take care of, but he excused her, at least having gleaned some useful info to go on. Cody, however, put his hand on Becky's arm to signal her to wait.

"Miss Becky, what do ya remember about Big Bart's horse?"

"Well, nothin' partic'lar. He was a sweet gelding, big— maybe sixteen hands—a bay with a blaze, a stockin' on his left foreleg, an' socks on t' others. An' there was the buckshot, like I said."

Tom shook his head in disbelief and muttered under his breath just loud enough for Mason to hear, "Eight years at this job, and you'd expect by now I'd know the right questions to ask a witness." Then in his normal volume, he thanked Cody for his assistance. Cody nodded in response before Tom turned his attention back to Becky, who was rhythmically rotating the doorknob from side to side. "Miss Becky, what did the other horses look like?"

Clearly tired of questions, she was standing at the door like a schoolboy sentenced to stand in the corner. Not turning toward him this time, she spoke to the door, saying matter-of-factly: "They were quarter horse mares, half-sisters, same sire."

Tom, Mason, and Cody colluded behind her back, eyeing each other and shrugging with palms up, silently wondering how she could possibly know that.

"The younger one was high strung. She didn't like that the gelding was in pain."

"Uh . . . of course not. What color were they?"

"Beautiful grays. The older one was dappled; the younger, more salt-an'-peppery." Becky spun on her heels. "An' now I recollect there was initials engraved on 'er saddle!"

"That's fine, Miss Becky, *very* fine. What were the letters?"

Becky had been rolling along like a trundled hoop, but now she hesitated. Undeterred, the sheriff asked her to close her eyes and imagine them.

She turned back toward the door and complied, but once again she sounded frustrated when she replied. "I'm not good with letters!"

Since Becky's back was to the others, Mason took the opportunity to nod his head and mouth the words, "that's true" to Tom.

"That's all ri—"

"An M or a W an' a B or a D."

Mason queried Tom. "Matt Dade?"

"Could be, Mace. He rides with his cousin Roy Dade. They're young men, lean and clean shaven. Roy has a deep scar on his chin from where a bullet grazed him.

"I believe I'll mosey around town. Would you care to join me?" Tom rose from his chair, and Mason did likewise.

Cody held up a finger to the sheriff, indicating he should wait. "Miss Becky, are Big Bart's horse or the grays in town?"

She snorted and shook her head like she couldn't believe the question, but she answered anyway. "No. I would know if'n they were."

"I believe her, Sheriff."

Tom didn't know what to believe, but he thanked her for the information and said she would receive a reward if it led to the bandits' capture. Then he thanked her again for returning the earrings. "Miss Becky, I think you deserve something to replace your earrings." The sheriff offered her some of his own money to buy herself a new pair at Sam Hill's, but she declined with a refusal that made him hold his breath to keep from laughing: "Earrings are pretty, but they're jus' 'bout as useful as silk pantalettes."

Cody arranged to meet his pa at the bronc-bustin' corral at 12:30. Then he and Becky skedaddled toward Sam Hill's, and the men trailed behind them out into the sunshine.

Mason adjusted his hat to shade his eyes. "I told you she was good with horses."

"That you did, but I thought you were just 'horsing' around with me."

"Ha, ha. Aren't you the jolly wordsmith?"

Tom smiled at his friend. "She's unusual, Mace, but I like her, and Miss Elizabeth was right last night. It looks like Cody has taken a shine to her."

"Yes, I'd say he has. Let's leave it at that."

Respecting Mason's wishes, Tom headed out to look at horses and make his presence felt around town. Given Becky's adamance about the outlaws' horses not being in town, Mason left Tom to perform his sheriffing duties and sauntered over to the saloon to down a beer and register for the contest. A twenty-five-dollar entry fee gave each contender the chance to win thirty-five dollars per horse he broke, but the stallion was the big draw, at two hundred dollars. Townsfolk could get in on the action by placing bets on the riders, and truth be told, it was those potential winnings that attracted the entrants more than the prize money. Mason wouldn't bet on himself or others. For him, the contest wasn't about the money. It was a way to test his skills and prove his riding abilities, plus, although he would never admit it, showing off for the ladies had crossed his mind.

*   *   *

The boardwalks in front of the buildings were crowded with folks, so Cody and Becky opted to walk at the edge of the road, winding around horses and wagons. Becky touched each horse, either on the rump, down the neck, or between the nostrils. The horses nickered in apparent pleasure. As they neared Sam Hill's, Becky grabbed Cody's arm and pulled him toward her.

"Take care, that Appaloosa kicks."

Cody had no idea how she had determined that, but he believed her and heeded her warning. "Thanks."

They made a wide berth around the horse, and then Cody removed Becky's hand from his arm and held it in his own as they continued on their way. At one point they brazenly walked between two horses coming directly at them, causing their riders to have to veer around them. Becky abruptly dropped Cody's hand and reached her arms out, making her body like a "T" so she could touch both horses on their rumps as they passed. Then she took up Cody's hand again. The rough-looking riders were not amused, shouting at the "jackasses" to get out of the road. A little later, Becky directed Cody to squish between the gray mare and mule that were tied to Sam Hill's hitching post and then to duck under the post. Like before, Becky patted both animals on their way past. The windy path wasn't the path Cody would have chosen, but they were, at long last, where he wanted to be. A couple of his schoolmates were just inside the door: Gordo and Travis. The boys greeted Cody, and then Cody led Becky toward Miss Elizabeth, who was standing behind the counter. As they were walking, he could hear Gordo and Travis snickering and whispering, presumably about Becky. He paid them no mind.

Sam Hill's was a large store specializing in hardware, but with two stories, there was room for an eclectic assortment of items, including clothing, food, jewelry, medicines, and saddles. The store was owned by Sam Hill and his wife, Clara, but one day it would belong to Miss Elizabeth. Cody saw that she and several clerks were busily attending to customers' needs. When Miss Elizabeth looked up from writing in her ledger, she met eyes with Cody and Becky and motioned for them to come over. Cody led them through a maze of displays and customers. When they reached Miss Elizabeth, Cody tipped his hat to her in greeting. She responded by presenting two peppermint sticks. Cody thanked her kindly and wasted no time tasting his, but Becky stashed hers inside her purse after saying her thanks.

"Is your pa in town?"

"Yes, ma'am, Miss Elizabeth. He's likely in the saloon."

"Oh. I see." Cody heard the disappointment in her voice. He knew she was sweet on his pa, and he also knew that she didn't approve of the gambling and drinking that went on in the saloon.

"He's just signin' up for the contest." Elizabeth smiled at that news, and Cody was happy he had relieved her anxiety. He liked Miss Elizabeth and had secretly wondered what she would be like as a stepmother. He was particularly interested in her culinary skills. She sure had a way with pies. He shared some more information with her. "I'm meetin' Pa at 12:30, and Miss Becky is springin' for our supper tonight. You're invited with John McCoy—he's Miss Becky's brother—and Sheriff Claiborne for 5 o'clock at the café."

"Oh . . . I thought it would be only three of us. And Miss Becky, you're treating? That's foolishness! A young lady doesn't pay for grown folks' suppers."

"Mr. Campbell's plannin' on buyin' yers an' the sheriff's."

"Oh . . . well . . . that's all right then." Elizabeth raised one eyebrow, still wondering about the arrangement, but she didn't dwell on it. "Well, let's get down to business." She pulled the pantalettes out from a shelf behind the counter and held them up.

As she was explaining that she had unpicked the stitches in the waistband and resewn them using cotton thread, more snickering and giggling could be heard from the entrance to the store. "Would you like to try them on?"

"No, ma'am. Not now. Scuse me . . . uh, please."

Becky released Cody's hand and beelined toward Gordo, leaving Cody and Miss Elizabeth flummoxed at the counter. Elizabeth felt annoyed that Becky didn't appreciate her efforts enough to try on the pantalettes or to even thank her for her efforts. She silently berated Becky's social graces tutor.

Over at the store entrance, Gordo and Travis were in stitches. Gordo was leaning against an apple barrel, and Travis, a shorter, leaner, younger, and therefore more effeminate boy, was strutting, facing him, wearing a turkey feather in his hatband and swinging a drawstring purse by its cords. As Becky approached, embarrassment apparently overcame Travis, because he tossed the purse to Gordo and raced out of the building. Gordo, however, stood his ground, and Becky bellied up to the barrel to introduce herself.

"Howdy, my name is Miss Becky McCoy. What's yers?"

"Miguel Contreras."

"Well, I'm right pleased to meet ya, Master Miguel." She held out her hand, and when he shook it, he was surprised at the muscle in her grip and the strength of her arm pump. "I heard what you've been whisperin'."

"Ya did, huh?"

"Yep, I have 'specially good hearin', an' yer right: Master Cody's got a girlfriend. Have ya got any sisters, Master Miguel?"

"Sí, cuatro. That means four, Gringa."

"Are ya 'lowed to hit 'em or hurt 'em?"

"Course not. That would land me in the woodshed."

"Good. Then I'm speculatin' that so would hurtin' me." Becky grabbed Miguel by the forearm in a solid pinch. The more he struggled, the more pressure she applied.

"Ye-ouch! Lemme go!"

But she held tight. "Did ya see the bicycle out front?"

He nodded yes.

"Well, it's mine, an' in a bit, Master Cody's gonna ride it over to the schoolyard an' give young'uns a chance to try it. He'll let his pals ride fer free, but he'll charge others five cents. Are *you* his pal?"

"Sí! Yes, we're good amigos!"

"Then ya won't be whisperin' or laughin' or gossipin' 'bout 'im or me, will ya?"

"No, ma'am, Miss Becky!"

"It's been a pleasure to meet ya, Master Miguel. See ya 'round." She winked as she twisted Miguel's skin clockwise between her fingers. Then she released him from her hold.

Miguel rubbed his arm where she had bruised it.

"Uh, one other thing: that bay mare out front, she's yers?"

"Sure is. So what?"

"She's got worms."

*   *   *

While Miss Becky and Miguel were talking, Cody had informed Miss Elizabeth that Becky needed traveling clothes and a party dress and had the cash to pay for them. Elizabeth had set aside several choices, including accessories. When she returned, Becky said they all looked fine, and she would make a final decision later. She asked Miss Elizabeth to leave the items in a pile with her name on it. She then proclaimed that those apples in the barrel by the door looked scrumptious, and to Elizabeth's dismay, her only purchase was a large bagful of the fruit. As they left the store, Cody was also disappointed. He had hoped to look for a birthday gift for Becky while she was trying on clothes.

The pair stood by the bicycle in front of the store. "Where to next, Miss Becky?"

She tossed an apple to Cody and took one out of the bag for herself. "Do ya believe in me?"

"Of course!"

"Do ya trust me?"

"Sure." But he wasn't sure his voice sounded confident, and apparently, she wasn't either because she clarified.

"I mean with horses."

This was different. Of course, he trusted her with all things concerning horses. This time he answered with enthusiasm. "Well, sure!"

"Then I could use yer help."

"All right. Tell me what ya need."

"I need a distraction an' a disguise so's I can sneak into the stable to talk to the broncs."

Cody's face erupted into a wide grin as Becky explained her plan. He wasn't one to cause trouble, but initiating a little mischief was well within his moral bounds and, he felt, was generally expected of boys his age. Cody figured his pa might *act* angry if he learned of his shenanigans, and he most likely *would* learn of them, but inside, Pa would be laughing and remembering his own horseplay. Cody fancied Becky's plan, and he willingly agreed to participate. He removed his hat, whose dark brown felt perfectly matched the color of his eyes, and offered it to her. "I'm partial to it, so treat it nice."

She nodded that she would. Becky grasped the hat upside-down by its brim and placed her purse inside. Then she positioned the sack of apples on top of the inverted hat and supported the stack with her arms under the brim and her hands cradling the sack. Unless someone looked closely, only the bag would be visible. She made a stop at the buckboard to collect some supplies from her carpetbag, which she stuffed into her shirt, and then she began walking on the boardwalk toward the livery stables as Cody walked the bicycle into the middle of the street. When he was well positioned, he squatted down and pinched the tires. A crowd of children began gathering around him like a herd of cattle huddling in the cold, and he encouraged them to touch the bicycle and ask questions. When Miguel's nine-year-old sister, María, requested a demonstration, Cody mounted the bicycle and rode around his audience in a tight circle before speeding off down the street toward the livery. The enthusiasts cheered him and followed behind like he was the lead steer in a stampede. If he gained too much distance from them, he dragged his boots to slow his progress, plowing up dust.

Meanwhile, Miss Becky made a quick detour into the sheriff's office, which was unoccupied, hung her purse and conspicuous pink hat just inside the door on Tom's hat rack, and donned Cody's hat. Then she continued walking, and right when she passed the smithy, Cody came pedaling by with the congregation of curious, raucous kids surrounding him. In the commotion, Miss Becky joined the crowd. The livery stable was essentially a long barn with the length paralleling the road. It was owned by the blacksmith and was located directly behind his smaller blacksmith's shop. It had two entrances, one at each end of the building, both visible from the street. Cody turned left to approach the livery. A heavyset wrangler stood smoking, leaning against the door at the entrance closest to him. Cody whizzed by the man, who waved friendly-like and shouted encouragement. Then Cody steered the bicycle to circle the building counterclockwise with his entourage still in tow. When the herd of children emerged around the building, no one noticed that one of them was hanging back. Cody sped up and aimed for a spot near the wrangler. When he deemed himself close enough, he applied his boot brakes, and the mechanical beast came to a stop just inches from the wrangler, covering him with a cloud of dust. The children roared with laughter.

"Why you little cuss! Get this contraption away from me and away from here!" The wrangler tried to grab the bicycle, but Cody outmaneuvered him, dodging away. Then he took off with the wrangler and screaming children in hot pursuit.

It wasn't long before Cody had a substantial lead and the wrangler abandoned the chase, but Cody figured it was enough time for Miss Becky to have slipped inside the stables. He slowed his pace and gave the children time to catch up with him. Then he announced riding lessons down at the schoolyard. As the horde ran past the saloon, Cody saw his father outside, standing with his arms crossed, frowning at the scene.

"What in the name of— Whoa, son!"

"Can't stop. Runaway!" Cody continued pedaling down the center of the street all the way to the schoolyard.

By the time Mason arrived atop Raven, Cody had arranged the thrill-seekers in line by size. He had recruited Gordo to assist with the smallest children, helping them mount the bicycle and pushing them around for short rides. Gordo had wanted to charge the children, per Becky's threat, but so few were carrying coins that the plan had to be dropped. Cody appeased Gordo by offering him a longer ride time than the others. Several youngsters had already finished their turns and were sitting in a cluster talking excitedly about their experiences. The bigger children stood calmly awaiting their turns or cheering on their younger siblings. The girls wore their shoes, but the boots of the boys who were planning to pedal the bicycle stood empty in front of them with their shafts bent over limply like the ears of hound dogs. Mason anticipated a run on boys' socks at Sam Hill's. Miss Elizabeth would be happy for the sales. But aside from the possibility of some holey socks, Mason was impressed. His son had established control over the situation. He had organized a safe, equitable system for the children to gain some skills and have some fun. And most impressive was the peaceable atmosphere. There was no pushing, fighting, bickering, or bullying. Once Mason discerned that all was well, he was able to relax, and that's when he became suspicious. He rode up to his son and cut him out of the herd of children.

"Cody, where's Miss Becky?"

Cody pulled his pocket watch from his front pocket and glanced at the time: noon. "I'm unsure, Pa. It's a might early, but she may be with her brother by now."

Mason considered the answer. It sounded truthful, but he knew Cody well and felt he was holding back. Still, the girl wasn't his responsibility, and Cody was. "Have you eaten, son?"

"A little."

"Well, let's go grab some grub before the contest."

"You go, Pa. I want to make sure everyone gets a turn." He motioned to the line of waiting cyclists.

"Okay, Cody. Just one more question: Where is your birthday present?"

Cody reached up to touch his hat before remembering he wasn't wearing it. "Uh, I lent it to Miss Becky, Pa. She looked right good in it."

Mason almost retorted that anything would look better on her than her pink, feathered hat, but he held his tongue. He was still processing that his son would allow a girl to *touch*, let alone *borrow*, let alone *wear* his prized possession. He would be reluctant to allow Miss Elizabeth to borrow his own hat. That thought reminded him of his relationship with Elizabeth, something he wanted to avoid pondering. He nudged his heels into Raven's sides and turned back toward town. Raven had barely begun the turn when Mason changed his mind and reined the horse full circle. "Cody!"

"Yes, sir?"

Mason motioned with his head at the playground. "I'm proud of you." He saw Cody's face take on a glow like a freshly lit lantern wick.

"Thanks, Pa!"

Then Mason tipped his hat up higher on his forehead as a farewell salute and once again turned his horse toward town.

Chapter 5

By 12:25 that afternoon, a crowd had assembled near the bronco-busting corrals. The sun was shining high in the sky, and the air was heavy with humidity. Clouds floated in thick formations off in the distance, but if a storm was approaching, rain wouldn't fall until late afternoon. Families were sitting in their wagons, where they were assured unobstructed views of the action. Older boys and men were leaning or hanging on the bigger corral, including Mason and Cody. Most of the competitors had arrived and were standing in small groups, recounting previous contests they had participated in or observed and injuries they had sustained or seen others sustain. They were young and old, scruffy and well groomed, local men and outsiders, but they were more alike than dissimilar. They were all brave, confident, macho. They were competing for the monetary prize, but more importantly, they were there to prove their manhood.

Before long, Cecil "Buck" Pruitt, the contest organizer, and Sheriff Claiborne strutted over to the corrals. Buck, a burly man with fingers as thick as beefy cigars, passed through Leaning Rock annually. He was well liked and considered to be an honest horse trader.

John McCoy, looking older than his seventeen years, was the best dressed man in sight, decked out in a pleated, white, pearl-buttoned shirt with a band collar, contrasting black pants, boots, and hat, and silver belt buckle. He followed a short distance behind Buck and the sheriff. Miss Elizabeth Hill was even farther back. Her parents had already joined the audience, but she had lagged behind to hang the "closed" sign on the store door and to lock up.

As Buck and Tom reached their stations on an elevated platform near the junction of the corrals, John muscled in next to Mason and Cody at the larger corral. They exchanged howdys, and Cody asked him if Miss Becky had met up with him. She had, and she'd be along shortly. Miss Elizabeth arrived and squeezed in between Mason and Cody. She had overheard Cody's inquiry and mentioned that she had just seen Miss Becky down by the doctor's office. Cody strained his neck to look for her but couldn't see around or over the crowd. He considered going to find her, but he decided to give her a few more minutes. Then the event began.

"Howdy an' good afternoon, good folks of Leaning Rock an' visitors, an' thank y'all fer comin' out today. My name is Buck Pruitt, an' fer those who don't know me, I'm the owner of the broncs that'll be green-broke today. The sheriff here is the official judge of the contest. It's up to him to make sure the rules are followed, an' if there's any disputes, his word is law."

The sheriff waved, and the onlookers clapped and cheered in response. A heavyset drunkard with thick reddish-brown sideburns shouted out, "Ya sure that ain't my wife?" and the crowd roared with laughter.

When the noise died down, Buck continued his speech. "We got Doc Ritter an' Doc Prescott here to tend to any rider or horse that gets hurt." The two men climbed the last steps to the platform to join Buck and the sheriff, and once there, they waved to the audience, which again responded enthusiastically.

"Before my wranglers drive the first ten mustangs into the holdin' corral, I want to explain some things. The mustangs were part of a large wild herd roamin' east of here an' over to New Mexico Territory. Me an' my men rounded up the stallion an' nineteen mares. The horses need to be green broke so I can sell 'em. Green broke means they walk easy under saddle with a cowboy on their back, so stayin' on eight seconds ain't the goal. We'll break half today an' half tomorrow. This is a freestyle competition, meanin' there's no restriction on how the bronc buster does the job or holds on. If a horse ain't broke in thirty minutes, we'll move on to the next one. The order of the riders is the order they signed up. Fifteen of the bravest an' best bronc riders in the territory are in line. Let's show 'em our appreciation."

The contestants doffed their hats and waved to their wives or girls or friends, who clapped and yelled encouragement. Miss

Elizabeth grasped Mason's hand and gave it a squeeze. "Good luck, and don't do anything foolish. You don't need to impress me. You've already done that."

He squeezed back, and then dropped her hand. "Thanks."

After the crowd quieted, Buck resumed talking. "If anybody else plans to enter, pay yer fee to Manuel over there by the chute before the first horse is saddled. Manny, wave to the nice townsfolk." An old-timer with a long, white beard and wearing a sombrero held up his hand. "The first horse out will be El Diablo, the stallion. The rider who breaks him earns two hundred dollars!"

The spectators cheered their approval. The contestants were particularly vocal, whooping it up. This time, Buck talked over the din. "The other broncs bring thirty-five dollars. After we get to the final entrant, we'll start the rotation over. Lastly, bettin' on the riders is encouraged. If ya have a favorite cowboy, Manny's the bookmaker. All bets on a rider must be placed before he's got one boot in the stirrup."

A thunderous roar of hooves erupted as wranglers drove the first ten broncs down the street from the stables toward the corrals. El Diablo, black and sleek, his ears laid back and voice screaming, saw the gate to the holding corral and dodged to his right, narrowly missing some bystanders, who barely leapt out of harm's way. A few mares could not turn in time to follow him and ran into the holding corral, but the rest of his harem veered and followed their leader as he galloped past. Two wranglers pursued him and lassoed him almost simultaneously, causing the stallion to jolt to a halt when the ropes tightened around his neck. Other wranglers rounded up and contained the loose mares as El Diablo reared angrily, pawing his front legs in the air. The wranglers held tightly to their ropes and deftly repositioned their mounts to pull and herd the uncooperative stallion back to the gate. The stallion called to his mares, and they responded by frantically trotting from one side of the corral to the other or in circles around the inner perimeter of the corral, trying to reach him. Those folks leaning against the posts or standing on the rails of the holding corral jumped back to stay out of the mares' way. The crowd went as wild as the horses, sensing danger and excitement.

The scene was a riot of noises and motion until the wranglers forced the stallion into the holding corral and then into the chute. While the same two men held the ropes, another one strong-armed a halter over El Diablo's face, and yet a fourth cowhand threw a blanket and saddle over his back. He cinched the saddle up tight, and to make sure the horse wasn't bloating, kneed him in the belly. When El Diablo exhaled, the cowhand tugged again on the cinch strap, tightening it another inch. Next, the wranglers loosened their holds and slipped their ropes back over his head.

Buck announced the first contestant, a first-timer named Clay Jenkins. Clay was a local cowhand who looked barely old enough to shave. He was as skinny as a scarecrow and had the same straw-like hair, which hung to his shoulders. He doffed his hat and waved it in greeting to the spectators. Buck yelled through the din, "Last chance to place yer bets on Clay!" as Clay strode over to the chute. He climbed onto a rail, eased his left boot into the stirrup, and quickly threw his right leg over El Diablo's back and into the other stirrup. Someone thrust the halter lead into his hand, and another wrangler pulled the gate door open, allowing the horse and rider to enter the larger corral.

A half second later, Clay landed on the ground with a thud. He rolled out of the way of El Diablo's hooves, and wranglers rushed in to contain the still-bucking beast. Someone picked up Clay's hat and handed it to him after he had jumped over the rails to safety. The audience applauded politely for longer than the cowhand had sat the horse, and when their clapping ceased the drunkard yelled out, "Way to wear 'im down, Clay!" His comment received considerably stronger applause and louder cheers than Clay had.

Competitor number two was also a local. Pedro Rivera had grown up in the barrio and had bedded down in bunk houses at various ranches in the last decade, most recently at the Circle G, about fifteen miles north of town. He was of medium height and sported a meticulously groomed black mustache. Pedro had broken a few horses in his time, and a couple of them had broken parts of him.

The wranglers did not attempt to move El Diablo back into the chute. Pedro and the subsequent competitors would have to mount him from the corral rail. The wranglers worked hard to steady the black stallion near the rail. Standing on the bottom rail, Pedro grabbed the lead rope from a wrangler and held it tightly in his gloved left hand. Then he leaned forward and placed his left foot in the stirrup. Still grasping the rope in his left hand, he lunged up and forward, taking hold of the saddle horn with both hands, the right cupping the left. He had barely placed his other foot in the stirrup when the wranglers released their hold, and the bucking began. He lasted through a series of ups and downs, but when El Diablo reared, cycling his front legs, Pedro lost his balance and came out of the saddle and off the stallion's rump to the ground. His total time clocked on El Diablo was less than two seconds.

Third up was a slightly older man, in his mid-thirties, from Tucson. Rod Collins stood six feet tall and weighed in at 210 pounds. His broad shoulders, tight biceps, and easy smile made him attractive to womenfolk, and they cheered loud and long when he was introduced. El Diablo surprised the cowboy, jumping straight up, rather than bucking. When that failed to dump his rider, he jumped again, this time kicking his hind legs out behind him. He landed poorly, in a sitting position, and when he stood again, he shook like a dog emerging from a swimming hole. That did it, and Rod flew off and into the dust.

The fourth contender fared no better, nor the fifth. The sixth rider, a handsome black man named Isaac Williams, had won prize money in several bronco-busting competitions in California. He was one of the favorites in the betting circle, owing to the fact that he was a proven prize winner, and also because he had a perceived advantage of good position—the stallion should be worn down a bit from the first five contestants.

Isaac hung on for seven seconds before El Diablo tried his rearing trick again. This time, his cycling was slower, and Isaac pulled back hard on the rope, turning the stallion's head backwards. The horse stood up straighter on his hind legs, and the crowd gasped in horror as he began to fall over backward. He tipped completely over, landing on Isaac, who released the rope. When the horse regained his feet, two wranglers kept him separated from Isaac for the few seconds it took for two others to drag the felled rider to the side of the corral and under the lowest rail. Doc Ritter met him there and asked Isaac questions as he lay panting on his back. In a moment, the doc offered him a hand up. When he stood, the crowd showed their appreciation by also standing, in effect giving him a standing ovation.

And so it went, young and old, green and experienced, all riders thrown in a matter of seconds, and El Diablo showing no signs of fatigue or acquiescing. Although the total amount of time cowboys had spent sitting on El Diablo was infinitesimal, more than fifteen minutes had passed since Clay had first sat in the saddle because of the time it took to catch El Diablo between contestants and readjust the stirrups. The thirty-minute-per-horse rule was fast approaching. Buck called the next contender. "All it says is 'McCoy.'"

Mason nudged John. "You're up." He was thinking John's pristine clothes were going to look like rags at the end of his ride, but he kept silent.

John turned and looked down the street. He was tall enough to see over most folks and saw Becky sitting on the bench in front of the doctor's office. He shouted for her to join him. Then he made his way over to Buck and the sheriff. "It's not me that's entered. It's Beck." Buck, not knowing "Beck" was a girl, made a second announcement, this time for Beck McCoy.

"Now hold on." The sheriff *did* know that Beck was a girl, and he had no qualms about disqualifying her either on the grounds of her gender or her age. No children were allowed, period. John joined the officials on the platform and tried to make his case. When Buck became aware of Beck's gender, he sided with the sheriff. A discussion among the three of them became a quarrel, and it sounded to Mason like John was becoming mighty riled and might throw a punch. He sidled onto the platform and grabbed John's arms from behind, pulling them behind his back. The lanky seventeen-year-old was no match for Mason.

"Cool down. Let the judge do his job."

John nodded. He relaxed his stance and called for an official copy of the rules. The sheriff judged that the written rules should prevail, so Mason released his hold, but he stood ready to restrain John again if need be. Buck didn't carry the rules with him and had to ask Manny where they were. Manny pulled a worn, folded paper from the bottom of his bookie clipboard and passed it to his neighbor, who in turn passed it to his, and so on, as though the men belonged to a bucket brigade.

Meanwhile, Becky approached the holding corral, and the mares stopped their fidgeting and stood quietly for a long moment. Then one of the older mares whinnied and trotted up to her. Her sisters and cousins and distant relatives followed her lead, and soon they were all bumping into each other, edging their way as close to Becky as possible. Becky reached out and patted those nearest her and spoke to them all in such a quiet voice that had people been trying to listen, they might have thought that she was not even whispering, only mouthing words.

The rules had reached the sheriff, and he was reading them aloud to John and Buck when he realized that a hush had spread through the audience. He looked around and saw that people were pointing at the holding corral. Tom craned his head to see what had captured their attention. He saw that Becky had entered the holding corral and was moving through the waiting horses across its length. The nine horses followed her, slowly, calmly, as though they were being guided by a lead rope. She then climbed between the rails that separated the two corrals and entered the bronco-busting corral. She stood motionless for a moment, staring at El Diablo, and then her lips began to move again.

If the crowd had been hushed before, it was now so still that a horsefly could have been heard buzzing in the stables down the street. Mothers had no need to quiet squirmy children, for the babies sat stock-still, like dolls in their laps. Everyone's eyes were fixated on the slight girl with a ball of curly red hair flowing out from under a dark brown hat.

"It looks like Beck made the decision for you, sheriff, but as you can see, there's no mention in the rules about gender or age. I checked with Manny before I entered her in the contest, and I have legal papers showing I'm her guardian for the duration of our travels." He produced some papers from his back pocket. "As such, I'm taking responsibility for her safety."

"Are you ruling that she can ride, Tom?"

Buck needed an answer. Tom recalled the stories Mason had told him just a few hours before about Becky's abilities with horses.

He had seen how the waiting broncs had reacted to her. And he thought he understood why she had stayed so far away from the contest thus far. In essence, he believed in her. "Mother of God help me if something happens to her. Yes, Buck. Yes, I am."

John thrust his hand forward for the sheriff to shake, as though they had agreed on a mutually beneficial contract, but Tom shook his head no, refusing to grasp the other's hand. John let his arm drop and turned to Buck. "Announce her as 'Miss Becky McCoy.'"

John returned to his position at the rail. While Buck made the announcement, John concentrated on his sister's safety. "Beck, you're official. Can you do this?"

Still staring at the horse named "The Devil," she nodded yes to her brother.

"Do you need anything?"

"Yer shirt."

He instantly tugged the tails out of his slacks and pulled up from the bottom, popping the pearl buttons off in the process and revealing his pale, mostly hairless chest. A young girl bent to retrieve the buttons. John paid her no mind. Instead, he loped over to the rail and eased his shirt to Becky. She gave him Cody's hat in exchange. "Mind this."

Becky tied the shirt's sleeves loosely around her neck. As she was making the knot, John moved to where the wranglers were holding tightly to El Diablo. He motioned for them to let go of the stallion and back out of the corral, but they held their positions, not being paid to take orders from strangers. John called up to Buck Pruitt on the judge's platform, "Mr. Pruitt, Beck needs more space. Order your wranglers out of the corral."

Buck gave the word, and the wranglers let go of their holds and moved away from El Diablo. The mustang felt his freedom and let the world know it. First, he nodded his head violently up and down as though testing to see if the rope end was truly unsecured, and then he shook his head from side to side, breaking the stillness with loud complaints, looking like a tot yelling, "No, no, no!" Becky kept staring and talking, but she also began walking, and when she was in the center of the ring, she sat down cross-legged. El Diablo pawed the ground and ran at her, and the crowd gasped. Just when it looked like the stallion was going to run Becky over, he skidded to a stop. The girl reached toward him, revealing an apple in her hand. He knew the smell, having eaten an apple within the hour, and he knew her smell and feel. His ears twisted to hear her voice, and somehow satisfied that she was not a threat, he tentatively stretched his lips toward the apple. She did not release it to him immediately but waited until he sank his teeth into it. As he did, she stood and unclipped the lead rope from the tie ring of his halter, and she wound it around her waist, tying it off in a big bow. El Diablo was nodding his head again as he munched, but this time the motion was generated by his pleasure from tasting the sweet treat. Becky walked around to his left side and loosened the cinch. She slid the pad and saddle off his back and walked backward with them until she bumped into a corral post, at which point she eased the saddle onto the top rail and once more approached the stallion. She produced another apple from between her shirt and body, and as he ate it, she stroked his neck. Then she removed John's shirt, and holding one sleeve in each hand, twisted the body a few times into a roll. She placed the roll above El Diablo's eyes, allowing several inches of shirt to hang down over his face; then she maneuvered the shirt's sleeves under the crownpiece of his halter straps and tied them together behind the horse's ears.

Once he was blinded, all the residual tenseness drained from El Diablo. Becky took hold of his mane at his withers and pulled herself onto his back. She slung low, hugging his neck, all the while whispering. His ears twisted, sometimes together, sometimes independently, to catch her voice. The audience maintained its silence, either from amazement or fear that loud sounds would break the spell. And then El Diablo began to walk. Becky gripped him with her knees, and using pressure, guided him in a circle around the corral. After completing a full lap, he turned and walked the perimeter in the opposite direction. Then Becky sat more erect with her hands on her thighs and nudged him into a trot. At the halfway point, he broke into an easy canter. Once back at his starting point, he slowed, walked to the center of the ring, and stopped. Then, to the delight of the spectators, he began taking steps backward. After a half dozen steps, he started forward again but stopped in midstride and reversed, taking a half step back, but he reversed again and moved forward, then back, then forward, as though he were dancing. When he finally stopped moving, Becky leaned forward and gave his neck a long hug, after which she sat erect and looked around. Her face was glistening with moisture, and her bangs lay plastered to her forehead. Her clothes were soaked with sweat—both hers and El Diablo's. The glare of the sun's rays shone in her eyes. She wiped her face first on her left sleeve and then on her right, ultimately leaving her hand at her forehead to shield her eyes as she squinted into the sea of faces.

"John? Good 'nough?"

He shouted up to the judge's platform. "Sheriff, Beck's asking if she can dismount and get credit for breaking El Diablo. So, Mister Judge, is he broke?"

The whole audience was now looking at the sheriff, holding their breaths in anticipation. Before Tom could answer, Buck reminded him of the rules. "Sakes alive, Sheriff! I ain't never seen anything like that, but he's only broke if he walks easy under saddle with a cowboy on his back."

The sheriff agreed. "Someone has to test him."

"John?"

Her brother heard the question as a fatigued plea and gave her the nod. "Beck, go ahead and dismount. You're good."

With that affirmation, Becky lifted her right leg over the stallion's neck and dropped down to the ground. Her legs buckled beneath her as she landed, and she sat in the dirt looking dazed. The crowd exclaimed when she went down, but it was Mason who reacted first. He bounded over the top rail and into the corral and scooped her up. John was directly on his heels, opting to bend between the rails rather than climb over. El Diablo stood quietly by, periodically swishing his tail at a persistent fly, apparently oblivious to the newcomers in his space.

John spoke first to Mason, then to his sister. "Much obliged, Mr. Campbell. Beck, are you all right?"

"Jiggly legs is all. They took a lotta squeezin'."

"Do you reckon you can stand, Miss Becky?"

"Mayhap."

Mason set Becky on her feet, holding his arms out for her to grab if she began to fall, but her legs held. At that moment, Buck announced that Miss Becky McCoy was a potential winner, and the crowd erupted in cheers.

John tapped Cody's hat onto Becky's head before wrapping her in his arms in a bear hug. "You were terrific! Take a bow, Beck."

"Do I hafta?"

"Yes! And smile big."

"Well, since ya say so." She turned toward the left and with a sweeping gesture removed Cody's hat and swung it toward the ground as she bent forward. As the cheering erupted anew, she turned to the mid-section of the crowd and circled the hat over her head a few times as though it were a lasso. The crowd's appreciation rippled to that section like a wave, but by then she had repositioned to face the folks on the right. This time she spun the hat on her finger before tossing it in the air, giving it a twirl, and flipping it over onto her head. Now everyone was on their feet, standing in ovation. And finally, Becky smiled.

Before the clapping died down and the folks reclaimed their seats, Becky turned her attention back to her work. She pulled the bow ends, loosening the rope around her waist, and clipped it back on the halter. Next, she removed John's shirt from El Diablo's face. She folded it neatly, and as she handed it to her brother, she told him he was in the way. He tipped his hat to her and climbed between the rails back into the audience. Then Becky led the horse over to the saddle and was about to heft it onto him when Mason took it from her and placed it on El Diablo's back. Becky stood back and let him fasten the cinch.

"As long as I'm here, I may as well be the one to test him. Is that okay, Judge?"

"Yes, but for this to be a fair test, I'm thinking Miss Becky needs to go sit on the doc's bench."

"Excellent point." Mason looked to Becky. "Are your legs feeling strong enough to walk down to the bench?"

"John can help me." Her brother nodded that he would.

Mason lowered the left stirrup and then walked behind the stallion, keeping his left hand on the horse's rump, to adjust the other one. He spoke to Becky over El Diablo's back. "Any advice?"

Becky looked up to meet Mason's aquamarine eyes. Her hair was a packrat's nest, and her face was covered with dirt and dried sweat. She shrugged her shoulders in response, but then her lips spread into her mysterious, crooked smile, her eyes twinkled, and she gave him what he asked for. "Talk to 'im."

"Right." Though he answered with a touch of sarcasm in his voice, he was not feeling mean-spirited. For the first time, he thought he had an inkling of what his son was attracted to. In addition to her unusual abilities with horses, this young Miss Becky could look beautiful even when she was a mess, and odd as it was, she had a subtle sense of humor. He chuckled and smiled back.

*   *   *

As Becky exited through the corral rails, Cody caught up with her. "That was the bravest thing I ever saw a girl do. I wouldn't have believed it if I hadn't seen it!"

"Why, thank ya kindly, but jus' so's ya know, I was never in any danger. El Diablo is spirited but not ill-tempered." She presented Cody's hat to him. He examined it carefully before positioning it on his head.

John muscled his way in and took Becky by her elbow. "Let's get you a drink."

She shook him off. "In a minute."

Becky made her way into the crowd, followed closely by Cody and John. As she passed, some folks patted her on the shoulder or offered their hands in congratulations. She stopped in front of a brown girl of about nine wearing a strained, shabby dress and playing with John's pearl buttons. The girl would shake them in one hand, then pour them into the other, then repeat the action in reverse. "What's yer name, miss?"

The girl looked around. "You mean me?" As she spoke, she pointed to her chest with her thumb.

"Shorely. What's yer name? Mine's Miss Becky McCoy."

"I know that. Everyone knows that. You're the bronc buster."

"Well, what's *yer* name?"

"I'm María Contreras."

"Master Miguel's sister?"

"You mean Gordo? Yes'm, I'm his sister."

"Pleased to meet ya, Miss María."

"Likewise, I'm sure."

"Miss, I believe those buttons belong to my brother." Becky indicated John by throwing her chin in his direction.

The youngster immediately held the pretty trinkets out for Becky to take. "Sorry." She hung her head, but Becky didn't take them from her.

"Can ya sew?"

"Yes'm."

"I'll pay ya ten cents if'n ya can sew these on nice an' proper by 4:45 today."

María lifted her head and smiled, revealing an arch of perfectly aligned teeth. "Oh, yes, ma'am. I can do it."

Becky tried to borrow a five-cent piece from her brother, but he balked, saying he wasn't carrying such a small coin. Becky gave him the stink eye, and John laughed in response. Cody could tell that Becky was annoyed. He stepped up, handing her a coin from his own pocket. She thanked him for it and vowed to pay him back as she passed it on to María saying, "Here's half." Then Becky seized the shirt from her brother and gave it to the girl. "Bring it to the boardin' house to get the balance."

"Yes'm. Thank you, ma'am." And María skipped happily off.

"That was right nice of ya to give her work, Miss Becky. In the Contreras family, cash is a rare crop. I doubt María's ever had ten cents of her own."

"I'll be mindful o' that."

Cody thought her answer was a bit odd, but much about Miss Becky was a bit odd. By now, the three of them had reached the bench. Becky sat down with a thud. Then John left in search of some water for her and a shirt for himself. "Ya best go watch yer pa ride, Master Cody."

"Do ya think El Diablo is green broke?"

"I wouldn't set jus' anybody on his back, but shorely yer pa can ride 'im."

"Then I'll sit here with ya." He plopped down next to her. There's nothin' special about seein' Pa ride."

While Becky rested, Cody related the fun he'd had giving children bicycle rides. He explained that they had been unable to pay. She was not disappointed, replying that she never expected them to. She had just been incentivizing Master Miguel.

"Ya want to tell me how ya came by the bicycle?"

Becky's lips turned slightly upward. "Shore 'nough. I saved a life, a person's life. Ya know Mr.—" But Becky stopped her story short. John had returned. He was wearing a fine tailored shirt that was better than most of the townspeople could afford but was a step down from his pearl-buttoned one, and in his left hand, he was carrying her tattered carpetbag. He had a five-cent piece in his right palm and without saying a word, he flipped it in the air over to Cody, who, though surprised, caught it reflexively. John reached into the bag and pulled out a red neckerchief and a canteen. Becky drank greedily, like a parched desert sagebrush during the summer's first downpour, and like the plant, within minutes she appeared to blossom before their eyes. Then she soaked the neckerchief in water and patted her face and neck before pulling her shirt away from her chest and dribbling a stream of cool liquid down her front.

"Beck, proper young ladies don't do that in public, if ever!"

"When are ya gonna learn I'm not like other ladies?"

"Well, if you don't start acting like one, I'm going back to calling you Spooky. And Papa isn't going to like your lazy way of speaking, so you had better stop slurring your words and dropping your g's before he arrives tomorrow afternoon."

Their spat was interrupted by hootin' and hollerin'. They looked toward the contest and saw Buck waving at them from atop the judge's platform. "Let's go, Spooky. Mr. Campbell must be finished." Becky rose and took a swing at him, but John caught her fist in his hand and laughed. She made a very unladylike face and growled at him, but by then she was addressing his back.

When they arrived at the platform, Buck invited Becky up. The sheriff announced that she was the winner of the two-hundred-dollar prize. Buck presented the money to her with his left hand, while extending his right to her in congratulations. The crowd cheered and whistled appreciatively, and when it quieted, the drunkard yelled, "Girlie, would ya buy me a drink?" Some folks laughed; others booed, but Becky took his request in earnest.

"Shorely, sir. I'd be happy to oblige ya."

A stunned silence followed her words. Surely a child would not buy a drunkard, a stranger, anyone, whiskey. On the other hand, if she would buy him a drink, maybe she would buy a round for all the men. At a dime a shot, two hundred dollars would go a very long way. The crowd began to murmur their thoughts, but John's stern voice could be heard above them.

"*Beck!* What were you thinking?"

As Becky began to answer, the audience hushed to hear her. "Well, John, I was thinkin' not with this here prize money. I'm givin' it back to Sheriff Claiborne," which she did with great flourish, "to mind. I want the money to go to Leanin' Rock School to buy some books or desks or slates. I can buy the thirsty gentleman a drink with my spendin' money. Or if'n that's a faux pas, *you* can buy 'im one, John. Have ya got a dime on ya?"

The crowd roared once more. They let Becky know that they valued the donation, and they also liked that she showed respect for their itinerant town drunk. Hank Starley would make an appearance in town now and then and bum drinks from anyone he could. Cody especially liked that Miss Becky proposed John would be the one buying the "gentleman" a drink. Cody liked John, but he didn't always like the way he treated Becky. He sure seemed cheap for someone who dressed duded up. Cody thought Becky clever to turn the tables on John, pressuring him to pay for the drink. He supposed if his sister had lived, he might needle her now and again, but he wouldn't aggrieve her the way John did Becky. While Cody was thinking about the McCoy siblings' relationship, to everyone's delight, John agreed to fund the gentleman's drink.

*   *   *

Becky's win being settled, Buck Pruitt called for the next bronc to be readied. Because Becky had successfully broken the previous horse, her turn had not ended. This time, Becky chose to mount the horse from within the chute. Manny waved his sombrero, encouraging people to place their bets. John and Cody followed Becky over to the holding corral, which she entered. Eight of the nine mares jockeyed for positions near her. They acted as though they were bees and Becky was a pollen-laden flower, swarming around her to glean some sweetness. One bay seemed immune to Becky's spell. She stood by El Diablo, nervously twitching her tail and shifting her weight from foot to foot. Because she was an easy target, a wrangler twirled his lariat toward her. He expertly roped her and hustled her into the chute where he held her while a cohort fitted her with a halter.

Becky could certainly be aggravating, but John didn't want to see her hurt. He had been tasked with keeping her safe. "Beck, can you do this? Of all the horses, he chose the 'Anxious Alice.' "

Becky answered without looking at him. "Alice won't try to hurt me, John, but I don't know if'n she'll lemme sit 'er. She's missin' 'er mother."

"Do you want out?"

"It would help if'n ya could bring the older version of 'er over here from the stables, but there's not 'nough time." She slipped through the huddle of horses and between the rails, and walked to the chute, still followed by her brother and Cody. "Lemme have my gloves."

John opened the carpetbag, and she reached in with purpose. First, she drew out a bright pink ribbon, which she used to quickly tie her unbridled hair into a ponytail. Next, she extracted her leather gloves and a brown, corked bottle. She handed the bottle to John before wiggling her fingers into place in the gloves and ordering him to pour a generous amount of the liquid into her palms and over the fingers. He hadn't realized that she was going to ruin her brand-new pair of custom-made gloves and fleetingly thought about the cost of another pair, but he obeyed nonetheless. As Becky rubbed her hands together completely saturating the gloves, a flowery lavender fragrance, or maybe it was citrusy, wafted in the air. At that moment, the wrangler signaled that he was ready for her.

"Stay safe, Spoo—uh *sis*." John tipped his hat to her as she climbed into the chute.

Cody had remained silent during Miss Becky's conversation with her brother, not wanting to interfere with her preparations. Now he offered his encouragement with "I believe in you!"

She ripped off her right glove and threw it to him. "Put this as near to El Diablo as ya can."

Cody wended his way through the crowd back to the holding corral as fast as he could, while Becky balanced on the fence, ready to mount. A boy in the audience starting chanting, "Bust 'er, bronco buster, bust 'er, bronco buster." Other children joined in until their voices overtook all the chatter emanating from the adults. John tried to call for quiet, but it was of no use. The children were unified in their exuberance. He and other folks nearby saw Becky whispering under her breath. Although no one could hear her words, John knew they wouldn't have understood them anyhow. John recognized that the mantra-like technique was Becky's primary method to calm both the newly dubbed mare and herself. The purpose of the liquid, he wasn't so sure about.

All eyes were on Becky as she hurriedly stretched over and rubbed her left palm back and forth on the anxious horse's neck. Then she took the halter lead from the wrangler, who helped fit her left boot into the stirrup. She threw her right leg over the horse and grabbed onto the saddle horn with both hands, all the while whispering. The assistant on the other side slid her right boot into the corresponding stirrup, then he opened the chute, and Alice leapt into the corral, angry and afraid and letting the world know it. The chanters shortened their cry to "Bust 'er, bust 'er," but the slogan itself was busted by the general roar of the horde as Alice bucked back and forth and called her frustrations to El Diablo, who whinnied to her. He and the other mares danced around their corral, bumping into each other and making a raucous commotion. Alice stopped bucking for a moment and galloped across the corral toward El Diablo, making the onlookers wonder if she would try to jump the fence to join him, but she skidded to a stop, almost dumping Becky over her head. The townsfolk gasped, and some covered their children's eyes, thinking Becky would be thrown into the fence, but the girl used her right arm to stop her tumble. She pushed hard against the nearest post and sprang back into the saddle, which evoked cheers from the spectators. Alice spun on her hind hooves and started bucking again. Through it all, Becky whispered and hung on. Before long, Alice had bucked her way close to El Diablo again. Becky was still whispering, but to close observers, she seemed to be addressing the stallion, not the mare. Becky began to look more relaxed. She moved like a rag doll, her head and shoulders rolling with the changes in direction. El Diablo settled, ignoring Alice's antics. Then his herd settled. With their calmness, Alice also quieted and came to a standstill. Becky kicked her gently in the sides, and Alice followed the instructions. After a trip around the ring, Becky, who was still whispering, stopped the horse again. This time, she stood in the saddle, putting her full weight into the stirrups. After a long moment, she raised her right arm in victory and exploded "Yeehaw!" Then she sat and rode Alice back to the chute amid cheers of jubilation and amazement. The wrangler helped her down, and John helped her out of the corral. She immediately dropped onto the ground and rested. Folks nearby patted her shoulder in congratulations, and someone handed her a wet cloth to wipe her face.

Acting as the official contest judge, Sheriff Tom Claiborne called for Becky to join him and Buck Pruitt on the platform. John hoisted the bedraggled Becky from her position on the ground and pointed her in the right direction. She wobbled through the crowd, looking like she might collapse. When the girl reached center stage, the sheriff pronounced Alice broken and declared Miss Becky the winner of the thirty-five-dollar prize by raising her arm in triumph. Becky took a bow per his suggestion. After the exhilarative applause but before she could say anything, a familiar voice rang out: "Girlie! Girlie, over here!" Becky shaded her eyes with her hand and searched for the drunkard, spotting him at the edge of the crowd. "Whisper to my wife there an' tame 'er fer me, will ya?" The crowd laughed heartily, but the sheriff did not look amused.

"Hank Starley, pardner, you're disturbing the peace. If you don't cork it, you'll be spending the night in jail."

A woman of surprisingly similar build to the sheriff came up behind the drunkard and whacked him on the head with her parasol. He yelped in surprise and prepared to punch his assailant, until he recognized the aggressor as his wife. "See, Girlie, see? She's a wild one!" The woman poked him with the parasol tip and stomped off toward town.

"My papa always says to know yer limits, an' I can tell ya plainly, mister, no amount o' me *whisperin'* is gonna tame yer wife. Have ya tried *yellin'* at 'er?" It was impossible to tell whether Becky was being serious or poking fun, but either way, her words brought another howl from the crowd. They were particularly jovial because they were unaware that Hank even had a wife. This was turning into the most entertaining day many of the folks had ever experienced.

When they quieted, to everyone's astonishment, Becky declined the prize money, donating it to the Leaning Rock church. The congregation showed their appreciation with a heartfelt "hurrah" and "God bless you." Pale and shaky, Becky was still on the platform being acknowledged when Buck Pruitt rose and ordered the next mare to be saddled, declaring that Becky would be first up on her. The contestants who had not yet had the opportunity to compete grumbled among themselves, wondering if they'd blown their entrance fees, but the crowd was ecstatic, seeing the potential for a repeat performance by Becky and, thus, an opportunity to make some money on a sure thing. Manny didn't have to wave his sombrero to encourage bets. Townsfolk who wouldn't normally risk their hard-earned money eagerly began moving toward him with bills in hand. Buck saw the movement and announced that the betting was closed. He, too, saw the potential for a repeat performance and was concerned that Becky's success would break the bank.

"Point of order, Judge!" It was John yelling. "The rules state that betting stops when the contestant's boot enters the stirrup, not before." He had everyone's attention. Buck looked at Tom for help.

"That *is* the rule. You pointed it out yourself."

Buck was looking grim and was weighing his options. "I could cancel the contest an' hire Miss Becky to bust the other eighteen." The crowd booed at his idea, so Buck tried to appease the people. "Y'all could come an' watch. It's not what ya counted on, but it would be entertainin'. Yes, sirree! I could just about guarantee that." The townsfolk had no choice but to accept the change, but Becky saved the contest and Buck's reputation.

"Mr. Pruitt, I'm plumb tuckered out. I'll walk away from today's contest an' rest in town."

Thus, Buck happily announced that Miss Becky was bowing out and that anyone who had bet on her for the next mare would receive a refund. He told Becky to take another bow, and when she did, the audience showed their appreciation once again by cheering long and loud. This was quite a wondrous day for them, seeing two unusual but successful rides by the young girl, and receiving a windfall for the school and church because of her.

Before exiting the structure, Becky searched the audience once more. "Hey mister! Mr. Starley!" When the drunkard's bleary eyes met hers, she continued, "How 'bout I get ya that drink now? No need to wait 'til the contest is over."

"Aye, Girlie! Aye! I'm itchin' fer a whiskey."

Unlike before, if the townsfolk were aghast by Becky's offer, they paid it no mind. Either they had come to accept the girl's peculiarities, or they were just eager to get on with the show.

Looking spent, Becky turned to Sheriff Claiborne and asked for a dime. He reached into his pocket and handed her a quarter. "Thank ya kindly. John will make ya good." Down in the audience, John folded his arms across his chest and sighed, but he nodded at the sheriff, signifying that he would honor his sister's debt.

Becky departed the platform holding tightly to the railing, while Buck announced the next contender. When she reached ground level, her brother pulled her aside. "*Beck*, what were you thinking? Riding the other mares would be as easy for you as riding your bicycle."

She kept walking, heading toward the bench she had rested on earlier. John stayed even with her, matching her pace, while

Cody followed behind at a respectful distance. The drunkard waved at Becky from afar, and she motioned for him to join her. While she waited for him, she plunked down on the bench. They heard cheering from the corrals. It sounded like someone had successfully broken a mare. At last, she answered her brother: "I'm thinkin', John, I'm thinkin' I'm tired an' dirty an' need a drink. I'm thinkin' 'easier than the first two' isn't the same as 'easy.' Leave me be. Go watch the contest."

John knew there was no sense in arguing. If she wanted to be alone, it was best to leave her to herself. "All right, then, I'll see you at supper. In case I didn't say it before, nice ride, Beck." He turned on his heel and left. Cody stepped up in his place.

"Miss Becky, I'll sit with ya."

"Thank ya kindly, but no thank ya. Go watch yer pa ride. Ya can come fetch me at the boardin' house afore supper." As she spoke, mild groans and polite cheers emanated from down the street. No doubt the successful rider had not been so with his second mount.

Cody felt disheartened by her rejection and was reluctant to leave her looking so depleted, but he followed John's lead. "All right." He reached over and patted her hand. "You were amazing!" He could see Hank Starley approaching and wondered if he, too, would get the boot. Then he heard the crowd gasp and groan. He guessed that the next unlucky entrant had been injured. He hoped it wasn't his pa.

* ~ * ~ *

The day was hot and humid, and Miss Becky was overheated. A breeze would have been nice, but the air was as still as a cup of three-day-old coffee. About the time Hank arrived at the bench in front of Doc Ritter's office where she was sitting, Becky could see the doc himself en route with two muscular men carrying a litter and Mrs. Ritter running behind, her beehive tilting precariously one direction and then the other with the movement of her hips. One of the men was Mason Campbell. The groaning man on the litter was young Charlie Reeves, a drifter. She hadn't met him, but she'd heard gossip that he'd spent his last dollar entering the contest on the hopes he could make some fast money.

Becky grabbed onto Hank's arm and pulled herself to standing. "Let's go! I can't stomach moanin' an' groanin'." She led the drunkard across the deserted street to the Rustler's Stoop saloon, stopping to pat the line of horses hitched in front of it. They responded with soft nickers or louder vocalizations, depending on whether she had greeted them before. Although horses were plentiful, people were nowhere to be seen. Almost all the townsfolk were at the bronco-busting contest, leaving Leaning Rock as abandoned as a worked-out gold mine.

Becky peeked through one of the dirty windows located on each side of the saloon door. She couldn't see anyone, but the establishment appeared to be open. Hank pushed the slatted swinging doors inward, and she followed him inside. The room was considerably dimmer and cooler than the outdoors. It smelled of alcohol and sweat and mustiness. Some of the odor could have emanated from Hank, being more noticeable indoors. The odd couple wound their way around the large round poker tables with mismatched armed chairs shoved under as far as possible, and they bellied up to the bar, where an open bottle of whiskey was sitting near a line of a half dozen shot glasses. "Whiskey costs a dime a drink, an' I got a quarter."

Hank licked his lips in anticipation. "That's three drinks."

"Two an' a half. I have readin' an' writin' deficiencies, but I can figure well 'nough."

"Aye, so ya can." Even so, Hank felt short-changed when Becky poured whiskey into three glasses, filling the third only halfway. Setting aside his annoyance, he struck up a conversation in an attempt to be sociable. "The paint lived. Likin' yer bicycle?"

"Best gift I ever received!" Becky set the quarter on the bar and settled herself on a stool. When she looked up, all three glasses were empty.

Hank couldn't tell from her expression if she was disheartened or angry or something else, but she didn't look happy, even though she had sounded happy. His thoughts were interrupted with a baritone "Howdy."

He and Becky were both startled by the voice behind them and instinctively looked in the large wall mirror behind the bar to see who had spoken. Hank recognized the barkeeper and turned to face the slim, mustachioed man of about forty-five who was coming toward them. Hank spoke first.

"Howdy, Fred. This here is . . . is . . . ."

"Miss Becky McCoy. I know. I saw her at the contest."

She turned to meet Fred with an extended hand.

He took it and gave it a gentle squeeze. "Howdy do, miss? My name is Fred Mercer." Then using the same arm, he removed his hat, divulging a full head of thick wavy hair the identical bronzy shade of his mustache. "I'll be remembering your name the rest of my life." The corners of his mouth edged up after he spoke, though his smile was difficult to discern, being partially covered by the hair hanging over his upper lip. If Fred was expecting Becky to reply, he was disappointed. Getting down to business, he sauntered behind the bar and fetched a white apron from a hook. He hung his hat in its place and then wrapped the apron strings around his waist a couple times before forming them into a bow in the front. "I heard her say you were coming here."

"I paid, Fred. Look-y here." Hank pointed at the quarter.

Fred plucked up the coin and dropped it into his apron pocket. "You buying more?"

"Uh . . ." Hank looked to Becky.

"That's all the money I have on me, but I'd be obliged fer a glass o' cool water afore I head back out into the heat."

"You can't stay long, Miss Becky. It ain't proper for a girl to sit in a saloon." Fred pulled out a pitcher of water from behind the counter next to his pistol. "It ain't fresh, but it's wet. And all my bigger glasses need washing." He sounded apologetic as he poured her a shot of the water and indicated where she should sit, which was a dark two-seater table in the corner by the entrance. She took the glass and pitcher to the table, while Hank stayed at the bar rubbing his fingers inside the used shot glasses and then sucking on them to consume the last drops of alcohol.

Becky poured and gulped a second and third and fourth shot of water before she hefted the pitcher and guzzled directly from its mouth, slopping water on her shirt in the process. With her head tilted back, she noticed a clean-shaven young man do exactly like she had: peek through the dusty window to determine if the Rustler's Stoop was open for business. Surely the man had seen Fred and Hank at the bar, but he had apparently changed his mind about wanting a drink. His heels clacked and his spurs jingled as he strutted off in the direction of the bank next door.

Fred hollered to Becky, saying she'd best be moving on. She left without hoopla, simply walking out through the swinging doors into the sunny afternoon. She used her hand as a fan to create air movement near her face. Standing there fanning, she eyed the street, taking in the sounds and smells, sensing her surroundings. Then she knew. Her lips began to quiver and words formed, but no audible sound emitted from her throat. Somewhere to her left, a horse whinnied, then another in reply, and yet another. She did an about face to re-enter the saloon, but as she pushed the doors, they hit Hank in the belly as he was trying to exit.

"Easy there, Girlie! Comin' back with more money?"

"Listen, Mr. Starley, I'll make a bargain with ya. I'll give ya a dollar to run over to Doc Ritter's office an' tell Mr. Campbell to come right quick."

Hank weighed her offer. He wanted drinking money, but it was hot, and he was middle-aged with extra pounds hampering him.

"Ten dollars!"

The higher amount worked. "Aye. I'll—"

"Jus' be on yer way!" And as an afterthought Becky added, "Tell 'im Big Bart's in town."

"Yes'm." Hank worked his way around her and departed doing a trot of sorts, since he couldn't muster a full run.

Becky turned now to the barkeeper. "Mr. Mercer! I need help."

"What's wrong Miss Becky?"

"Outlaws. I sent Mr. Starley fer Mr. Campbell across the street. Can ya ride down an' fetch the sheriff from the contest?"

Fred reached under the bar for his pistol and spun the cylinder to make sure it was fully loaded. "We'll be safe in here. I'll close and lock the exterior doors. Keep away from the windows." He started moving toward the doors, but rather than accept his offer of safety, Becky ran.

Like the man she'd seen, she also headed down the boardwalk toward the bank. The man was not visible now, but she saw the Bennett gang's horses standing untethered at the hitching post in front of the bank. The two gray quarter horses were closest to her, and Big Bart's big bay was on the far side. She strode over to greet and quiet them. While she worked the horses, Becky heard clinking noises generating from inside the building. Because the window shades were down, she couldn't peek in to confirm wrongdoing. Nevertheless, she sprang into action.

* * *

Mason Campbell was just leaving Doc Ritter's office with Isaac Williams, the bronc buster who had helped him carry Charlie Reeves on the litter, when Hank called to him from the street.

"Mr. Camp-bell, Mr. Camp-bell!"

The rancher hurried out and over to Hank's side. The drunkard was bent over, breathing heavily.

"What is it, Hank?"

"Gir-lie." He pointed toward the bank.

Mason's eyes followed Hank's finger. He couldn't see Becky. "Is she sick? Hurt? Where is she?"

"Big Bart!" Hank looked as though he were going to collapse. As Mason eased him onto the familiar bench, Isaac Williams opened the doctor's door and called in for help.

"Mrs. Ritter, Doc has another customer!"

"Coming!"

Hank was still breathing hard but managed to speak. "She said you'd gimme ten dollars." He held out his hand unabashedly.

"Don't that beat all!"

Mason agreed with Isaac but placed a ten-dollar bill in Hank's hand. He turned to Isaac. "Take my horse and quick fetch the sheriff. Something's amiss. Mention 'Big Bart' to him."

"Where's your horse?"

"Black gelding." He pointed toward the sheriff's office where he had left Raven secured to the hitching rail. They shook hands, and then with a clenched jaw and look of determination on his face, Isaac set out with long, businesslike strides.

Mason heard Mrs. Ritter's skirt swishing from inside the office before she reached the doorway. Staring through her spectacles, she quickly assessed the situation. "Looks like heat sickness. Help him in."

Mason maneuvered Mr. Starley through the door and into a chair in the waiting area, but he was eager to find Becky. "Sorry, Mrs. Ritter, I can't bring him farther." Then he took his leave and started across to the Rustler's Stoop.

Mason was surprised to find the saloon locked up. He knocked on the door with no response but saw movement of the curtain at one of the windows. He spoke through the glass, identifying himself and asking Fred if Miss Becky was with him. Fred pulled the curtain aside, and even through the dirt on the pane, Mason could see that he was holding his pistol ready for trouble.

"She ain't here, Mason. She left in a hurry. You want to come in?"

"Thanks, no, Fred, but you stay safe." Mason knew he would. Fred was not one to purposely put himself in danger. On the rare occasions when bar brawls erupted, he had the reputation of being the first out the door to fetch the sheriff or the first to dive for cover behind the bar. He mainly managed trouble by preempting it, making sure undesirables didn't overstay their welcome, but when his life depended on it, he could shoot fast and straight.

Mason remembered Miss Becky's description of the robbers' horses, and seeing the trio in front of the bank, he surmised that Big Bart's gang was robbing it. He drew his gun and crept over to the building, staying close to any cover he could find. Looking around, he spotted Miss Becky, or at least her legs. She was up the street a bit, apparently hiding between a pair of sorrels. Then he saw her flit over to another group of horses, and he wondered if she was on a greeting spree. Whatever she was doing, he was glad she was away from the bank and out of harm's way.

The gang's horses were standing quietly, tied to their rail. Mason heard metallic sounds emanating from the building, just like Becky had. He was cocksure that robbers were trying to force the safe open. Mason hoped Tom would arrive noiselessly and before the gang succeeded in cracking the safe and departing the bank.

He looked for Becky again, and to his bewilderment, she was walking slowly down the middle of Main Street toward Sam Hill's with her arms outstretched in a V shape at shoulder-height. He wanted to call to her to take cover, but he didn't want Big Bart to know he was just outside the bank. Then, to his utter amazement, he realized that every horse that had been tethered on the street was following Miss Becky. She must have been untying them when he had seen her earlier. There had to be two score horses lined up behind her, all as silent and calm as the day itself. They didn't jostle for position, just spread themselves wider across the street if they were about to overtake other horses around them. Dust was beginning to accumulate in the air from all the hoof action on the rutted road; but for that, a person would hardly have known of their presence.

Because Becky was walking slowly, it didn't take long for the front line of horses to catch up to her. The girl could easily have been run down by them, like a calf in a stampede, but without missing a step she gracefully grabbed the saddle strings of the horse coming up on her right, hopped a foot into the stirrup, and swung into riding position. Mason assumed she was taking the horses out to the churchyard or schoolyard, but he was unclear of her purpose. Meanwhile, the horses in front of the bank had become unsettled, tugging on their tethers in an apparent desire to join the Pied Piper parade.

Mason could see Tom in the distance, riding Raven up from the corrals. He waved his hat to him. Seeing Mason with his gun drawn, Sheriff Claiborne knew there was trouble, plus, like Mason, he recognized the gang's horses from Becky's earlier description. He was quick to put two and two together. *What better time to rob a bank than when everyone is occupied elsewhere?*

The sheriff dismounted at the veterinary office next door to the bank, dropping the reins to the ground, a signal for Raven to stay in place. He quietly approached Mason and when they were near enough to converse, he needlessly put a finger to his lips to indicate they should speak softly.

"It sounds like they're hammering on a chisel to try to pry open the safe door."

Tom hoped that was all they would try. If unable to pry the door open, gun powder would likely be their next course of action, and the powder could blow up or burn down several buildings if not used with expertise. "Best to wait until they come out. If they suspect we're here, they'll hole up."

Mason nodded that he understood. Tom instructed his friend by pointing and gesturing for Mason to go to his office, secure a rifle from the weapons cabinet, and then situate himself on the roof, which would provide him with an unobstructed view of the bank. Tom lobbed his office keys to Mason and motioned for him to go. Mason crouched low as he ran across the street while listening for the sound of breaking glass, the tip-off that a lookout was taking aim at him, but no such sound occurred. If it did occur, he trusted his friend to keep him safe by getting a shot off before the lookout did.

The town was eerily quiet but for sleek Raven trotting up the street in the dust of Becky's ragtag herd. Mason had hoped Raven would stand pat where Tom had left him so that one of them could use the horse to pursue any gang member who escaped. Raven had been ground-tie trained and should have stayed put, but Mason spent no more time thinking on it. He hurried to follow

Tom's directions and position himself on the roof. From there, he could see Tom waving at him from the roof of the bank.

Before long, the two men could see Raven cantering back down the street toward them with Miss Becky riding atop him. To their chagrin, the girl stopped directly in front of the bank. They watched her jump down from the saddle and slap Raven on the rump, encouraging him to run off. That done, she unwound the reins of the three horses from around the rail, leaving them lying loosely over the rail, precisely like she had originally found them. Just then, the door to the bank opened, and the three men rushed out, pistols drawn, to make their get-away. Sheriff Claiborne recognized Big Bart Bennett and the Dade cousins. Each cradled a bulky leather saddlebag over his left arm and carried a pistol in his right. Big Bart packed a second pistol in a holster tied to his left thigh. Becky was standing sandwiched between the bay and a gray. One of the young, clean-shaven cousins shoved her to the ground as he positioned himself to mount. Both cousins threw their bags over their horses behind the cantles of their saddles. They grabbed the reins and saddle horn with their left hands and the cantles with their right as they rammed their left boots into the stirrups, but when they put weight in the stirrups, the saddles slid down, ultimately hanging beneath the horses' bellies. The men lost their balance and landed hard with thuds. Becky narrowly missed being crushed by forming her body into a ball and rolling under the big bay, where she lay like a turtle with its head pulled into its shell. Big Bart had reins in hand, but he had seen his partners fall and realized that his own saddle cinch had been tampered with. He was tightening the cinch when Sheriff Claiborne yelled to the trio from the roof of the bank.

"Hands up! Toss your guns into the street!"

Matt and Roy Dade looked up to see two shiny Colt Peacemakers aimed at them.

"You're surrounded." The sheriff nodded upward toward Mason in case they needed proof. "Last time, boys, put your hands up!"

The cousins hesitated for a moment, no doubt deciding if they could win the fight or were willing to die in the street, but unlike the Dades, Big Bart had the means to escape. He raised his pistols and fired first at Mason and immediately after at the sheriff, missing his targets but blasting wood splinters from the buildings. Matt and Roy rolled over to lie prone on the ground supported by their elbows, one man facing Mason and the other, Tom. They started firing away, distracting their adversaries from Big Bart. The horses provided cover to Becky and the Dades. They pranced around them but did not flee. Mason and Tom fired only a smattering of shots, taking care not to hit Becky or the horses. Sacrificing a horse was acceptable to both men in dire circumstances, but neither of them wanted one to collapse on Miss

Becky, splatting her like a cockroach under a boot or pinning her underneath a half-ton or more of dead weight.

Big Bart secured his saddlebag, then hoisted his 230-pound frame onto his big bay horse and leaned his chest forward, parallel to his mount's back, to make himself a smaller target. His mustache and beard were practically buried in the horse's mane, his face was so low. As Big Bart's horse twirled on his hind legs to turn toward the road, Becky remained huddled below him. Big Bart took off heading toward the church. Neither Tom nor Mason could shoot at him without exposing themselves to the Dades. Big Bart's departure left Becky coverless, still rolled in a ball. Matt was nearer her, lying beneath his horse, and Roy was lying between the two grays. Tom could see Becky's mouth moving and wondered if she was praying or even cursing under her breath. He felt a bit like cursing, himself.

Matt pointed his pistol at Becky and yelled to the sheriff. "Drop your guns or I'll kill her!"

Tom immediately tossed his guns into the street below. Just as they whumped one after the other in the dirt, he saw Becky arise and take the gun out of Matt's hand. Then she walked behind his horse and took possession of Roy's gun. "They're secure, Mace. Come on down!" Tom reached the ground in a split second, retrieved his weapons, and relieved Miss Becky of the outlaws' guns. "You can get up now, boys."

But they could not get up, and when Mason arrived, he discovered why. Each mare had stepped on her owner's upper back, immobilizing him. The pressure had caused the outlaws to flatten to the ground. Mason approached one of the mares and attempted to lift her leg off Matt Dade in the same manner he would lift a leg to clean inside a hoof. He pushed the horse, trying to throw her off balance, but she would not budge.

Miss Becky came forward and patted each mare in turn on the shoulder, at which point the horse removed her hoof from her prisoner and held it in the air until each man made his way clear. Becky rewarded the horses with apples that she let roll out from under her shirt.

The sheriff and Mason shrugged at each other, silently asking how the horses' catch and Becky's release of the robbers were possible. Aloud, the men meekly thanked her for her help. Then Mason volunteered to lock the Dades up and take control of the money in the saddlebags until the bank owner arrived from the contest to retrieve it. Tom's task was to ride down to the contest and rustle up some deputies to go after Big Bart with him. As he saddled the Dades' gray mares, he thought to himself that the townspeople must have heard the earlier shots. He was surprised, but glad, that none had ventured near to help with the gun battle. He and Mason had managed fine, either because of or despite Miss Becky's interventions.

Becky stood with her head down, lips moving as though in a conversation, but as silent as a mute. She looked a mess: tired, tousled, and filthy, with curly red bangs clinging to her forehead and her clothes torn and looking like rags.

"Miss Becky, why don't you head over to the boarding house and wash and set a spell until Cody comes around for you?" The sheriff handed her the reins to one of the horses, and she mounted up.

"Listen. He's comin'!"

Tom, still on the ground, turned to look down the road but didn't see Cody or anyone coming their way from the corrals. A rumbling sound and shaking of the ground from the other end of town caused him a moment of confusion. He wondered if he was living through an earthquake. Tom had heard of such things but had never experienced one.

"My herd blocked an' turned 'im. Big Bart'll be here right quick. Be ready."

Sure enough, Tom saw Big Bart sitting straight in his saddle, racing toward them with both guns raised for action and a whole herd of saddled horses galloping in his wake. Behind them was a cloud of dust rolling down the road like a pack of tumbleweeds.

"Move!" Tom reached over to pull Becky's horse out of danger, but Becky dodged him and trotted the mare to the center of the road, where she sat facing the danger head on, eyes closed, arms outstretched with palms facing outward, as though she were trying to stop the horses by pushing them backwards. Her mouth was moving, yet no sound emanated from it.

Big Bart aimed at the sheriff and fired, but just as he squeezed the trigger, his horse reared, causing the bullet to pass high of its intended mark. Tom returned fire, but his shot flew high when Big Bart's bay dropped his forefeet to the ground and Big Bart took the opportunity to, once again, lean forward, parallel to the horse's back. This time, however, he positioned his head and upper torso to the left of the gelding's neck rather than planting his face in his mane. In that way, Big Bart's upper body was mostly blocked from the sheriff's line of sight, but his orientation also blocked Big Bart's sight of anything directly in front of him or to his right. While he was repositioning, the herd had stopped dead in its tracks causing the dust cloud to stagnate in the air.

From Big Bart's sideways position, he could no longer spur his gelding on with kicks to his side. Big Bart's horse did not stop, but he slowed from a wild gallop to an easy canter. Big Bart blindly began blasting away, some bullets zinging toward the sheriff, but most zipping perilously close to Becky, who was still sitting atop the gray with her eyes closed. For her part, Becky looked amazingly composed, not spooking from the booms of the shots or the whizzing of the bullets flying by.

Mason, who had completed his jail tasks, joined in the fray. His shot missed its target but distracted Big Bart from shooting toward Becky. More shots were exchanged with no apparent injuries, and finally, the gun battle ended when Big Bart's weapons clicked, signaling that they were out of ammunition. With three men's guns trained on him—Sheriff Claiborne's, Mason's, and even Fred Mercer's from behind a post at the Rustler's Stoop—Big Bart conceded. He reined his horse to a stop a few yards from Becky and put his hands in the air. The sheriff then dragged Big Bart down from the saddle and hauled him to jail.

Becky opened her eyes. Her domestic herd began moving down the street again at a good clip, heading toward the end of town where the horses' owners were watching the bronc riding. She dismounted unsteadily, and Mason approached her. He grabbed hold of her shoulders and shook them.

"You almost got yourself killed! What in the name of—" Then feeling how limp she was, Mason caught control of his temper. He steadied her and let go. He didn't say it, but he knew if his son had pulled anything so dangerous, he would have whipped him. In general, he didn't believe in hurting children, but sometimes you had to beat sense into them. Still, he regretted touching someone else's child. "Sorry, Miss Becky." He knew by now that Becky was an unusual girl. He recalled John's way of speaking to her and tried again. "Miss Becky, what were you thinking?"

Becky stood a little taller and smoothed back the stray hair from around her face. "Well, Mr. Campbell, first I was thinkin' I needed help, so's I sent Mr. Starley fer ya. Offered 'im ten whole dollars to find ya. Later, I was thinkin' I could stop Big Bart's bay. The herd stopped 'im, like I planned, but they turned 'im, instead o' holdin' 'im. They was s'posed to surround 'im. The bay knew me. He liked me, but there was too many others to talk to. The bay kep' on a comin'. He wouldn't listen. I didn't think Big Bart would get so close." She paused for a breath. "An' afore that I was thinkin' to get all the horses outta town so's if'n the gang excaped, they could block 'em. I left the gang's horses so's the robbers wouldn't suspicion they were found out, but I loosed their horses' cinches to stall 'em. I got two undone but not the last, so's I had to make a new plan. I knew from afore that the grays didn't much like the Dades, so's it was easy to talk 'em into helpin' me."

"Hmm. I see." Mason accepted her explanation whether he believed it or not. Clearly Becky believed it. "Well, in the future you should let the law handle the outlaws. You need to stay out of the sheriff's and harm's way. Understand?"

"Yes, sir."

"Good. Now why don't you go prepare for supper?"

Becky didn't answer. She just started trudging toward the boarding house.

In the meantime, the herd of horses had reached the vicinity of the wild horses being broken. The contest had ended for the day, so some of the contestants, wranglers, ranchers, and townsfolk worked to capture the domesticated horses, sort them out, and ride them back into town to tie them up and to make sure it was safe for the women and children to return. Once back in town, many of the folks would disperse to the Rustler's Stoop to drink and reminisce over the day's strange competition, head to the Leaning Rock Café to eat vittles, or rush to Sam Hill's when it reopened to spend their money on necessities and, perhaps, indulgences.

Elizabeth Hill, John McCoy, and Cody Campbell walked into town together after the bronco busting had finished for the day. A welcomed breeze had kicked up, making their journey a bit more pleasant. Elizabeth set a fast pace, eager to return to Sam Hill's. Her parents should be there already, having hitched a ride back to town just prior to the end of the contest. They could handle the first comers, but they would need her help waiting on folks when the second wave of customers hit. It was an excellent day for making profits.

Elizabeth mentioned to John that his sister had left a stack of clothing for later purchase. John rolled his eyes, but he agreed to come take a look at the items. He knew that Becky was a poor shopper with no sense of style, or as his papa would say, "an inexperienced shopper with an eccentric style." Becky's social deficiency grated on him because he prided himself on wearing stylish clothes and didn't like being seen with her when she dressed inappropriately for a girl her age, which was most of the time. As her chaperone, he had taken responsibility for Becky's health and welfare, and that broadly included seeing to her appearance. He figured she still needed something appropriate to wear to supper this afternoon and a party dress for tomorrow. He didn't know that Becky had just been to Sam Hill's and purchased an outfit.

Cody walked with Miss Elizabeth and John because his father was nowhere in sight, and he was looking to make a purchase at Sam Hill's himself. During the long trek, Elizabeth filled the time chattering about the highlights of the day. Of course, Becky's amazing rides and her generosity to Leaning Rock topped Elizabeth's list. She then expressed disappointment that Mason hadn't been around to take his turn at breaking a bronc. She was eager to hear how he and Tom Claiborne had spent the afternoon. Everyone had heard gunshots and seen the horses stampede, but the commotion had ceased, so they assumed that all was fine. Cody's mind wandered as Miss Elizabeth carried the conversation and John periodically grunted an acknowledgment. For once, Cody was glad social conventions prescribed that children be seen and not heard— not that he was a child—well, maybe he was age-wise, but he didn't feel like one—especially when he was with Miss Becky. He was eager to make his purchase and catch up with her.

Chapter 6

"Miss Becky!"

Mason heard the alarm in his son's voice and turned abruptly to determine the cause. He and Tom were standing outside the sheriff's office, people-watching. He saw Cody running from the direction of Sam Hill's toward the boarding house. At first, he didn't see anything amiss, but when he strode into the road to get a better view, he saw a body, presumably Becky's, lying on the ground between two horses hitched at the post in front of the lodging house.

"What's wrong, Mace?"

"It looks like Miss Becky is on the ground. C'mon!"

They started to run toward the boarding house, taking the road rather than the boardwalk to avoid pedestrians.

"Do you think she was caught in the crossfire?"

"Can't be. I spoke with her. She was fine. I tell you, she was fine."

"Okay then, but she's not fine now."

They were moving fast, but Cody was far ahead of them, so he reached Becky first. He lifted his arms into a T and shoved the horses' rumps, forcing the geldings to move away from Becky, who lay still as a possum. Mason and the sheriff arrived a moment later, and Mason scooped Becky up. The skirt of her stylish two-piece gray dress billowed gently in the breeze, and a pair of shiny black patent lace-up boots poked out from beneath its hem. Cody's first thought was macabre—how beautiful she would look in a coffin.

Mason examined her. "She's breathing. I don't see any blood."

"Hurry, Pa. Take her to Doc Ritter's."

"Go ahead, Mace. If the doc finds anything criminal, send Cody to fetch me. Otherwise, I'll see you at supper."

Mason hurried off down the street with Becky cradled in his arms, Cody trailing closely behind. The sheriff turned to the business of keeping the bustling town peaceful.

When Mason reached the doctor's office, Cody moved past him and flung the door open. "Doc! Mrs. Ritter?" He and his pa entered through the office door and heard the click-click of a woman's heels coming down the hallway.

"Stay with Charlie Reeves, dear. I'll take this. Let me know if he wakes up. I'll call if I need you." The clicking sounds retreated and were replaced by the thuds of Doc Ritter's boots. Then he appeared. "Bring her through. What happened?"

They all filed into the same examination room where Cody and Becky had met with the doctor earlier that day, and Mason set her down on the leather cushion on the examination table. He removed his hat and wiped the sprinkling of sweat off his forehead with his forearm.

The doc started gently smoothing back the hair from Becky's face. "Cody, run and fetch her brother."

Cody hesitated, wanting to stay. He wondered if the doctor was just trying to shield him from bad news.

"You heard him, son."

"Yes, Pa."

"When John gets here, you wait outside on the bench."

"Yes, Pa." Cody forced his words to sound natural, not wanting his father to know how disappointed he was to be isolated from the action. *When will you accept that I'm not a little boy anymore?* As he left to find John, his mind turned to Becky. He hoped with all hope that she would be all right.

The doctor lifted Becky's eyelids and placed his head to her chest. "Mason, fetch me those scissors." He nodded toward the top of the cabinet. "And the smelling salts. They're in the right side of the cabinet."

"What's wrong with her, Doc?"

"There's no name for it, but I've read about it."

That didn't sound good. Mason handed him the items and took a seat.

The doc rolled Becky onto her side. "An English doctor named Langdon Down has described the symptoms. As socially awkward as she is, Becky is highly functional and has some amazing, rare abilities. The best thing for her is to allow her to experience activities with people. That's probably why her folks sent her on a long trip to unfamiliar places."

"You know I meant her being out cold."

"Yep. Just thought I'd give you more information than you're paying for." The doctor smiled as he used the scissors to cut the back of the dress from the neckline to the waist. Mason cringed at the waste of new clothing, but he knew the price of a life could not be measured in money.

"It does explain a lot."

"Her brain works differently than ours, but if folks give her some allowances, they'll see she's a fine young lady. She has a difficult time understanding people, but she's trying, and she does particularly well with your son." When Doc Ritter pulled open the back of the dress, another layer of clothing could be seen underneath.

"That can't be a *corset*? What possible use could she have for a corset?"

"It's *not* a corset. It's binding cloth." He started to cut through the layers of thick bandages.

"What's it for?"

"I suspect she prefers to look like a boy, even in these fancy duds." With the final snip, there was an audible improvement in

Becky's breathing. The doctor turned her onto her back and waved the smelling salts under her nose.

Mason first felt confused by the doctor's suspicion, but then he reasoned out that a young lady traveling across open country with a man barely old enough to be called a man could be an invitation for unwanted attention. Maybe John or her parents had wanted her to look more masculine, and that's why she had shown up at his door wearing boys' clothes. Maybe she wanted to be called "Miss" because she felt like a lady on the inside, even though her outward appearance suggested she was a tomboy.

Becky awakened with a start.

"Whoa, girl. Lie right back. You've been unconscious. Look at me. Do you know your name?"

"Miss Becky McCoy."

"And how old are you, Miss Becky?"

"Fourteen."

Mason kicked the leg of a chair, creating a disturbance, and the doctor turned his head to look at him. Mason shook his head no, and then he flashed ten fingers and another three at Doc Ritter.

"Have you ever passed out before?"

"Twice."

Her answer surprised Mason, but he kept quiet.

"In the last three months?"

"No, sir."

"What did you eat today?"

"An apple noonish an' an egg an' a slice o' bacon 'round sunup."

"Do you hurt anywhere?"

She indicated her lower abdomen, and he palpated the area.

"Ever hurt there before?"

Again, she answered "twice," but this time she said the pains were in the last few months.

"When did this pain start?"

"Last evenin'."

"Did you do anything for it?"

She avoided his eyes while answering. "Whiskey in the night."

"Did it help?"

"Fer a while."

"Do you *like* whiskey?"

"'L no."

The doctor gave her a disapproving look—his first. The usually jovial man had seen many unusual cases and heard uncountable odd tales during his tenure as a doctor. His primary concern was helping folks, but he had raised two daughters of his own, and that had included putting the kibosh on foul language. "What's that, young lady?"

She grimaced. "I mean, no, sir." Then she blurted, "Asides, I don't much like the idea o' growin' hair on my chest."

Mason wondered if John had told her whiskey would do that. It was a commonplace notion used to encourage teen boys to drink, but he'd never heard of folks using it to discourage girls from doing so. He turned his attention back to the doctor's voice.

"Don't fret that, Miss Becky. It's an old wives' tale. Did you drink any today?"

"No sir. Mr. Starley beat me to it. But I took a warm bath this mornin'."

At this point, Mason was feeling like a fool. Miss Becky had held her cards so close to her chest that he hadn't even realized she'd been playing a game with him, and she'd won two hands! Rather than asking him for whiskey straight out, she must have rightly assumed, especially after his reaction to her petition for coffee, that he would not have allowed her any, so she'd invented that celebratory story following the foaling and acquired her whiskey in a roundabout way. And who ever heard of a bath as a gift to a child? He wondered what other sleights of hand Miss Becky had pulled on him.

When Mason rejoined the present, the doctor was asking, "Did it help?"

"Not so much as the whiskey."

"You've been out breaking horses today feeling poorly?"

"Tryin' to stay alive kinda took my mind offa it."

The doctor and Mason both smiled at her statement, finding it mildly humorous, but Becky had worn a straight face and spoken matter-of-factly. Mason reconsidered. He surmised from the doctor's earlier comment that Becky might not totally understand humor, and then her explanation hit him like a punch in the gut. He had been there, close up and personal, and saw her amazing feats with the mustangs. He had seen the sweat trickling down her face and soaking her shirt. He had seen her wobbly legs. And it had not once occurred to him that she had consciously been trying to not get herself killed. Of course, all the wranglers knew there was a risk of death when attempting to bust a bronco, but he doubted any of them were thinking about trying to stay alive when they slid their boots into the stirrups. He certainly hadn't been when he'd test-rode El Diablo.

"Okay, Miss Becky. Let's sit you up." Doc Ritter eased her up and held onto her hands as she swung her legs over the edge of the table. "Here's your medicine: No more tight binding cloths. Mrs. Ritter is going to draw you a nice, warm bath. You soak twenty minutes and then go eat a hearty, and I mean *real* hearty meal. And Mason, you make sure she does. She needs an adult looking after her, not a half-grown one. And afterward, Mason, you sneak a shot of whiskey out of the saloon for her or buy a bottle for yourself and discreetly give her a couple of swigs."

"Really, Doc? You got all educated back East and you come up with a hick-ish remedy like that?"

"It's a dirty little secret between doctors and their female patients. If your dear departed Emma were alive, she'd probably be drinking, too." He paused for a moment and then added an addendum: "But perhaps for a different reason." His lips curved into a sly smile as he let Mason absorb his innuendo. It didn't take long.

"Thanks, Doc. I can always count on you to make me feel better."

And the doctor laughed full force with his belly jiggling and eyes twinkling. A knock at the door interrupted him, and they heard John's voice call out.

The doctor answered him. "Come on in."

Mason was glad to relinquish responsibility for Becky and placed his hat on his head. "This is my cue to exit." He hesitated momentarily, then quietly asked the doctor if he could speak to him after he was finished with Becky. The doctor indicated yes, just as the door opened and John made his way in. Mason started to pass through the threshold going the opposite direction. The men nodded at each other by way of a greeting.

"Thanks for your help, Mr. Campbell."

"Didn't do much, but you're welcome, John. See you at five o'clock." He turned to face the patient. "You too, Miss Becky."

"Well, ya can 'spect I'll be late. Let Master Cody know?"

"I shorely will."

His response brought a hint of a smile to her face, and Mason hoped she knew that he was attempting to cheer her.

After Mason closed the door, John stepped over to his sister and took her hand. "What's ailing you, Spook? Mama and Papa aren't going to like it if I didn't keep you safe and healthy."

"Don't call me Spook. An' nothin' is wrong with me. I fainted from the heat an' jus' need ya to bring me some clothes. Tell 'im, Doc."

"That's about the gist of it, John. She'll be fine. Mrs. Ritter will fetch Becky when her bath is ready. You can stay here with her until then. You can pay Mrs. Ritter on your way out."

John turned to his sister. "You have money. It's your illness. You're paying."

Becky answered without a fight. "O' course. I never 'spected elsewise."

"Now that you've settled that, do you have any questions?" There being none, the doctor left the room. He found Mason loitering in the hallway. "Just what is it you want to see me about?"

Mason steered him away from Becky's room so their voices wouldn't carry. "Well, Doc, I just wanted to make certain you knew that Becky is thirteen today, not fourteen. Are you sure she's okay?"

"Well, now, Mason, I expect a girl knows how old she is."

"Are you saying she lied when she said she was turning thirteen today?"

"You'd be surprised how many females in this town fudge their ages down a bit."

"Yes, I guess I would. Thanks." Mason shook the doctor's hand and left him standing in the hallway. On his way out the door, Mason was wondering particularly which women the doctor was referring to. He even wondered if Elizabeth was one of them. Then he felt ashamed for thinking such an uncharitable thought. Elizabeth had no reason to misrepresent her age, besides which she'd been born right here in Leaning Rock and many folks had known her since that day. She just seemed older because she was sensible and mature in her thinking.

Cody was obediently waiting outside on the bench. "Pa, how is she?"

"She'll be all right. The doc's going to keep her a little while, but she'll be coming to supper with us. She said to tell you she'd be late."

Cody nodded his thanks for that information. "Pa, what's she got?"

"Well . . . Doc didn't rightly say."

"I'll bet it's female problems."

Mason's eyebrows rose to the brim of his hat. "Son, what do you know about 'female problems'?"

"Just that lots of girls at school are sent home or excused 'cause of their monthly. I sure wouldn't want to be a girl."

Son of a gun! Somehow Cody had learned at fourteen what Mason hadn't known at eighteen, and Mason had three sisters. He figured he was well overdue for a man-to-man talk with his son, but not just now. All he had the presence of mind to say was "And I'm sure glad you aren't one."

*   *   *

The same folks who ate supper at the Camp Bell Ranch the previous evening, with the addition of John, had reservations together at the Leaning Rock Café for 5 o'clock. As guest of honor and hostess, Becky was assigned the seat at the head of the rectangular table. If she had been present, she would have been flanked by Cody and her brother, but she had not yet arrived. Elizabeth Hill sat at the table's foot, with Mason on one side and Tom on her other. The arrangement placed Cody next to his father and John next to the sheriff. John was wearing the same fancy shirt as earlier, the pearl buttons aligned neatly in a perfect row.

The café was crowded, filled with extra tables and people. The sole waitress, twenty-year-old Miss Louisa, had been helping in her parents' café since just out of babyhood. Her parents, former slaves, had made the café a success with tasty basic food in generous portions. Louisa knew her business well but was wearing holes in her ankle boots trying to keep up with the demands of the customers. The room was noisy with friendly chatter and occasional callouts to Miss Louisa. Tales reliving the excitement of the day rang around the room; animated children rocked in their chairs, acting out motions of wild mustangs or using their fingers as guns shooting in the air; mugs of beer kept the cowboys happy and talking freely; in a far corner someone was playing "Oh, My Darling Clementine" on a harmonica, and he had a good following of people singing along.

John was ravenous after a busy day in town, and he anticipated having a long wait for food. "There's no need for us to delay ordering 'til Spooky appears. I pre-ordered a special meal for her yesterday."

"That was real brotherly of ya, John. Now maybe you could do somethin' else brotherly, like callin' her *Becky*. There's nothing spooky about her. It's all science and knowledge and experience. And if ya can't remember her name, I'd be happy to remind ya."

Mason wasn't particularly surprised to hear his son stand up for Miss Becky: Cody had never been one to allow a perceived injustice to go unchallenged. He was, however, astonished at the insinuation in Cody's tone—that he was willing to fight John. Although Cody had been in a few scraps with schoolmates and had even come home with a black eye once, he had always tried to avoid altercations. Mason looked at Elizabeth, and she, too, had apparently caught the meaning in Cody's tone because she winked at Mason as though they shared a secret.

"Well, well." John raised his eyebrows and smiled. "Did she tell you all that, Master Cody? More important than her words, what do your own eyes tell you after seeing her with the broncs this afternoon? For as many times as I've seen her work, it's still spooky to me."

Cody opened his mouth to answer, but Miss Elizabeth used the momentary silence to voice her opinion.

"Impressive is what I'd call it. Very impressive."

"Well, Miss Hill, I believe we can all agree on that. Maybe drink to it. I brought this bottle of Kentucky bourbon whiskey to share." He held up a bottle that had been sitting on the table in front of him. "Any takers?"

Mason and Tom responded in the affirmative, but Elizabeth declined the offer. In truth, everyone there would have been thrown off their horses if she had said yes. Mason fretted briefly that Cody would ask for a nip after his experience with whiskey the previous night, but to his relief, Cody politely abstained without mentioning his introduction to alcohol. Mason was fairly sure that his son had not imbibed previously, but Cody was at an age when curiosity and peer pressure could trump good sense, so he did not know for certain. Mason was glad that Becky wasn't there. Who knew if she would want a drink or if her brother would even allow her one? Yet, if she consumed a few swallows of alcohol with dinner, his dilemma of how to slip some to her later would be solved.

As Miss Louisa shot by, skillfully balancing trays laden with plates of steaks, John caught her attention. She scurried over soon after. He requested three whiskey tumblers, and everyone placed their food and beverage orders. It took just a few minutes for her to bring the tumblers, milk, and coffee, but in an instant, she was off again. The adults toasted "to Becky's impressive riding feats," and since Tom and Mason expressed their approval of the bourbon, John poured another round. Just then, Becky appeared wearing the same simple, drab dress as the previous evening. John frowned at her, since he had spent considerable time with Miss Hill choosing an appropriate print dress for her to wear this evening, but the room went wild, and she received a standing ovation. The diners stood until Miss Becky was seated at the table, which was accomplished with the help of Cody pushing in her chair.

"Are you feeling better, Miss Becky?"

"Yes, ma'am, Miss Elizabeth. By the way, that frock John bought fer me has intoler'bly itchy lace cuffs. I didn't have time to cut 'em off afore comin' here. An' 'bout those clothes ya set aside fer me? I reckon folks'll be giftin' some of 'em to me tomorrow fer treatin' their horses when I'm workin' with Doc Prescott. Anything they don't, I'll buy offa ya, so long as they don't scratch me up."

"Well now, Miss Becky, that's fine, and I'm glad you remarked on the subject of gifts because I have one for you."

"Ya do?"

Elizabeth was surprised at how astounded Becky sounded. "Of course. It's your special day. Happy birthday!" She reached under her chair and extracted a box wrapped in newsprint and trimmed in bright pink ribbon. "Could you pass this down?" She handed the box to Tom, who relayed it to John, who in turn gave it to its intended recipient.

"Open it, Beck."

Becky gently eased the ribbon from the box. "I lost my pink ribbon earlier today. I can find a use fer this. Thank ya kindly." Then she lifted the lid and presented two handkerchiefs for all to see. Both were white with crocheted trim and embroidered flowers in their centers: one a long-stemmed red rose; the other, a pair of tulips. "Miss Becky" was handstitched in a corner of each cloth.

Becky rubbed the cloth of the rose handkerchief between her fingers.

"They're for waving. Try it." Becky looked confounded, so Elizabeth took her own handkerchief from her reticule and demonstrated.

"Oh, now I know. I've seen ladies do that when they leave train stations."

"Precisely, dear."

"They're the best gift I ever received."

Elizabeth beamed. "Why thank you, dear. I'm glad you like them."

"I have something for you too, Miss Becky." The sheriff pulled a small box tied with a piece of twine from his shirt pocket and tossed it across the table to her.

Becky caught it two-handed and shook it before hazarding a guess: "A pair o' dice?"

"Now what would a young lady be needing dice for?" Tom warmed as her mouth formed a smile, apparently as a reaction to being called a lady. Becky smiled so infrequently, it was a pleasure to see when she did. She opened the box to reveal a pair of earrings.

"Ooh!" Her eyes lit up like sparkling stars.

"I know you said earrings aren't useful to you, but maybe you meant diamond-and-ruby ones aren't useful."

She nodded. "Shorely that's what I meant." She held them up for the others to admire. The silver dangles were about the size and shape of a thick postage stamp. The bottom half of each earring was designed to look like a stall door. The doors were exquisitely detailed, with vertical lines etched to represent the wooden boards of a stall door, hinges on one side, and a lock on the other. The upper half looked like a picture frame with the center cut out, and from that opening emerged a sculpted horse's head and neck that hung over the stall door with ears erect, as though the animal had come over to greet someone. Cody recognized that the horses were positioned very much like the ones in the Campbells' barn when they scuttled to meet Becky as she entered. There was clearly a left and right earring, so the horses on them could be worn facing each other. Becky expertly strung one wire loop, then the other, into the correct lobe and shook her head back and forth to try them out. They hung near her jawline, a quarter inch down from her ears, perfect for some movement but not too long to catch in her hair.

"Let me see, Beck." She turned to face her brother, and the earrings swayed with her head. "They suit you."

The others nodded their agreement.

"Very nice. Clearly you had them made special, Tom."

"Yes, Mace. It's the first time I've had occasion to visit the silversmith. I met with him this morning. He's part Navajo and is a master of his trade."

Cody agreed. "He's a real artist."

"They're the best gift I ever received."

Tom smiled, happy that Becky appeared to love them but also wondering if she had been trained by her social graces tutor to say that phrase every time she received a gift, since she apparently received so many. "They are courtesy of Arizona Territory for your role in capturing Big Bart and his gang."

"What do ya mean?"

"Paid for with part of your reward money."

"Ah! Aren't they fine! Way better'n money." Becky fingered the dangles and played with them until her brother told her to stop.

The food was slow to come, but the wait presented the opportunity for Mason to extract a gift he had hidden behind his back when he sat down. "From Cody and me. Cody, please pass this to Miss Becky." As Cody did so, Becky slapped her thigh.

"A lavender ribbon, an' I know that shape: bath oil!" She unwrapped the item, and sure enough, it did contain bath oil. Becky uncorked the bottle and took a whiff. "Lavender, like the ribbon! My favorite. Thank ya both kindly. It's the best gift I ever received!"

The sheriff chuckled, and Elizabeth warned him to behave with a discreet kick to the shin under the table.

"Actually . . ." Cody paused, and everyone looked at him expectantly. "Well, actually, it's not really from me. I got ya somethin' separate, Miss Becky. I'll give it to ya later. It's in the buckboard."

"Oh?" Mason eyed him suspiciously. He was hoping Cody hadn't spent his savings rashly.

"Now don't get angry, Pa, but I came by the money from bettin' my gold half eagle on Miss Becky breakin' El Diablo."

"You did *what*!"

"It seemed like a sure thing, Pa, and the odds were fifty to one."

Miss Elizabeth was the first to do the math. She didn't say anything, but she smiled broadly, clearly delighted at Cody's pluck and good fortune. The sheriff was more vocal. "Holy mother of, uh . . . cow. Holy cow! Your boy made a two-hundred-fifty-dollar killing, Mace!"

John stood and reached across the table, his arm extended for a congratulatory handshake. "Well done, boy. Well done!"

Cody gripped John's hand and shook it. "It was Miss Becky that did all the work. All I did was to believe in her." He turned toward Becky and acknowledged her with a nod, but she didn't seem to be caught up in the excitement.

John marked her mood. "Something's eating at you, Beck. What are you thinking?"

Sounding annoyed, she laid bare her concern. "Don't y'all know that talkin' money at a meal is a grievous faux pas?"

"A proper point, Miss Becky, and it stops here." Although Mason was happy for his son and didn't want to spoil his moment, he also didn't want Cody gambling, nor did he want his son's windfall to become public knowledge. He made his voice sound stern when he told Cody they would talk about it later, but Cody took the admonishment in stride. He suspicioned that his pa was secretly pleased.

Miss Louisa carefully wriggled her way between some tight tables, her hands held high, each balancing a large, round tray loaded with baskets. She stopped by Mason. "Mr. Campbell, could you lend me a hand? Here's some complimentary bread for folks while they're waitin'. It's gonna be a while yet."

Mason rose and removed two baskets of warm bread from a tray. The aroma was enticing. He handed one basket to Cody to pass around and offered the other to the patrons at the next table. He removed two more baskets and distributed them to other hungry diners at nearby tables. Once the first tray was emptied, he left Miss Louisa to distribute the rest by herself and returned to his seat to hear Cody turning the conversation in a new direction.

"John, do ya know any good horse tales?"

Miss Elizabeth passed the bread to Mason.

"Shorely." John winked at his sister, but if she realized he was teasing her pronunciation, she didn't react. "Here's one of my favorites."

Mason scanned the table and determined that the basket had made the rounds and that everyone was apparently waiting for him to take a slice before they began eating. He obliged them, and the eating commenced as the story commenced.

"About five years ago, Beck decided she wanted to drive a team, but Papa wouldn't allow it because he thought she was too young and too small, plus Mama thought no self-respecting girl ought to learn such a thing. Beck has always been a runt, so back then she must have weighed only about a sack and a half of grain. She was determined, however, and one day when we had visitors, she launched her plot."

Becky rolled her eyes. "He's makin' it all up, like he did 'bout my dotty ol' godmother comin'."

"Beck, Miss Reba *is* coming. I didn't fabricate it, and this other story is also swearable true." John was about to continue the tale, but before he could utter a syllable, Mason broke in.

"I checked the manifest, Miss Becky, and a gal named Miss Reba Martin is ticketed to arrive on the 3:30 stage tomorrow along with four McCoys. If Miss Martin is your godmother, John spoke truly."

"Oh no! Please no! I thought fer shore John was teasin'."

Elizabeth tried to help ease the girl's distress. "Now don't you fret, Miss Becky. She must be a sweet matronly lady to send you such fine clothing all the way from Paris, and she must love you very much to travel here to celebrate your birthday."

While Elizabeth was speaking, John motioned to the sheriff to pass the breadbasket to him, which Tom did. John withdrew a slice of bread, tore off a bite-sized piece, and ate it.

Mason added his support to Miss Elizabeth's logic. "Yes, Miss Becky. It's a long, hard trip for an elderly woman to sail across the Atlantic."

"Oh, she's not old!" Everyone turned to look at John. He popped another bite of bread into his mouth and smiled as he chewed it.

"She's *not*?" Becky had verbalized what they were all thinking.

Imitating her recent action, he rolled his eyes. "Goodness gracious, girl, she's your *godmother*, not your *grandmother*. She's not some ghastly old biddy. Miss Reba is barely older than Mama. She's coming all the way from Paris to help Mama with our newest brother or sister, and she may stay permanent."

Becky looked horrified to the others, but John either didn't take notice of her expression or didn't care. Cody did, though. Like when they were on the way to town, he patted her knee to comfort her. Mason saw the action, and astonished though he was, he was pleased to see his son showing compassion toward Becky. He would have made the gesture himself had he been sitting next to her.

Undeterred by the interruption, John forged ahead with the horse tale. "As I was saying, Beck launched her plot: A pair of young brothers had driven out to look at our quarter horses for their father. The father had bought from us before, but it was the first time he had allowed his sons to make a purchase without him. It was my job to sit the horses and put them through their paces while the men looked on. Beck was along too, well, to do what she does. So, while I was demonstrating, Beck approached their team, which was hitched to a wagon. She whispered to those horses all the while the men were choosing out their stock. The men knew their father put great confidence in Beck's horse abilities, so when they were finished selecting, they asked her opinion, and she rightly said the horses they chose were sound and in fine condition. Satisfied, the brothers were ready to return to our house and finish the deal with Papa. One brother lifted Beck and set her on the buckboard seat. She slid over to the side to make room. Then both men climbed aboard, but before they could take up the reins, Beck said in barely a whisper, 'They want *me* to drive.' The men had been previously entertained, seeing how Beck could quiet a barn full of horses or roust them up by simply walking through the barn, so they knew she talked to horses—and they believed the horses talked to her. The one lifted her again and set her between him and his brother. Then he handed the reins over to her without a second thought, and they proceeded on their way. Since the ploy worked, Beck has repeated it more times than I have fingers, but she's crafty. To my knowledge, Papa and Mama still don't know that she can drive."

When Miss Elizabeth giggled at the story, Cody and Tom joined in chuckling. Then full-fledged laughter broke out from nearby. Everyone in the Campbells' party had been listening with rapt attention, so none of them had noticed the silence that had pervaded the area around them. With the much-welcomed bread to keep their mouths occupied, the diners at the tables nearest them had turned their ears to John's story. They were now laughing jovially at the account. Some were hurling comments to Miss Becky, congratulating her on her ingenuity; others clapped or whistled. Tom turned toward the interlopers and gave them his best sheriff's "don't mess with me" stare. The eavesdroppers quickly looked away and began talking among themselves again.

Mason felt the color rise in his face. How had he been so stupid to fall for that trick? He looked at Becky questioningly, but she did not lift her eyes to meet his. Cody was all smiles, and Mason was particularly annoyed that he looked foolish in front of his son.

"That's a dangerous trick, Miss Becky. If folks find out you're being dishonest with them, they won't believe you when you're being honest. You'll lose your credibility."

The sheriff knew his friend well and was good at reading situations. He surmised that Mason had been caught in the snare and chuckled again, but he supported his friend: "I can attest to that."

John spoke for his sister, who had remained silent. "The thing is, no one but Beck knows what, if anything, a horse says to her, so there's no way to prove she lied." He reached for the basket and snagged the last piece of bread.

While Mason and his friends digested John's statement, Cody again turned the conversation. "I'd like to know when ya first knew ya were a horse whisperer."

And once again, John took the reins. "Master Cody, that's like asking, 'When did you first know you could see?' You never thought about it because you could always see. Well, Beck has always known she was a horse whisperer, from the time she first encountered a horse."

Cody encouraged Becky to speak for herself. "Is that so, Miss Becky?"

Becky took a deep breath before answering. "Well, I 'spect so, but it took a long while afore I reasoned out that other folks don't have horse sense."

Everyone laughed at Becky's unintended joke, and she sighed deeply in response. "Did I commit a faux pas?"

John placed a hand on her shoulder. "No, Beck. It's okay. You just said something funny. Laugh with us." And she did. When the moment passed, John turned his attention back to Cody.

"The better question, Master Cody, would be, 'When did *other* people first know that Beck was a horse whisperer?' and I can answer that because I was there."

Becky shook her head. "Not again. Ya always tell it wrong."

"You were too young to remember, Beck."

"Ya don't know what I can remember, John!"

"She always says that, but she never offers her version."

"'Cause ya wouldn't believe me!"

Cody didn't like seeing Becky riled. "*I* would believe ya, Miss Becky."

"Then mayhap I'll tell *you* later." She smirked at her brother.

"Go on, John, tell us your version."

"Certainly, Miss Hill." He was about to begin the story when some of their meals finally arrived, steaming and exuding a mouthwatering aroma. Miss Louisa served Becky first, a plate piled high with fresh fish, hushpuppies, and fried green tomatoes. "Happy birthday, sister!"

Upon seeing the plate, Becky's mood swung round. "John, ya got this special fer me? It's truly the best gift I ever received!"

John grinned. It had not been easy keeping weight on his sister. She was a picky eater, and much of the food they had encountered on this peregrination had been unpalatable to her. He had gone to considerable effort to hire a local boy to go fishing, and he had provided recipes to the café's cook, not knowing that she was well-versed in Southern cuisine. He now noticed that while he had downed three slices of bread, his sister's single slice remained untouched in front of her. He would have prodded her to eat it, but he knew that doing so would give rise to another mention of faux pas. Of all the proprieties that her social graces teacher had tried to instill, the only one that his sister had seemed to latch onto was avoiding faux pas. John was eager for tomorrow when his papa would arrive and take back the responsibility for Becky's health and welfare.

Miss Louisa set plates loaded with steaks and mashed potatoes in front Elizabeth and Tom and then retreated to the kitchen to fetch the final three meals. When everyone had been served, Becky pronounced her standard prayer to her brother's disapproving look. Nevertheless, he amen-ed along with the rest. Then Becky tentatively forked a piece of fish while the others reached for their knives. She had swallowed only one morsel when a weathered-looking woman approached the table. Her skin appeared dark and leathery, presumably from decades of outdoor work, and she was missing her top two front teeth. Her dress was faded and dirty, and parts of its hem drooped from stitches that had torn loose and hadn't been resewn. She may have been thirty-five, but she looked closer to fifty.

"Beg pardon, folks. I need the horse gal ta talk ta my Appy gelding." She moved toward Becky.

John stood to block her way. "I'm John McCoy, her brother and business manager, ma'am. She can see your Appaloosa in the morning. Come by Doc Prescott's. He and Beck will be working together 7:30 'til 11:30. That's your only opportunity because starting at 12:30, she'll be busting broncos 'til every last one of them is rideable."

The woman wrung her hands. "I can't wait 'til mornin'." She tried bypassing John and appealing directly to Becky. "Please, miss."

Now Tom intervened. "Miss Hannah, can't you see we're eating our supper?"

As if on cue, Mason filled his mouth with steak and began working it with his teeth. As he chewed, he stabbed the beefsteak with his fork. When he sawed off a section, bright red juice trickled out.

"I'll have to ask you to leave us be."

Hannah persisted. "I got a long ride ta get my chillun home tonight an' can't come back in the mornin'. I gotta know if my horse is safe fer 'em." Her eyes focused on Becky, waiting for a response. "Girl, yer green!"

John saw that she was right. "Look at me Spooky. *Spook!* Don't look at the blood. Look at me. That's it. Don't you be sick, Rebecca Ann McCoy! Hold your breath!"

Becky covered her mouth with both hands and started to rise. Cody jumped up to help her with her chair, and the men at the table rose out of politeness and concern.

"Now close your eyes and exhale slowly. That's it."

"I don't understand. This girl is anything but squeamish. I've seen her around blood."

"I can't explain it, Mr. Campbell. The sight of bloody meat turns her stomach."

Cody clutched Miss Becky's elbow and announced that he was taking her outside for some air. "Come on, Miss Becky. Let's go look at Miss Hannah's horse."

Hannah visibly brightened. This unfortunate event for Becky was a stroke of good luck for her. She led the way through the maze of tables and out the door.

After the trio had gone, Elizabeth reminded John that he had been about to tell them the story of when other people realized Becky was a horse whisperer. "You were saying?"

Before John answered, he flagged down Miss Louisa and instructed her to take Becky's and Cody's plates back to the kitchen. He apologized to Miss Elizabeth, saying he was famished and would tell the story after he made some headway on his meal. They all ate for a few minutes before John felt ready to talk.

"Well, as you may know, our family consists of four older brothers, Becky, and three younger siblings, but what you may not know is that there were other children. Mary and Ruth came between me and Beck. Sadly, they both died of measles the winter they were but two and one."

"I'm so sorry. It must have been awful for your whole family, but especially for your mother."

"Yes, Miss Hill, Mama was understandably distraught to lose both of her baby girls, so when Beck was born, Mama was overly protective, and it became my job, as the next older sibling, to keep an eye on her."

The café was clearing out, and Miss Louisa found time to bring a pot of coffee to their table. After she poured them all drinks and left, John continued his account.

"Well, Beck was a difficult baby to love. She was colicky, crying hour after hour for no reason. She never learned to sleep through the night—still doesn't—and she couldn't tell anyone what was wrong because she was a real slow learner. She didn't speak one word 'til she was three. The only person who could tolerate her was Papa.

"Mama was afraid to take Beck anywhere, such as to town or on a social call to a neighbor's, because she didn't want her to be exposed to illness like Mary and Ruth had been, and she didn't want anyone gossiping about this unhappy, slow-witted baby, so she kept Beck to the house. Beck never took a buggy ride or even went near a horse 'til one day Mama reached her limit. Beck was fussing and whining, and Mama was exhausted, being preggers with the twins. So, she told me to take Beck out to her papa, who was working with the horses in the stables.

"I grabbed Beck by the hand and dragged her outside kicking and screaming. When we entered the stables, I saw and heard Papa several stalls down. He was cracking a whip over an uncooperative, barely broke breeding colt. I knew enough not to interrupt him, so we stood at the stable door waiting, Beck barefoot in a shift, crying. The colt was foaming at the mouth, and the dozen or so other horses nearby were pacing in their stalls and blowing and pawing, so that the stable was filled with frenzied movement and a cacophony of sounds. And then, suddenly, as though a decisive battle had ended, all was quiet and still, and out of the quietude I heard Beck's first words. She said clear as a bugle playing 'Taps' on a cold, still night, 'Spooky. I spooky.' And that's when we knew she was a horse whisperer, and that's how she obtained her nickname."

John paused a moment to gulp a swallow of coffee while his audience murmured their amazement to each other, but he didn't let them chatter long. "And for the record, my siblings and I have called her that for most of her life. I don't mean any disrespect by it. It just doesn't come natural to call her Becky, and for sure I'm not going to call my sister *Miss* Becky. But back to the story, Beck had barely spoken before the horses' eerie silence ended, and a new phenomenon occurred. All the horses in the barn, and there had to be two dozen or more, approached their stall gates and started whinnying and nickering and calling—I thought to each other—but

Papa realized it was to Beck. Our family folklore held that Papa's great-grandfather Daniel Sullivan in Ireland was our family's first horse whisperer. Then came an uncle, and later still, a cousin who lived in France. Papa knew the stories of their abilities by heart and recognized the signs that Spooky and the horses were communicating."

"That's fascinating."

Mason was skeptical about the tale, but he agreed with Elizabeth that it was fascinating. Before he could ask any questions, Cody and Becky returned. Becky pranced in, sporting a bright pink knitted shawl across her shoulders. She looked invigorated to Mason, as though helping Hannah had revitalized her.

John pulled out her chair for her. "What was it, Beck?"

As she sat, so did Cody. Mason was surprised neither of them seemed to notice or care that their meals were missing. He spotted and made eye contact with Miss Louisa. She signaled to him that she had seen the pair return, so he refocused to hear Miss Becky's answer.

"I knew what it was even afore I went out—I talked to 'im earlier. He can't see right, an' he's kickin' at shadows. All she hasta do is keep blinders on 'im."

"I doubt Miss Hannah can afford blinders."

The sheriff disagreed. "I reckon she can, Mace. She was selling her wares this afternoon and looked to have a steady stream of customers for her preserves and quilts and knitted baby items."

"Miss Hannah gifted me this splendid shawl. It matches my hat perfeckly. It's the best gift I ever received."

The men seemed at a loss for words, so Elizabeth complimented Miss Hannah's skills and said the shawl looked fine.

"And don't forget the jerky."

"Yep, she gifted that too, but we already ate most o' it."

"Well, your supper is being kept warm for you in the kitchen, and Beck, I expect you'll polish your plate when it comes." John glanced up and saw Miss Louisa heading their way with a plate in each hand. "Which is now."

The doctor's words had settled forward in Mason's mind, and he silently hoped that Becky would do as her brother commanded and eat a hearty meal. Becky did not look cooperative, however. She rolled her eyes. Then she whispered loud enough for all to hear, "That's a faux pas on ya, John."

*   *   *

The meal had taken longer than any of them had anticipated, and Becky was picking at her food. Finally, unable to bear any longer delay, Miss Elizabeth spoke up. "I hope you'll excuse me, Miss Becky, but I have work to do at Sam Hill's before morning.

I'll see you tomorrow afternoon at your party, if not before. Happy birthday, again! Thanks for the supper, Mason." She threw him a quick smile. "Good night, all."

"I'll walk you to the store, Elizabeth." Mason started to rise, but Tom jumped to his feet.

"No need, Mace. I'd be happy to escort her. It's time for me to go, too. I have duties to attend to: prisoners to feed and rounds to make. The town sounds quiet, but I expect it to liven up in the coming hours. Those prisoners will likely be breakfasting with company."

"Okay, Tom. Cody and I will see you in the morning."

"Thanks again for your assistance today and for the meal. Good night, everyone." Tom helped Elizabeth with her wrap, took her by the elbow, and steered her toward the door.

Cody and John echoed goodbyes to them as they left. Then John displayed his irritation. "Beck, hurry it up! I have things to do, too."

Becky scrunched her face and growled at her brother in response. Then she returned to stirring her food around her plate. Mason and Cody pretended not to notice her behavior, though Mason was thinking it was past time to declare supper over if she wasn't going to eat. So much for a hearty meal.

"All right, Beck. Can you just tell me what's eating you?"

Thankfully, she had an answer.

"Where am I sleepin' tonight, John?"

"So that's it. I was figuring on the boarding house."

"Ya know I can't sleep in a town!"

"Well, you may have to make do. I don't see many options." Perhaps he was hoping Mr. Campbell would invite her for another night in his barn. When Mason remained silent, even with Cody's eyes begging him, John suggested another location. "I'll see if Mr. Pruitt will let you bed down in the stables with the mustangs. They're at the edge of town, plus you've already met all the horses. Would that satisfy you?"

"Oh, John, would ya do that fer me?"

"I'll go ask him right now, but I doubt he's going to want you making friends with those broncs the night before you're to break them."

Mason thought John had a good point, but he didn't want to offer his barn until all other options were off the table. If John knew his silence was a bluff, Mason would surely be hosting her again tonight. He had come to like Becky, but he didn't want her overnight again. "Cody and I will stay with Miss Becky until you return, but we have chores to do back at Camp Bell, so please don't dillydally."

"No, sir!" John pressed his hat onto his head and picked up his bottle of whiskey.

"Would you mind leaving the bottle?"

John looked surprised, but he slid the bottle down the table to Mason. "I'm glad you like it."

"I like it well enough I'd like to keep it."

"For sure." Now John looked pleased. "I lugged several bottles from home to gift to people. It gives me dual pleasure to be rid of one."

"Then we both benefit. I'm much obliged."

John tipped his hat as he strutted past Miss Louisa and out into the street. Miss Louisa stopped at their table and started to clear some of the dishes that were no longer needed. "Can I bring you anything? More coffee? Fresh apple pie?"

"I could eat pie, Pa. Could you, Miss Becky?"

"I reckon I could try, Master Cody. Leastways, it's gotta taste better'n this warmed-over fish. Coffee would help me down it."

"Miss Louisa, two pieces of pie and another coffee, please."

"Right away, Mr. Campbell." She reached for his empty whiskey tumbler, but he waved her off, so she left with the other dishes that she'd collected.

"Miss Becky, this may be a faux pas, but I need to talk to you before Miss Louisa or John returns."

"Shorely." She placed her fork on her plate and gave him her full attention.

He lowered his voice, though no one was seated near them anymore. "Did Doc Ritter mention to you that a shot of whiskey tonight would be good medicine?"

"Yes, sir."

"Good, because now's your chance to take one." He poured a finger's width of whiskey into his tumbler. "If you think you need more for tonight or tomorrow, I could let John think I was taking the bottle back to Camp Bell but make sure it ends up with you." Mason didn't like being underhanded, but the doctor had given him, not her brother, the responsibility of Becky's pain management. When Mason was seventeen, he wouldn't have wanted to know about his sisters' female problems, and he was trying to do both John and Becky a favor.

"This'll do fer now, an' I'll take ya up on the bottle."

Mason instructed Cody to pass the glass to Miss Becky. "We'll talk about this later, Cody, but don't take it as my permission for you to drink any." He thought to himself of the growing list of subjects he needed to discuss with his son. How was it that just two days around this girl caused so many issues that needed immediate attention? Maybe he'd been lax with his fatherly talks while thinking about his own relationship with Elizabeth.

Becky held her nose against the alcoholic odor and took a deep swallow. She repeated the action and shuddered involuntarily.

"And that's supposed to be the good stuff." Cody recalled that she hadn't shown any reaction to the swig she'd taken the night before.

"There could be a higher concentration of alcohol in it. Are you doing all right, Miss Becky?"

She slid the tumbler to Mason, just as he spotted Miss Louisa coming their way with their order. As soon as she received her coffee, Miss Becky drank several sips. She hadn't spoken since downing the whiskey.

Mason was glad to see Miss Becky attack the pie with gusto. Having food in her belly would help with the alcohol absorption. After a few heaping bites, Becky quietly uttered that she also had a faux pas item to discuss. Curious, Mason nodded for her to go ahead.

Becky recounted her morning visit with Doc Ritter and disclosed that he had given her the results of the equine mucus test at the conclusion of her afternoon office visit. "It's kinda rare, but yer brood mare Stella has yeast. Ya gotta treat 'er with a vinegar flush. Have Doc Prescott retest 'er afore ya breed 'er next summer. Yer lucky—she could o' had much worse."

"Son of a gun! Thank you, Miss Becky." He flashed a grateful smile her way.

"Uh, Pa . . . it wasn't free advice. I told Doc Ritter you'd pay for the test."

Mason's mood had improved in the last minutes with Becky's eating and drinking and a solution to his mare's problem. He laughed at his son's revelation. "Well, it's not the first time you've committed my funds to others, but it is the first time it wasn't for your own benefit. Do you remember that candy you charged weekly to my tab at Sam Hill's for two months without my knowledge?"

Now it was Cody's turn to laugh. "I was just a kid, Pa, but I knew Miss Elizabeth would forgive me the debt if ya wouldn't pay. Sometimes I think she likes me more than she likes you!"

"Whoa, that was low." He sounded serious, but his eyes were glimmering.

Miss Becky sat wide-eyed and silent.

"You remember how I made you work off the debt when I found out what you'd done?"

"I sure do. Rather than switch off our weekly floor-moppin' chore, ya made me do all the moppin' for two months. What do ya think of that, Miss Becky?"

"I think it's fun listenin' to tales 'bout other folks instead o' 'bout me." Then she laughed harder than they had ever heard her, and they couldn't help but join in.

*   *   *

John returned to the table to find the three remaining diners in a jovial mood. He was not feeling jovial, but he was pleased to see that his sister was and that she was polishing off the last of a piece of apple pie. More apples, one of her staples, but at least she had eaten something.

Mason asked what they all wanted to know: "What did Mr. Pruitt say?"

At that moment, Miss Louisa approached them again. With just a few people still supping in the café, her service had improved immensely. She asked if John wanted pie and if anyone needed anything else. After receiving a negative answer, she told Mason the amount of the bill. Mason paid it using a combination of his money and Miss Becky's and told Miss Louisa to keep the change. She thanked him, gathered the remaining dishes, and left the group to finish their conversation.

After Miss Louisa was out of sight, Mason returned Becky's surplus birthday money to her. She seemed surprised, but he was the one taken aback when she took care to count it, and he wondered if she thought he had cheated her. But then she handed the money back to him, rooted around in her silk purse, and counted out enough more money to total ten dollars.

"It's fer yer payin' off Mr. Starley. I don't reckon John's gonna foot that one." Before Mason could respond, she moved on. "John? What o' Mr. Pruitt?"

"Oh, right." Her brother removed his hat and ran his fingers through his dark, wavy hair. "Well, Beck, he was tough, but we worked out a deal: you can sleep with the broncs, but you can't participate in the contest tomorrow, and you have to stay away while the contestants ride."

"Fine."

And she really did seem fine with the arrangement, so with that settled, Mason was eager to leave. "Okay, son, we can go back to the ranch." He stood up to encourage the others to do the same and started backing slowly toward the door.

Cody was disappointed with the deal. He druther Miss Becky spend the night in the Camp Bell barn and the two of them ride into town together in a repeat of this morning. He wanted to see her put on a show and tame all the remaining broncs. He liked watching the crowd's reaction as Miss Becky worked, and he liked hearing the cheers when she bestowed the prize money.

John rose next and shadowed Mason, leaving Cody to help Miss Becky from her chair. "Mr. Campbell, you'll most likely be the first contender at 12:30. Mr. Pruitt is going to talk to judge Sheriff Claiborne about putting you up first because you missed your turn when you were helping with Mr. Reeves and with the bank robbery."

That was welcome news. Mason had been concerned that he wouldn't get a turn because the contest had circled through the other contestants and made it back to the beginning of the list before it had ended for the day. "It's a safe bet that Cody and I will be in town before noon. I wouldn't want to be late for my ride."

Cody helped Becky gather her things, being sure to nab the whiskey bottle. "Uh, Miss Becky? Since ya won't be allowed to watch, would ya like to go with me to the swimmin' hole at noon? It's not too far from here." Belatedly, he asked his father for permission. "Can I, Pa? Sorry, but I'd miss yer ride."

Mason didn't answer directly. Now that everyone was standing, he turned around and paraded the group to the door, where they lingered for a minute. He felt conflicted. He would like Cody to see him in action, but with his son elsewhere for a few hours, he might catch a little alone time with Miss Elizabeth. In addition, he wasn't sure if it was appropriate for a young lady and a young man to go unescorted to a swimming hole, and he did think they would be alone. The bronco-busting contest only came once a year, and anyone who could be there would be there, especially since they were expecting to see Miss Becky ride.

"Master Cody, ya know I'm deficient at swimmin'.

Mason smiled. Maybe Miss Becky would settle the matter without him having to say anything, but Cody was persistent.

"Ya don't have to swim, Miss Becky. It's a peaceful place. Ya can write a song, and I could bring my guitar. Me and Pa would ride into town, and after you're finished workin' with Doc Prescott, ya could borrow Raven, and the two of us would ride to the swimmin' hole." When Miss Becky was slow to respond, Cody sweetened his proposal: "And I'd bring burnt bacon." After hearing that, Miss Becky seemed to be doing some serious considering. Cody saw her left eyebrow raise and her lips scrunch together.

"Go, Beck. Let it be your play time. Just be back before the stage comes in at 3:30." John turned to Mason. "I mean assuming it's all right with Mr. Campbell." He looked at the man questioningly.

The outing meant so much to his son, how could Mason refuse? Although he wasn't one to lend his prize mount to just anyone, he trusted that Miss Becky could handle the large horse. And he trusted Cody to behave like a gentleman. "Fine." More importantly, he wanted to hear Becky's approval.

"Miss Becky?"

"Fine."

Mason noticed that she said it in the same tone as her agreement to Mr. Pruitt's terms, with no hesitation but no enthusiasm. On the other side, he thought his son looked like he would burst with happiness. If they hadn't been indoors, he reckoned Cody would have let out a joyous, "Yahoo!"

Becky was difficult for Mason to read. Her interest in going with Cody was clearly more veiled than Cody's interest in going with her. It was sad to think that she may be mostly interested in the bacon, but that had been one reason he had given permission to Cody. The other reason was that John had encouraged the encounter. Surely, he wouldn't have done so if he had any doubts about Cody sullying Becky's reputation.

With the swimming matter resolved, the group stepped outside to find the air thick with humidity. The sun shone low in the sky, hidden by a layer of cloud banks that were periodically flashing with lightning. Soon folks would begin lighting their lamps. Tinkly piano music emerged from the Rustler's Stoop, along with raucous laughter. The cowboys were obviously having a good time, drinking and whooping it up. Almost immediately after Miss Becky exited the café, horses in the street began to vocalize and turn toward her as far as their reins allowed them.

Mason sent Cody for the buckboard while he went for Raven. John was to walk with his sister as far as the boarding house, at which point they would wait for Cody, who would drive Becky to the stables. John found walking with Becky to be slow business. She wanted to greet all the horses, or they wanted to greet her, he didn't know which. By the time John and Becky reached the boarding house, Cody was driving toward them. He came to a halt and hopped down. John handed his sister off and said he'd meet her at Doc Prescott's at 7:30 the next morning.

Miss Becky climbed aboard and took a seat. She whispered away to the team as Cody took a moment to reorganize the items in the wagon. During this process, he collected the birthday gift he'd bought for Miss Becky and brought it around for her to see.

"Sorry it's not wrapped in paper, but I hope ya like it."

"A new big travelin' bag! It's the best gift I ever received!"

Cody grinned, happy with her response. "Made from genuine oriental carpet." He tossed it up to her. "Take a gander inside."

She was caressing the colorful sides like the bag was a pet dog and even rubbed her face against them, inhaling deeply. "It smells so clean an' new!"

"Sure, but look inside."

With his second request, she removed the key from a string attached to one of the handles, put it in the lock, turned it, and pulled the bag open. "Ooh! A doctor's bag!" She tugged it out of the carpetbag.

"It's a leather Gladstone bag, but it's not new. It's an older one that Doc Ritter was castin' off, but I cleaned it up and got yer initials branded onto it, 'R.A.M.,' for Rebecca Ann McCoy."

"I see that! At first, I thought it said 'A.R.M.' an' couldn't figure the meanin', but now I see the letters are fer my name. I'm real glad ya didn't go with 'B.M.' fer Becky McCoy. My brothers tease me 'bout that."

Cody nodded. "I thought of that, too. Best to use all three initials."

By now Miss Becky had opened the doctor's bag. She squealed, spooking the team hitched to the buckboard. Cody grabbed onto the harness and kept them from pulling forward, while Miss Becky sat with her back against the seat and closed her eyes, apparently trying to calm herself and the team. When the horses settled, she whispered the contents into the evening air: "Veterinary tools!"

"If ya look closely, you'll notice they're mostly yer old ones. I took the liberty of movin' 'em from yer tattered bag to this one. I didn't know what ya needed, but Doc Prescott added a few things, mostly supplies. When ya work with him tomorrow, he might gift ya more."

"Oh, Master Cody, this is truly the best gift I ever received. Thank ya kindly!"

"There's one more gift."

"What's that?"

"I'll give it to ya tomorrow at the swimmin' hole."

"Shore. That would be fine."

"Oh, I almost forgot. Here's the whiskey." He stretched out his arm to hand it to her. She placed it in her bag, and then Cody reached up and grabbed the frame of the buckboard to hop aboard. Miss Becky clicked to the team, and off they went clip-clopping down the road with half the town's horses making a ruckus. The pair of them saw Sheriff Claiborne on the street and waved. He was shaking his head like he couldn't believe all the noise was caused by one slight, red-haired girl.

As the buckboard approached the sheriff's office, Mason trotted over on Raven and rode alongside. His horse whinnied and danced with knees high but kept moving in the right direction. Miss Becky drove to the stables, where they met burly Mr. Pruitt, who had prepared a stall for Miss Becky to sleep in. Becky entered the big building first, and all the broncs immediately went wild. Behind her, Cody pushed her bicycle, and Mason carried her old and new bags. The Campbells dropped off her belongings and said a quick goodbye, eager to get home and take care of their stock. Mr. Pruitt followed them out into the air.

"Son, tie Raven to the back of the buckboard." Cody got right on it. Once he was out of earshot, Mason spoke briefly with Mr. Pruitt. "Buck, you're a better man than I."

"Hogwash. Happy to have her. It's only fer one night, an' it saves my contest. An' like I told her brother, she'll be safe here. No one will bother her." He offered his hand to Mason. "All's set with Tom. You'll be up first tomorrow at 12:30."

Mason grasped the other man's thick fingers and firmly shook them. "Thanks, Buck. I'm beholden to you."

As Mr. Pruitt headed back into the building, Mason climbed aboard the buckboard in one smooth motion. He reached for the reins, but Cody hesitated.

"What?"

"They want *me* to drive." There was a second of silence before both Campbells broke into laughter. Mason playfully pulled the brim of Cody's hat down over his eyes. After Cody had repositioned his hat, Mason motioned with his fingers to hand over the reins, and Cody complied. Mason thwacked the reins, and the horses lurched forward.

When Mr. Pruitt reentered the stables, the broncs were eerily quiet. El Diablo had been quartered as far from the mares as possible, near one end of the stables, and Miss Becky had entered his stall. She was standing there brushing his neck and whispering to him.

"Miss! Miss Becky! Ya shouldn't be in there. Go back to yer own stall." To Mr. Pruitt's relief, she gave the stallion's neck a final brush and slipped out of the stall. She returned to her own, as he had ordered, and began reorganizing her belongings, arranging her clothes and ribbons and things in her new bag.

*   *   *

It wasn't long before the Campbells' team was out of town and on the dusty road home. The cloud banks on the horizon continued to flash in the distance, but the sky overhead was mostly clear. The moon and stars provided sufficient light for Mason and Cody, but the Campbells kept a lantern in an emergency box in the buckboard in case they got caught in the dark. Things could happen: a wheel could break; a horse could throw a shoe. The road was familiar and well worn, and the horses had no trouble navigating it. Their hooves sounded a steady rhythm with each step of their quick-paced walk. No doubt they anticipated going home to food and the comfort of the barn. Anyone who ever owned a barn-sour horse knew that horses had such thoughts.

Mason wanted to talk to Cody about many subjects, and the drive home afforded him a good opportunity because they were alone and in a confined space, not that he expected trouble from Cody. The worst he could imagine was that his son would ride off in a rage on Raven, but he reckoned the probability of Cody's doing that was about the same as a poker player being dealt a full house with no draw; that is, possible but unlikely.

He contemplated where to begin: Cody's concealing his knowledge yesterday of how horses react to Miss Becky's presence? In all honesty, Mason knew he wouldn't have believed Cody if the boy had spoken up. The horses' reactions had to be seen to be believed. Maybe he should start by asking what happened on the porch this morning when Miss Becky was in tears? Or maybe that was best kept between Cody and Becky. He was curious about the bicycle-rides-distraction in town, and he was positive the lessons *had* been a distraction. Had Cody done anything that required disciplining? What was a fair consequence for Cody's actions, especially his gambling? And something needed to be said about alcohol consumption. And what about the swimming hole tomorrow, appropriate gifts for girls, girls in general, and more specifically, Miss Becky. Yes, she was the subject he wanted to address. All the other topics came down to her.

Mason clicked to the horses to encourage them as they approached a slight incline. As he was about to speak, Cody broke their silence.

"Uh, Pa, what do ya think of Miss Becky?"

Mason chuckled to himself at the timing. "Well, son, I'm pleased you introduced the subject. I wanted to talk with you about her."

"No foolin'!"

"No foolin'. What do *you* think of her?"

"I like her, Pa! She's the most remarkable person I ever met, but what do *you* think?"

Mason took care before answering. He wanted to be honest, but he didn't want to tarnish Cody's first infatuation. "I like her, too, son. She has many fine qualities, but I have concerns about her."

"Is that why ya wouldn't allow her to stay another night in our barn?"

"I would have allowed her. She's been traveling with her brother for weeks, and I'm sure he has arranged for her to sleep in many different places. I wanted to give John an opportunity to find a suitable place in town before I offered our barn. I think Miss Becky is dangerous, son.”

“Dangerous?” Cody sat up straighter and looked at his father defensively. “That’s—”

“Yes, dangerous. For one, she shot off a pistol in our barn. For—”

“That was—”

“Before you defend her, let me finish explaining without interruption.”

“Yes, sir.” He had said it respectfully, but Mason could tell from Cody’s posture that he was riled. He had crossed his arms, and instead of continuing to look at him when he spoke, Cody was looking straight ahead into the night.

“For another, she has trouble controlling her emotions, like when she punched you without warning. For a third, she does things that could get her killed, such as riding broncs and trying to capture bank robbers.” Mason could think of additional behaviors that were concerning to him, but he stopped after the three he ranked highest in importance. “Go ahead, Cody, I’ll hear you now, but uncross your arms first.”

In the moment it took Cody to comply, his father’s words seemed to hit him like a hoof to the face. His entire demeaner changed. “I see what ya mean. I was goin’ to say that she had good reasons for doin' those things, but now I see that even with good reasons, they're dangerous."

"Good. I'm glad you didn't let your feelings override your sense. Did *you* do anything dangerous today, Cody? Anything I should know about?"

"No, Pa. I played a little mischief, but nothin' lawless or harmful."

"Good. I just want you to be careful, Cody. Miss Becky doesn't always think first, so when you're with her, like at the swimming hole tomorrow, you must be particularly mindful. Things can happen when a couple is alone, and I trust you to make sure nothing does."

"Pa!" Cody's voice raised a notch. "You don't think I would try anything untoward, do ya?"

"There's no reason to get riled. No, I don't think that or I wouldn't allow you to go, but she can't swim, and she may not know her limits. I don't know if she'll even touch the water, but she likes to have fun, and it will be up to you to keep her safe."

"Sure, Pa. I'll be mindful of safety."

Mason felt better with that assurance. He didn't say it, but he was glad Miss Becky was passing through and wouldn't be settling in Leaning Rock. She'd be gone in a day or two.

They were close to home by now. Visibility was good. The outline of the two heads of the Dos Cabezas Peaks twenty miles ahead acted as a landmark. To the southeast, the much farther away but much larger Chiricahua Mountains dominated the landscape. The land on either side of the road was covered in grass and brush, the perfect cover for rabbits. A pack of coyotes yipped eerily from somewhere ahead.

"Cody, I wanted to talk to you about drinking and gambling, too."

"Pa, I'm level-headed. You're always saying that. Didn't ya take notice I didn't ask for any whiskey or even coffee at supper? Someday, when I'm ready, I reckon I will. Miss Becky is ready, but she's not proddin' me to join in. There's been times ya don't know of when I've been prodded by schoolmates to do things like smokin' cigars behind the church and drinkin' hard cider, but those are part of growin' up, aren't they? And I always had enough horse sense to know when to stop. You smoke and drink and gamble some; don't ya expect I will too?"

"Of course. I just don't expect you will at fourteen." Mason turned the buckboard through the Camp Bell entrance posts and heard Shep bark a joyful greeting. "I was thinking you should have a consequence for betting on Miss Becky, but—"

"What did I do wrong?"

"I was going to say, 'but I've reconsidered.' You put forth a good argument that shows you're growing into a man. I just didn't count on you growing up so soon."

Cody beamed, happy that he had skirted any consequences, but happier that his father understood his thinking and approved of it.

The night was darker now, and so was the trail. The blotchy shadows of the trees lining the long approach looked like ruts in the roadway. The horses knew the difference and handily avoided the real ruts they knew so well, as they headed toward the house.

Mason felt happy, too. He thought that their conversation had gone particularly well, thus far. This next part should be easy.

"Cody, I also wanted to talk to you about giving gifts to girls. I think you did fine with Miss Becky's birthday gifts. You stayed within your means, and you didn't give her any expectations."

"Expectations. How do ya mean?"

"For example, jewelry is off limits to boys your age. It's unsuitable because it symbolizes future commitment. It creates the expectation in a girl's mind that you intend it as a stepping-stone to a wedding band."

"Oh!"

"You don't want to spend much money, or the girl thinks you are overly fond of her. And you don't want to give something on a special day, like Saint Valentine's Day, because that also creates expectations. Timing and cost are the basics. It's better to give nothing than to over-gift. Do you understand?"

"Yes, sir. No jewelry, no special occasions, no costly gifts."

Mason expressed his approval as he drove the horses past the hitching rail near the corral and reined them in at the barn. He climbed down from the buckboard, eager to unhitch the team and begin the nightly chores. As he worked, the horses in the pasture came trotting in, some neighing greetings.

Without needing to be told, Cody climbed into the wagon, lit the lantern from their emergency box, and set it on the driver's seat to help his pa see. Next, he jumped down from the buckboard and gave Shep a quick pat. Boy and dog headed into the barn, where Cody fetched another lantern, lit it, and went back outside to hang it on a barn peg designed for that purpose. Then Cody walked over to help his pa with the team. While performing his lantern duties, he had given more thought to his father's gift advice, plus he had worked up some courage. "Um, Pa, there's one more subject I'd like to talk to ya about."

Mason could hear the hesitancy in his son's voice. Late as it was, the chores would have to wait. It was his responsibility to lead Cody in the right direction when it came to girls, or specifically, Miss Becky. "Sure, son. What is it?"

"Miss Elizabeth."

That threw Mason. "Miss Elizabeth? What about her?"

"Well, Pa, you've been friends with her for years."

"Yes, she's a good friend."

"Are ya courtin' her, Pa?"

"Well, of course I am! I thought you were fine with the idea! Your ma, God rest her soul, has been gone five years now." He didn't mean to sound so gruff, but it was late, and he was tired, and he thought he was going to be discussing Cody's girl, not his own.

"I have nothin' against it, Pa. I like Miss Elizabeth. I was just wonderin' if she knows it?"

"That you like her?"

"No, that *you* do. Have ya given her any gifts with expectations?"

"Cody, what are you getting at?"

It was now or never. "Pa, I saw her and Sheriff Claiborne kissin'."

Saturday

Chapter 7

Sheriff Claiborne lived with his tubby tabby, Catrina, in the second-story room of the widow Grayson's house. The room was a perk of being sheriff, paid for by the town coffers. Widow Grayson's house was conveniently located on Granite Street, which crossed Main Street between the sheriff's office and the telegraph office on the one side and the saloon and bank on the other. So as not to disturb the widow with the tenant's comings and goings, the room had a separate stairway entrance on the side of the house.

The sheriff's room was sizeable, with a fireplace in one corner and a picture window that provided light and a view. It came furnished with a rug, bed, nightstand, armoire, small pine dining table with two matching chairs, and a cushioned rocking chair, but the rocker was of little use because Cat had commandeered it. Although there wasn't a cook stove, the room did possess a basin with a hand-pump faucet for water. Tom had added a few personal items, such as curtains, his vibrantly colored, tasseled Mexican blanket on the bed, a framed oval mirror above the basin, and some wall art, making the room feel comfortable and inviting. Moreover, he kept his place tidy and respectably clean.

Well before sunrise on Saturday, Tom awoke from the sound of a fist banging on his door and the calls for "Sheriff! Sheriff! Tom, wake up!" He was a light sleeper and was fully roused before Cat had even stirred. Disturbances like these were common for Tom, and anyone friendly enough to be using his first name was welcome. Besides, he recognized Buck Pruitt's booming voice. Thankfully, Mrs. Grayson was hard of hearing and would likely sleep through the racket.

"Come in!" Tom felt around in the dark until he located and lit the nightstand lamp. His loaded Colts were stowed under his bed.

The burly man tentatively peeked in before entering. "No lock?"

"Nothing worth stealing." Tom didn't bother to further explain that the lock had been broken before he'd inherited the room from the previous lawman, and he hadn't troubled himself to replace it. "What's happened, Buck? Am I going to be needing that coffee?" He stifled a yawn as he nodded toward the steaming porcelain pot Buck was holding out in front of him. Tom identified the pot as a fixture in the boarding house dining room and wondered if staff or Buck had made the coffee.

"Yes, sirree! It's a gift fer seeing me at this godawful hour." Buck set the pot on the table, freeing his beefy fingers to extend a hand in friendship.

Tom rolled out of bed to meet it.

"It's Miss Becky."

"What about her?"

"Dagnamit, Tom, she done stole El Diablo!"

"What! Are you certain?" Tom pointed at a chair. "Sit down and tell me about it." He knew Miss Becky was eccentric, but he couldn't believe she'd steal the stallion. That was a hanging offense. "Start from the beginning." He produced two cups and poured the coffee.

When Buck pulled up to the table, Catrina stretched and jumped up, friendly-like, onto its surface, so Buck petted the cat, triggering a low, rumbling purr. Cat's composure was contagious, calming Buck. While they waited for the coffee to cool, Tom dressed, including his signature black vest and a bola tie, and Buck explained that he had been fretful about the mustangs and had, consequently, incurred a fitful night at the boarding house. He awoke with a bad feeling and trekked down to the stables to check on the horses and Miss Becky. The mares were fine, but the stallion and Miss Becky were gone, as was her new carpetbag.

"Have you checked with her brother to see if she moved to other accommodations?"

"No, I came here directly. Didn't want to wake him."

"You're going to have to. Fetch her brother and bring him to the stables. I'll meet you there."

Thirty minutes later, it was still dark out, and the chilly night air caused Tom to pull his shirt collar up higher on his neck. From outside the door of the stables, he could see two men coming toward him with a lantern. Other than them, the streets were as empty as a ghost town.

John approached the sheriff. He looked a mess, nothing like his usual well-groomed self. "So, Beck stole the stallion." He ran the fingers of both hands through his hair, grabbed a section, and shook his head in disbelief. "Hell's bells!"

"G' morning, John."

Annoyed at his sister and at the sheriff's niceties, John didn't reply at first, but then he decided it was best to be mannerly and grumbled a greeting. "Morning."

"It's like I told ya, eh, Tom?"

"Yes and no, Buck. The girl and horse are gone, but I think she was abducted. See these tracks?" Tom walked away from the stable, pointing at hoofprints on the ground.

"I ain't a tracker, Tom."

"It's four small, unshod horses, plus one bigger one. The large prints are El Diablo's. Miss Becky is such a featherweight that I can't be certain she's on him, but I am certain those other tracks are made from Apache ponies."

"Apaches! Why would the Apaches want Miss Becky?"

"I'm guessing they didn't, at least not at first. They probably wanted the stallion, and her being in the barn was simply untimely. Maybe their ponies reacted to her, so the warriors thought she was mystical and took her along. Maybe the Apaches want to ransom her—or keep her."

While Buck and Tom had been talking, John had been standing by quietly with his arms crossed and fists in his armpits, trying to keep them warm. He was gladdened to know that his sister hadn't stolen the stallion. That would be awfully hard to explain to their father. On the other hand, so would an Apache abduction. Sleepy as he was, a different possibility formed in his mind.

John must have looked worried, or else Buck projected how he would feel in John's place. "Don't fret, son. The sheriff will get a posse together an' start trailing 'em at first light. I'll take part."

"I'll go too, but first I have some explaining to do about Mr. Starley."

Buck had to think for a second, but then the name came to him. "You mean the drunkard who was hecklin' Miss Becky earlier fer a drink?"

"None other." John saw the sheriff looking at him quizzically. "The Apaches know of Beck through Mr. Starley. I think they want her for the same reason everyone does: for help with their horses."

*   *   *

As the sun peeked above the horizon in the east, Tom loped his other perk, a buckskin gelding, through the entryway to the Camp Bell Ranch, reaching out to ring one of the cowbells to announce his arrival. The buckskin was sweaty from riding hard, but Tom knew his best friend would lend him another mount if this one was spent.

Even from this distance, he saw the glow of a light from inside the house, indicating that Mason and Cody were up and about. Drawing closer, he heard Shep bark from within the barn and figured at least one of the Campbells was doing chores inside. Upon arrival at the house, he hitched his horse near the water trough and headed to the door.

Cody answered his knock. "Uh, hello, Sheriff. A might early, isn't it?"

Years on the job had honed Tom's senses. He wondered what was wrong. Cody would normally have invited him in and offered him some coffee and even breakfast. In fact, he'd counted on it. "G' morning, Cody. Could I come in?"

"Best if ya don't. It's all smoky in here 'cause I've got bacon burnin'. Pa's in the barn." Cody started to close the door.

Tom could see and smell that Cody was being truthful, but he couldn't figure why he was being unneighborly. "Best to leave the door open. It'll help clear out the smoke. Any chance Miss Becky is here?"

"As far as I know, she's spendin' the mornin' with Doc Prescott."

It had been a long shot, but Cody's burning bacon suggested to Tom that Miss Becky was there for breakfast. He didn't want to alarm the boy. "That's fine. I'll go check in with your pa." When he arrived at the barn, he opened the door and called out to Mason. "Mace, hey Mace!" He didn't see his friend, so he walked down the aisle looking in each stall. When he was about halfway down, he received an answer from behind him.

"You need to leave, Tom. Get out of my barn and ride off my ranch."

"Are you holding a gun on me, Mace?" He realized by now that Mason knew about the kiss. Why else would Cody and Mason be acting unnaturally? "I'm going to turn around and face you." When he saw Mason, the man was not holding a gun, but Cody was standing at his side.

"I ought to punch you to a pulp."

"And I'd let you do it, except for one thing: Miss Becky has been kidnapped by Apaches, and I need to rescue her. I need *you* to help me rescue her. Buck and John volunteered, but Buck is too large and loud, plus he can't track, and John is a greenhorn who's never shot at a moving target. The two of us together stand a better chance to free her than I'd have with a full posse."

Well, that presented a dilemma. Mason took a moment to think. He was so angry about Tom and Elizabeth that he didn't want anything to do with either of them. He'd spent a restless night contemplating his relationship with Elizabeth, his relationship with Tom, and Tom and Elizabeth's betrayal.

Cody, on the other hand, didn't need any time to think. "*I'll* go! It'll just take me a minute to saddle Athena. I'm small enough to slink among the brush unseen, and ya know I'm a decent shot with a pistol."

Mason's most important relationship was with his son. He would do anything in his power for him. Cody would never forgive him if he didn't try to save Becky, and just as Tom knew, Mason would never forgive himself. Permitting Cody to go was not an option, and Cody would not likely take Mason's decision well. Mason was about to state his decision when Tom rescued him from having to deny Cody's offer.

"I'd take you at seventeen, Cody, but not at fourteen. Killing a rabbit or coyote can't be compared to killing a person."

Mason looked at his son sympathetically. "Never you mind, Cody. I'll go. I need you to stay here and take care of the ranch. We could be gone for days. Go serve up some breakfast for Tom while I saddle Raven."

"Pa—"

"It's too dangerous. Remember what we talked about last night. Now get moving."

Within twenty minutes, the men were on the road, heading toward the Chiricahua Mountains.

*   *   *

The leader of the four-man Apache band, dubbed "Hawk" by Miss Becky for his vigilance, kept a close eye on his hostage, his rifle at the ready. His captive was a strange being. She seemed old enough to have taken part in the Sunrise Dance, the ceremony initiating girls into womanhood, but he wasn't sure she was completely human or completely female. She seemed to be part spirit. She hadn't said a word to the Apaches since she had been with them, but they had noticed her whispering to the horses and observed the animals' reactions to her. It was spooky.

His hostage was currently leaning forward as she sat on a fallen log in their secluded campsite in the Dos Cabezas Mountains. Her feet were on the ground, her elbows were planted on her thighs, and though her wrists were bound, her face was cradled in her hands. She was either thinking or dozing. He suspected dozing, because of the short night and her long ride on El Diablo. She had used strong magic to control the wild stallion, and her strength was surely sapped.

She was wearing white-man clothing: trousers, a red plaid shirt, and boots, but she was also wearing female clothing—a bright pink hat with two magnificent, fluffy black-and-white feathers. He was watching the feathers as much as he was watching her. He and the others in his party had previously wondered aloud what kind of bird had produced the feathers and what power the feathers might endow.

Hawk had sent the brave whom Miss Becky thought of as "Thunder Voice" higher up the mountain, and he sent the one she designated "Freckled Pony Man" lower down than their position to act as lookouts from among the granite outcroppings. Their fourth member, "Little Hawk" was collecting firewood from around the shrubs and alligator junipers. The band's paint ponies were resting up the mountain a ways, at a nearby spring, along with a sorrel gelding with a snip on his nose, and the prize stallion, El Diablo. The animals were tethered at the hidden spring because the scrub bushes were thick, and anything that might be considered a trail was rocky and only wide enough for a single-file line. If enemies found them, the Apaches could move faster and better concealed on foot than on horse.

Hawk's small band of braves had been part of a larger tribe led by Geronimo, but Geronimo had surrendered to the white man and was being held at nearby Fort Bowie. The tribe would be relocated to a faraway land called Florida, but Hawk's band, one of several, had escaped. They would rather die than leave their sacred land.

Hawk and his braves were in their twenties or thirties. His son, who had lived sixteen summers, was as lean and fit as the others. They all sported long black hair held in place with brightly colored cloth headbands knotted in the back with dangling ends. The father's and son's headbands were cut from the same red-and-white cloth. They wore fringed buckskin shirts, leggings, breechcloths, wide belts, and moccasins that reached to their knees. The other two wore long tunics, baggy cotton pants tucked into their high moccasins, breechcloths, belts, and either a blue or green headband. In addition, each member of the band was adorned with necklaces and bracelets fashioned from shells and beads.

Little Hawk, who looked very much like his father in both features as well as outfit, returned with the wood and lit a low fire. While waiting for the wood to catch, he noticed Becky's closed eyes. A combination of brashness, bravery, and curiosity caused him to reach out and grasp the edge of Miss Becky's bright pink hat with one hand to see how it felt. He was more interested in the feathers than the hat, but he wouldn't dare touch them. To his surprise, Miss Becky jerked back, and he now held her hat in his hand. Her eyes had popped open, and for half a second, the boy and girl stared at each other before Little Hawk roughly pushed the hat back onto her head. That motion caused one of the ostrich feathers to come partially loose from the hatband. The plume tilted precariously and looked like it was going to drop to the ground. Little Hawk did not want the feather to fall, but he also did not want to touch it. As he pondered his options, Miss Becky must have seen the feather's movement from the corner of her eye. By contorting her elbows and hands, she was able to pull it from its casing. Suddenly, she became full of life. She held the feather out toward him. Little Hawk took a step backward. Miss Becky next waved the feather around, making the fluffy tendrils tickle the air. Then she began to twirl the plume in circles, faster and faster, until she abruptly jabbed the feather toward Little Hawk. He tried to dodge, but she succeeded in poking him. At the touch, Little Hawk jumped as though the feather had inflicted a scorpion sting.

With scrunched up eyebrows, Miss Becky erupted with strange-sounding syllables of the English tongue: "Go on, take it. I gift it to ya."

His eyes widened in alarm as he deduced that she had put a curse on him. Hawk had observed the whole encounter and felt anxious for his son, but he had experience with these matters and knew how to dispel the curse. The feather needed to be set free, but they could not take it forcibly. Little Hawk knew just the thing. He fetched his fringed buckskin pouch and pulled out his most treasured belonging, a tail feather from a young golden eagle. It was three-quarters white, with the tip-end quarter being dark, and the very tip decorated with a splash more of white. Little Hawk drew Miss Becky's attention to him. He then circled around her and conspicuously placed his feather on the log that she had recently vacated. Once it was placed, he stepped back a few feet. Miss Becky had watched his action but stood motionless. A little time passed before a gentle breeze caused the eagle feather to quiver. With the next breeze, it became airborne and floated to the ground. A stronger breeze followed, and this one lifted the feather enough for it to skim along the dirt, rising and sinking as it moved toward Miss Becky. Little Hawk was pleased that his golden eagle feather wanted to be with Miss Becky, and to his relief, Miss Becky bent down and scooped it up in her palms. He then pointed at her ostrich feather, and she understood. She placed her fluffy possession on the same log and stepped away. Once again, the breeze kicked up, but this time, the feather took flight and headed directly to the campfire, which was now producing flames and heat. Neither Little Hawk nor his father made a move when the feather wafted into the fire. Miss Becky ran to retrieve it before it was too late, but Little Hawk blocked her approach.

"Grr. Whatcha go an' do that fer? Why'd ya let it burn?" She shook her head and rolled her eyes.

Hawk was pleased, even though Miss Becky's words sounded harsh, and her tone sounded angry. The souls of both feathers had chosen their paths. The feather that had touched his son had been destroyed. The other had wanted to be with Miss Becky. All felt right with the spirits.

Then to both Hawks' surprise, Miss Becky freed the second fluffy feather from her hatband and set it on the log. When she moved away, she stood in front of the fire, with a clear message that she would not allow the second feather to burn. But the second ostrich feather did not move near the fire. The wind took it to the feet of her elder captor. With Little Hawk watching, Hawk ceremoniously incanted some words before securing his feather under his headband at the back of his head. While the Apaches were occupied, Miss Becky was busy trying to maneuver her new feather into her hatband, no easy task with her hands tied.

Now feeling more comfortable around her, Hawk addressed Miss Becky in his soft-spoken voice and used hand motions, inviting her to come over and warm herself. Although she didn't understand his words, she understood the offer and accepted it. Hawk announced it was time to eat, and his son produced a piece of smoked venison from his pouch. Little Hawk cut off two sections with his hunting knife, gave one to his father, and placed one in Becky's hands, keeping the rest for himself. As she grasped the meat, Miss Becky motioned with her head toward her carpetbag. The Apaches had never seen such a large bag and wondered what powerful medicines it contained. Out of respect, they hadn't looked inside.

Becky had earned their respect when Hawk had stealthily entered the stables to retrieve El Diablo. All was quiet when he set foot inside. He easily located the stallion, but when he opened the stall door, he discovered Miss Becky sitting bug-eyed in the corner, propped up by a carpetbag. She was fully clothed, including the curious hat. She hadn't cried out, hadn't made any noise, but suddenly all the horses in the building were wide awake and vocalizing. El Diablo had been the worst of them, screaming. Hawk sensed that somehow the girl was responsible. He moved quickly to accomplish his mission before he was discovered. The girl remained motionless, but now her eyes were closed, presumably to block out his image. Perhaps in her mind, if she couldn't see him, he didn't exist. But then she stretched out her arms and began to whisper, apparently to El Diablo. The horses' leader calmed, and the others followed. The girl was either damaged or favored, but either way, he saw no reason to harm her. He just wanted to take the stallion and go. He quickly slipped a rope around El Diablo's neck and began to lead him from the stables. Just as quickly, Becky was on her feet. She grabbed her bag and leapt from behind onto El Diablo's back. Once aboard, she held her bag in front of her and leaned forward for balance, continuing to whisper to the stallion as Hawk led him from the stables.

Freckled Pony Man had appeared on horseback from around the corner of the stables with a makeshift weapon he had found in a scrap heap. He swung the five-foot long board at Becky's midsection, but she blocked the blow with her carpetbag. Even so, the force of the impact knocked her to the ground, stunning her. By then, Little Hawk and Thunder Voice had ridden over from the shadows to join the group. With Miss Becky down, the Apaches were eager to leave. Hawk climbed onto his pony and tried to lead El Diablo toward the road, but the stallion refused to follow, and then all the ponies refused their riders' commands, instead forming a head-to-tail circle around the girl in the dirt and El Diablo. No amount of kicking would budge the four ponies. El Diablo's eyes bulged, expressing his anger. He bucked wildly and reared dangerously near Becky. Through it all, Hawk had continued to clasp El Diablo's rope, until, finally, it was torn from his fist. Apparently realizing he was free, El Diablo settled and stood quietly near Becky. Then the still-stunned girl sat up. She whispered words, and like a circus horse, El Diablo bowed down. Becky grabbed her bag and clambered aboard El Diablo's back. When she was in riding position, the stallion stood back up. Hawk had possessed the presence of mind to grab the lead rope, and like ice in a spring thaw, the four ponies had unfrozen. They began moving again, responding to their riders' commands. Recognizing that the girl possessed some kind of magical connection with horses and not wanting to delay their escape further, Hawk decided to let her accompany them. He had directed Little Hawk to bind her hands with leather cord, and then the band of Apaches had walked their ponies slowly and furtively out of town with Miss Becky atop the stallion. Thus, she had earned their respect with bravery and the ability to communicate with horses.

Miss Becky set the venison down, withdrew an apple from her carpetbag, and tossed it underhanded to Little Hawk. Her throw was bad, but his reflexes were good. He leapt for the fruit and caught it. After examining and sniffing it, he lobbed it to his father, whereupon Becky tossed a second apple to the young brave. Next, she brought out a handful of soda crackers. Hawk acknowledged her friendly gesture by having his son untie her. Thus, they all ate crackers, venison, and apples for breakfast. Becky made faces while chewing the gamey venison, and the Apaches did likewise at the dryness of the crackers, but sharing a meal was a step to building trust.

By chance, the Apache band was already somewhat familiar with Miss Becky. Three days ago, Hawk's band had been part of a ten-brave renegade band that was camping out in the Chiricahua Mountains. They had assembled to discuss El Diablo because white men had trespassed onto Apache land and captured the stallion and many of his mares. The Apaches were outraged, and at a minimum, they meant to take the stallion back.

Accompanying the larger band were Mischief Maker and her husband, Hank Starley. Mischief Maker might have been part

Apache, but her ancestry was unclear. She had lived with them on and off for many moons, coming and going as she pleased. The Apaches tolerated her because they thought she was touched in the head in a harmless way. They accepted such people as being part of the supernatural world and showed a certain respect for them, much as they respected Miss Becky.

Hank was not as welcome. Although he and his wife often wandered, they had a home, a shabby shack in the mountains. Hank was formerly a blacksmith, and he was an avid junk collector, which was evident in and around the shack. He had sometimes brought the Apaches useful implements or firewater, but those gestures did not make up for his laziness, drinking, and most recently, thievery. When the bands split, with Hawk and his party moving to the Dos Cabezas Mountains to be closer to Leaning Rock, and therefore, El Diablo, Hank had stolen one of their paint mares and taken off, leaving his wife behind with the six members of the band that remained in the Chiricahua Mountains. That band intended to catch and kill Hank to retrieve the mare and be rid of Mischief Maker's man once and for all.

In the late afternoon, after settling into his new camp in the Dos Cabezas Mountains, Hawk received word from a messenger that the larger band had hunted down Hank Starley. They had seized a fine horse from him and may yet come to recover the paint mare.

Mischief Maker had been reunited with Hank, and Hank had been banished from their land forevermore.

As it so happens, John and Becky McCoy had been sleeping under the stars in the Chiricahua Mountains three nights ago. While hunting Hank, the braves had discovered the white girl and a young white man riding double on a chestnut gelding, the girl in front. The girl was wearing two large, fluffy feathers in her hat. Feathers came from living creatures, signifying a connection to the Creator. The Apaches wondered how she had acquired them and what protection the feathers provided her.

As the Apaches spied on the people, they saw the girl whisper in the chestnut's ear. The horse reacted by whinnying, and before long, another horse countered with a distressed response. The girl directed the chestnut gelding toward the sound and quickened his pace. The two horses continued to call to each other until the white people came upon the missing mare stuck in the muck by a stream. The Apaches dismounted, spread out, and took cover in a stand of hoodoos. From there, they watched the girl instantly calm the anxious mare by whispering to her and blowing dust in her nostrils. Once she was calm, the white people easily rescued the mare from the mud, but the paint pony looked weak and ill. The girl took a feather from her hat and swept the paint's neck with it.

At that point, five Apaches stepped out from behind their cover to announce their presence, their rifles pointed at the intruders, ready to fire. The young man saw them and put his arms up in surrender, dropping the blanket he had been using to dry the mare. Although they saw no weapons and had no grievances with these people, the Apaches moved in cautiously. As they were climbing down and around the boulders, Hank Starley appeared from behind a hoodoo, sitting atop a magnificent sorrel gelding with a snip on his nose. The rifles turned toward him. Someone fired. Hank's horse reared, and Hank fell to the ground. The girl stopped ministering to the mare. She waved the feather over the downed man. Hank stood up. The girl went back to her business.

One of the braves called out to Hank, who spoke their tongue, requesting a parley. They did not want a sick mare. They wanted Hank's life, but they were now wary of Hank, since the girl had performed strong magic over him. In the end, they settled for the gelding with a snip and the promise of the stolen paint mare, if she survived. Hank received his wife and his life—but if he showed his face on their land again, he could expect no mercy. The girl and her companion were left in peace, since she possessed powerful healing magic and the ability to talk with horses, and the companion was, they supposed, her man. When the Apaches had departed, the girl was still tending to the mare. She had never looked up or otherwise acknowledged their presence.

All of that was factual from the Apache perspective, but John McCoy told Sheriff Claiborne and Buck Pruitt a somewhat different, yet swearable true, account back in Leaning Rock:

"Much of our travel from Kentucky has been by rail, but as the trip was nearing its final leg, Spook pestered me into traveling the final two hundred miles on horseback, so I purchased two fine geldings in Las Cruces, a chestnut for myself and a sorrel with a snip for Beck. We rode to Arizona Territory, camping out at night to accommodate Beck's sleeping peculiarities. You already know how she likes to sleep with horses and can't tolerate boarding houses." He paused as his audience nodded their understanding, and then he continued. "I intended to sell the geldings in Leaning Rock before Papa and the others arrive tomorrow—I mean, *today*. We'll be taking the train to California, so we'll have no use for horses." John stood taller and puffed out his chest. "I'll be enrolling in Woodbury's Business College in Los Angeles. Then I can take over the family business when Papa's ready. He wanted me to get exposure to different sorts of people and places first, and I have, though I'd say Beck outshines them all as the most unusual." He smiled weakly.

The sheriff was interested in John's chronicle, but not at the expense of quickly finding Miss Becky. "Can you jump to the part about Hank Starley?"

"I'm there: When Beck and I were eating breakfast in the Chiricahuas, we were surprised by Hank Starley stumbling into camp in a state of drunkenness and distress. He said some renegade Apaches had captured him and his wife. He had escaped on foot and was trying to get to Leaning Rock for help from you, Sheriff. He asked to borrow one of our horses. At the mention of Apaches, I wanted to pack up and leave immediately. It never occurred to me that they lived in the mountains, and my instinct for self-preservation is as strong as the next man's. Besides, I had sworn to keep Beck safe.

"Beck and I began to break camp. Mr. Starley excused himself, he said to answer the call of nature, but he took that opportunity to steal Beck's mount. I was livid and wanted to chase after him. Spook, however, knew in her odd way that another horse was in the area, and by using her horse sense, she quickly located the mare. The paint mare had become trapped up to her chest in mud overnight, but she had come close to working herself free. It didn't take us long to pull her out. Unfortunately, the mare was sickly. She was exhausted and had developed hypothermia during the night. Beck easily calmed her, and I was warming her with a blanket when Apache braves appeared from behind the army of tall rock formations, brandishing rifles. Beck was engrossed in her work, setting up to administer a warm enema, but I yelled to them, hands up over my head, telling them they could have the mare and begging them not to hurt us. Two of them mounted up, rode over, and took a gander at the paint. When they saw her condition, they looked angry. That's when Mr. Starley turned out to be upright. He appeared on horseback from behind one of those eerie rock sentinels to help us, but just then one of the Apache braves shot him in the arm, only a flesh wound, but with enough kick to throw him from Beck's horse, especially since he was already unbalanced. Beck went to check on him. She waved an ostrich feather over him because Mr. Starley had told her Apaches believe feathers hold strong magic. Mr. Starley arose with difficulty and began talking in Apache. I don't know what he said, but the two Apaches left with Beck's horse and rejoined the others. Shortly thereafter, Mr. Starley pointed to the direction they had gone and drew attention to a woman, his wife, walking slowly toward us.

"Becky's enema treatment was helping the mare, so Mr. Starley offered Beck a deal: We would take the mare to his shack, and he would give Beck a gift for saving his life. By that, he meant the Apaches would have killed him if he hadn't had a horse, *her* horse, to give them. He came clean that they thought he stole their mare, though he adamantly denied doing that. He allowed that if the paint survived, his wife would return her to them. He had convinced the Apaches that they were only entitled to one horse in exchange for his life, not the sorrel *and* the chestnut, which is what they were bargaining for. He used to be a blacksmith, you know, before he became a drunkard. He's uncommonly creative and found a way to improve on an invention he had seen at a traveling show. Fittingly, for the loss of her sorrel, Mr. Starley gave Beck something rideable—a bicycle."

*   *   *

Cody washed the morning dishes quickly and mechanically. His mind was on Miss Becky and her predicament. He told himself he was fourteen and old enough to make his own decisions. Just as his father could not forgive himself if he didn't try to help Miss Becky, Cody could not live with himself if harm befell her and he hadn't tried to help. He had never before recognized the strong moral influence his father had instilled in him, but now was not the time to think about it. Against his father's strict orders to stay home and to never use a firearm without his supervision, Cody loaded Mason's spare pistol and tucked it into the waist of his trousers. Barely ten minutes had passed since his father and the sheriff had ridden out.

Cody was saddling Athena when he heard the bell clang. Someone was coming up the long dirt road to the ranch. Rather than wait for the person to arrive, Cody packed a few necessities into his saddlebags, mounted Athena, and galloped down the road toward the visitor. It was John McCoy galloping up. Cody observed that Miss Becky's brother was dressed in his fancy duds but was rigged out with a pistol nestled in a holster. As they approached each other, John's steed performed a tight U-turn, with no bigger radius than an apple barrel. By the time the turn was completed, Athena had drawn up beside the chestnut. The horses' strides fell into unison, perfectly matched.

"Mornin', John."

"Master Cody."

"We're about twenty minutes behind 'em. They're headed to the Chiricahuas."

"She's not there. She's considerably closer, in the Dos Cabezas Mountains."

"How do ya know?"

"From Mr. Pruitt. Mr. Starley told him."

"You trust the drunkard?"

"Enough. He told Mr. Pruitt that his wife delivered a paint pony to the Apaches camped there." John then proceeded to provide a condensed version of the story he had told the sheriff and Buck Pruitt.

"Sheriff Claiborne and my pa are the best trackers you're likely to ever come across. They'll not pass by the turnoff."

"Well, I shorely hope you're right, because if they do miss it, we'll have to rescue Spook on our own. You any good with that?" He nodded toward Cody's pistol.

"We'll see."

 *   *   *

Mason Campbell and Sheriff Claiborne flew past the turnoff to Dos Cabezas Mountains. They had a long ride ahead and were heavily absorbed in their thoughts. Neither had spoken since they'd begun their pursuit, but that wasn't unusual, because it wasn't easy to converse while galloping. With heads facing forward, words often became lost in the thunderous sound of the hooves or in the wind, never making it to the intended recipient's ears.

The sheriff yelled that he was going to stop. Mason pulled on Raven's reins to instruct his horse to stop as well. When the horses had halted several yards down the road, the men dismounted and squatted on the ground, searching for evidence of the Apache ponies' unshod hooves and El Diablo's much larger tracks. They also looked for fresh horse manure.

"Mace, you know I'm not one to run on with words, but I've got to speak my piece about Elizabeth." He eyed some tracks and moved closer to them. Mason was busy wiping sweat from his forehead onto his sleeve, but he looked up. "Look, I'm truly sorry I've taken an interest in your gal. I should've said something earlier. I didn't set out to steal her from you or to hurt you. Our affections developed during our long rides together back and forth to visit you and Cody. We had to talk about something, and we discovered we had more in common than just our mutual friendship with you.

Elizabeth and I are just starting to test the water. If you put more wood on the fire, she would likely choose you over me."

Both men stood and gulped several swallows of water from their canteens. Then they mounted up. Tom didn't pressure Mason for a response, though he would have welcomed one. When Mason did speak, it was only to say that the trail had gone cold. They'd have to backtrack.

*   *   *

After breakfast, Little Hawk walked Miss Becky with her carpetbag up to the spring. She seemed happy to be near the horses, and they seemed happy to be near her. They greeted her loudly, like she was a reunited member of their little herd, and they pulled on their tie ropes, trying to get nearer to her, bending the branches of the sycamore trees to which they were tied. If the branches had been dead, they would have snapped from the strain. Miss Becky responded by approaching the animals one by one, whispering in their ears, blowing in their nostrils, caressing their necks, and feeding them apples from her bag before they settled, after which she sat on a rock in the shade.

Little Hawk had watched Miss Becky with fascination. He observed the individual attention she afforded each animal and, especially, her relationship with the stallion. The stallion that he was familiar with had been as wild as the wind, but now he acted as docile as a newly born cougar cub. Little Hawk motioned that he'd like an apple, and Miss Becky obligingly threw her last one to him. He then approached the stallion, hand outstretched, and discovered that El Diablo wasn't as tame as he had appeared. The horse pawed the ground and threw back his head in defiance. In his own show of defiance, Little Hawk wolfed down the apple and threw the core into the wilds.

It was time to move out, to return the great stallion to the canyon where he had been born. Little Hawk quickly prepared the ponies for riding, securing Spanish-style saddles with dangling metal stirrups onto their backs and slipping bits into their mouths. He also readied the sorrel with a snip, but he didn't have a saddle for El Diablo, not that he thought the stallion would accept one anyway.

The Apache boy heard the beautiful descending trill of a canyon wren's song. The wren was common in the area but was more often heard than seen because its song carried a great distance but its feathers blended well with the cinnamony colors and the salt-and-pepper patterns of its rocky habitat. He answered with a scratchy *tsee, tsee*. His call roused Miss Becky. She sat up taller and looked at him with scrunched eyebrows beneath the rim of her pink hat. She must have realized that the song had been a signal from another Apache, not an actual bird. She was smart, and he liked her all the more for it.

His father joined them at the spring. He told Little Hawk that four of their enemies were approaching. Two were almost within fighting distance; the other two were advancing rapidly behind them. The band would fight first and retreat if necessary. Little Hawk was confident that they would defeat the four white men. Their numbers were the same, but the Apaches had the advantages of better position, better knowledge of the mountain, and the mountain spirits guiding them. Their disadvantage was lack of modern weapons. The Apaches who stayed in the Chiricahuas were fully armed with rifles, but other than Hawk's one working rifle, the four tasked with returning the stallion had only bows and arrows and knives. The arrows were just as deadly, but a rifle had the advantage of greater distance and accuracy.

Buck Pruitt and Hank Starley were the first of the enemies to arrive. Buck felt responsible for Miss Becky's abduction, and he needed Hank to translate for him so he could negotiate her release, plus he wanted his stallion back.

Hank had been hard to rouse that morning, having spent a good part of the evening imbibing at the Rustler's Stoop, thanks to the ten dollars he had earned by fetching Mr. Campbell from Doc Ritter's. The money had also covered his room at the boarding house.

Hank was groggy when he finally opened the door to his room. Buck had stated his business matter-of-factly through the cracked door. Hank had wanted nothing to do with the job. Even in his stupor, he remembered the Apaches' threat to kill him on sight. Not knowing Hank's strained relationship with the Apaches, Buck tried to entice him with a crate of whiskey. That was a substantial amount of whiskey and could keep Hank happy for weeks. Buck could see Hank was considering the deal. He was waking up, and his eyes looked more focused. Using his right thumb and trigger finger, he scratched the growth of beard that had formed overnight on his chin.

"Well now, I like Girlie. I'd hep ya if I could, but I don't know where them A-pach are holed up." He yawned as he began to close the door in Buck's face. "What now? Whoa! Whoa, woman!" A commotion had commenced, and then the door had swung wide open revealing the wild wife with the sheriff's build. She took up a third of the opening to Hank's two-thirds. She was kicking his lower legs and jabbering in a mix of English and other languages. Hank aimed to kick back, but he missed, lost his balance, and grabbed the doorknob to keep from landing on the floor.

Buck turned to leave, but Hank called him back. "Hold up, mister. My woman says an A-pach band is camped in the Dos Cabezas Mountains. She's kickin' me into yer service, but ya still owe me that whiskey." He was dressed and out of the room faster than Buck had hoped for. Thus, shortly after Sheriff Claiborne had raced out of town for the Camp Bell Ranch, Buck and Hank had raced out, too.

Freckled Pony Man had easily spotted the loud trespassers from his low perch. He recognized Hank as the man who was banished from Apache lands and Buck as the man who had captured and stolen El Diablo and his mares. He whistled a bird call. The clear, dry, morning air carried the tune aloft and into their campsite, where Hawk was breaking camp, and over to the spring, where Little Hawk had heard it and responded.

While the two Hawks packed the ponies with their belongings from the campsite, the older one shared his plan, which was for Thunder Voice to descend from his upper lookout post and join Freckled Pony Man in the fight with the whites. One would take the left, and the other would take the right. Hawk would also descend, but not as low as the others, and he would be in the middle, positioned between the two warriors. His son would remain with the rifle at the highest point, the campsite, backing up the others. Miss Becky would be detained at the spring. Little Hawk, looking apologetic, tied her hands and feet with cord and left her on the rock, after which he returned with his father to the campsite.

Thunder Voice was too far away to hear Freckled Pony Man's bird-call message, but from his position, he should have seen Hank and Buck's approach. If he weren't already on his way back to camp, Hawk knew that a rifle shot would bring him running. It would also warn the intruders that they had been spotted. That could be a mistake, but Hawk decided to fire a bullet anyhow. The white men would learn that the Apaches had a rifle. If they thought all of them did, even better. Hawk aimed the rifle at the men and squeezed the trigger, then he tossed it to his son, picked up his quiver and bow, and disappeared down the mountain.

At the shot, the white men jumped from their horses and scrambled to hide behind granite boulders. Hank was panting from the effort when Freckled Pony Man saw an opening, nocked an arrow, and let it fly. Hank ducked just in time, with the arrow lodging in his hat.

Cody and John were minutes behind Buck and Hank, had heard Hawk's rifle blast, and had seen the men take cover. In fact, the men's horses had spooked at the rifle report, and in their hysteria, the horses had headed directly toward the younger rescuers. John looked panicked, but Cody reacted with purpose.

"Dismount and take cover! I'll catch 'em!"

John did as he was told without thought, while Cody drove Athena, who was trained to out-maneuver balky cattle, to round up the horses. Afterward, Cody dismounted to secure their reins. Large trees didn't grow this far from a water source, and the grasses, spiky yuccas, and scrub vegetation were impossible to tether reins to, so he improvised, pinning the reins on the ground by shoving weighty rocks over their ends. Athena was trained to ground tie, but Cody couldn't trust her to stay put through the anticipated roar of gunfire any more than the men's horses had.

Cody next zigzagged toward the nearest cluster of boulders for cover, cupping his pistol against his body to control its motion as he ran. When he scrunched behind the boulder next to John, his heart was pounding, beating as fast as a jackrabbit's being chased by a coyote.

During this time, a sprinkling of more arrows had been launched down on the men, but neither Hank nor Buck had returned fire. In essence, the men were pinned down. They couldn't turn back or go forward without exposing themselves, and if they leaned their heads out far enough to determine where the Apaches were, they risked much more than ruining their hats. Buck's goal was to retrieve Miss Becky and the stallion, not to kill the Apaches. He nudged Hank.

"Tell 'em we want to talk."

Buck tied his neckerchief to his rifle and poked it out from behind their cover, waving it erratically in the air. Hank hollered to the Apache braves, identifying himself and Buck, and requesting a parley. All the Apaches knew that Hank was banned from their land, and they would harbor no misgivings if he were killed; in fact, they would prefer if he were. They silently moved in.

With no response from the Apaches, Buck yelled for Miss Becky, but only a canyon wren answered his call.

Behind their cover, Cody and John conferred. If they proceeded forward, they'd become pinned like Hank and Buck. If they stayed put, they wouldn't accomplish anything.

"What do we do now, Master Cody?"

Cody wasn't sure. His plan to sneak up on the Apaches, locate Miss Becky, and secret her out of their hold was blown. He noticed movement to their left and pointed to Hank and Buck splitting up and making a run for new cover. The sound of arrows whooshing in the air caught their attention, and their sources were closer than they expected. The men dodged and rolled and crawled as they attempted to advance. There was only one thing Cody could see to do.

"Shoot!"

*　　　*　　　*

Miss Becky sat on the rock by the spring, her wrists bound behind her with leather cord, and her ankles tied tightly together. As soon as Little Hawk departed, she wriggled her fingers and tried to force her wrists apart, but Little Hawk had tied her well, and the cords didn't have much give to them. She looked around for a sharp rock to cut the cords, but she didn't see any. The only item she spotted was Little Hawk's discarded apple core in the vegetation on the other side of the spring. The water source for the spring was seepage from underground. The incoming water collected in a pool that was surrounded by granite boulders, like the one she was sitting on. When the water reached a high enough level, it began to flow into a stream that later became a waterfall. Beyond the circle of boulders, vegetation grew.

With no resources within reach, she tried to stand. She planted her feet hard into the ground and used her back and thigh muscles to push forward, but the motion didn't produce enough momentum for her to stand. She rocked backward and tried again, this time over-compensating. She became upright with her effort, but she immediately lost her balance and began falling to the ground. She twisted her shoulders just before she thumped onto moist dirt at the edge of the spring. Her right shoulder hit first, taking the brunt of the fall, but her head flopped and landed hard on a rock, also taking quite a blow. Never mind that her whole side was covered in a light layer of mud. She squeezed her eyes tightly shut to keep tears from leaking out from the smart of the fall. As she lay there resting, she heard the boom of a rifle shot. She started, and the horses fidgeted. El Diablo was the worst, pulling against his tie rope, severely bending the sycamore branch to which he was attached, and causing leaves to shake loose and fall to the ground. His feet pranced as though he were attempting to avoid stepping on the leaves.

Becky spoke to the horses in a subdued voice. She tried to calm them, but El Diablo did not cooperate, and the others fed off his emotions. If she could get closer to him, she could quiet him, but she needed to escape her bindings to do that.

She was positioned on her right side with her legs slightly bent and her hands behind her back. Her first instinct was to retract her knees into a fetal position to try to bring her feet to her hands, but that approach still left her appendages too far apart. There was only one other option: Becky uncurled from her position and arched her back into an uncomfortable arc so that her body formed a circle, and sure enough, her slender fingers could feel the ends of the cord. She inched her fingers along the cord until she found the knot. Her curved position was difficult to maintain, causing cramps in her upper left leg. She had to release from her position, stretch out her legs and try again, and yet a third time, before she managed to pick the knot apart with the ragged nails of her middle fingers and thumbs. The bindings loosened, and she was able to slip them from around her ankles. One problem solved.

Miss Becky carefully stood. The rocks made walking difficult without use of her arms for balance, but she made her way to El Diablo. She nudged her head against his neck and whispered something in his ear. He nickered softly and nodded his head down and up in a motion that made it look as though he were agreeing with her about something. Becky needed her hands free in order to escape, and El Diablo had given her an idea. Though she feared to tread through water, walking around to the other side of the pool was too arduous. Besides, wet leather might stretch a little.

Miss Becky waded into the spring. Before long, the cool water ran into her boots. She shivered and made a sour face from the sogginess it produced, but she continued onward, cautiously, step by step, feeling her way along the bottom so as not to slip. The water became waist high, then chest high. She raised herself to her fullest height and tilted her chin high into the air, and finally, she was at the deepest point, and soon after, she was dripping on a small stretch of land. The granite rocks were in lower clusters on this side. She made her way over them and found her prize. After retrieving the apple core by squatting down and grasping it behind her, she carried it clammed safely in her palms for the return trip. Now knowing the depth of the water, she was able to step with more confidence and speed. When she reached El Diablo, she was doubly drenched. She tried again to wriggle loose from her ties, but all she succeeded in doing was placing the apple core beneath them. She backed up to El Diablo's mouth and offered him the goody.

El Diablo didn't disappoint. He tried to snatch a bite of the sweet treat, but along with the apple, he also got a taste of the wet leather, and he liked it. He liked it a lot! He grasped the cord in his teeth and nodded his head up and down vigorously a few times, as though he were sampling a sugar cube. By the time he worked his way to the apple core, her hands were free. She rubbed El Diablo's neck and told him what a clever horse he was. He momentarily calmed.

Miss Becky could hear distant shouting, whoops, and occasional gunshots emanating from down the mountain. The Apaches' paints and the larger horses flinched from the resounding booms. El Diablo became distressed again. Becky needed to stop the fighting.

She quickly climbed over to her carpetbag and began rummaging through it until she located the item she was searching for. Then, still dripping, she silently made her way down the trail back to the campsite. From behind a juniper tree, she observed Little Hawk lying prone with a rifle sited down the mountain. A flash of light and a bang from someone's handgun informed her where one of the shooters and one of his Apache targets were hunkered down. Within a minute, she determined where the other people were located and that the Apaches had the advantage. Several arrows zinged in succession in the direction of one of the unfortunate men.

Miss Becky cocked her pistol and made her presence known. "Little Hawk."

The Apache rolled and aimed his rifle at the sound of her voice. Miss Becky stepped out from behind the juniper, pistol pointed skyward.

She lowered her voice to a whisper. "I know ya don't understand my words. Jus' try to understand my intent. We hafta work together. Please, don't shoot me. I'm not gonna shoot ya. I'm jus' gonna let 'em know I'm fine."

She slowly walked toward the center of the campsite, whispering to him all the while. With her left arm, she motioned for him to lower his rifle. He didn't, but she continued forward even under his threat, constantly motioning. When she reached her goal, she stopped. "I'm not gonna shoot ya. I'm gonna shoot into the air. Then I'm gonna yell. I'm not gonna be yellin' at ya. I'm gonna be yellin' to them folks." She pointed with her left hand. "Got it?"

Little Hawk liked and respected the spirit girl. He admired her abilities with horses and wondered at her magic. *How else could she have escaped her bonds, if not with magic?* He considered that she could have shot him in the back, but instead, she had shown remarkable bravery and walked toward him even though he had a deadly weapon pointed at her. He found her voice to be non-threatening, even soothing. He kept the rifle trained on her, but he waited to see what she would do next.

She looked him in the eye and raised her pistol straight up. "I'm gonna fire it now. See, I'm not gonna shoot ya." She closed her eyes and pulled the trigger, producing a loud bang. After the smoke cleared, she dropped the pistol to the ground, and with arms akimbo she began her promised yelling. "This is Miss Becky

McCoy. Stop shootin', do ya hear! I'm fine, but yer upsettin' the horses!"

Then Little Hawk was hit by inspiration. He yelled to his people. "The spirit girl escaped, and I am her captive. She wants to make a peaceful exchange."

The commotion down below ceased, as both sides considered the situation. Hank Starley was the only one who knew what both Miss Becky and Little Hawk had said. He loosely translated Little Hawk's message to his three allies. It was his turn to yell. "He wants peace!"

The two sides established an uneasy truce and made their way up to camp to negotiate. Meanwhile, Little Hawk placed his rifle on the ground and picked up Miss Becky's pistol. He pointed it at himself and handed it to her butt first as his way of showing her that he trusted her with his life, just as she had trusted him with hers. The corners of her mouth twitched and raised a little. He thought she was going to smile, but she surprised him by bursting into a delightful fit of laughter. Miss Becky took the pistol from Little Hawk with her left hand and opened the cylinder with her right, showing him that the gun was empty. Then he joined in the laughter. Becky spit into her hand and held it out toward him. Following her lead, Little Hawk spit into his, and they shook hands on their friendship.

Mason Campbell and Sheriff Tom Claiborne reined in their horses as they reached the turnoff to the Dos Cabezas Mountains. The mid-morning sun beat down on them, but rain clouds were looming above the peaks. It was promising to be another hot, humid day. The men gulped from their canteens and wiped the sweat from their necks and foreheads before dismounting and searching the ground for recent activity.

"Several horses passed here this morning, Mason. At least four in the last hour and some earlier."

"Agreed. Both coming and going." Mason frowned.

"What else do you see?"

"Athena has a distinctive print—just like this one." Mason traced the track with his finger.

"You don't think Cody—" Tom was interrupted by the boy himself.

He and Mason could hear hooves pounding on the roadway before Cody appeared around a bend. "Pa, Pa!" The men looked up to see Cody loping Athena toward them. When Athena skidded to a halt, Cody exchanged nods with them in way of a greeting.

"What's happened, son?"

"Everything's fine! Miss Becky escaped from the Apaches. She's bruised and battered and half-drowned, but she's fine. And she's still goin' to the swimmin' hole with me. And it's early enough you can still ride in the bronc-bustin' contest. And her party is still this evenin'. Today's goin' to be a grand day!"

Mason was happy for the good news, but he was also suspicious. It looked to him like Cody had been to the Dos Cabezas Mountains, but he wasn't sure enough to bet on it.

"That's fine, just fine. How did you occupy yourself this morning?"

Cody waited for his father to look him in the eye before he answered. "Chores. Cleaned the pistol since I never got around to it after target practice on Wednesday. Rode Athena some. Then John McCoy rode in with Miss Becky."

"Fine, fine." Mason looked back down at the dirt. He traced another track with his finger. Then he stood and mounted up. Tom followed his lead. The three formed a line side-by-side with Cody in the middle. They began walking their horses toward civilization.

"How are Athena's new shoes working out?"

"Fine, Pa. I was just discussin' 'em with John. The gelding he rides wears the same keg shoes with calks. They're becomin' popular. He says lots of horses are wearin' 'em now."

"Is that so?"

"Yes, sir."

Tom had waited patiently to speak, and now it was his turn. "How did Miss Becky escape?"

"She didn't rightly say."

"Was she riding El Diablo?"

"No, sir. She was ridin' double with John."

"Well, what happened to the stallion?"

"She didn't rightly say that either. Listen, Sheriff, she was tired to the bones, so I set her up in the barn to sleep. I didn't pester her with questions. John stayed a few minutes and then rode out."

"Well, Cody Campbell, if I didn't know you better, I'd think you weren't being completely honest. You can play innocent with your pa, but you owe the law the truth."

That was too much! "Goodbye, Tom. Cody and I are headed home." Mason kicked Raven in the sides, and his horse took off. Cody had been unprepared for the abrupt departure, but he gave Athena a couple of heels to her belly, and she soon caught up and matched Raven's stride.

Behind them, the Campbells could hear Tom yelling. "Sure, you do that, Mason, but I'm trailing you. I need to question Miss Becky."

*   *   *

By the time he and Cody approached the entrance posts to their ranch, Mason had cooled down. He knew Tom was right. Tom had been right about his lukewarm approach to courting Miss Elizabeth, and he was right that Cody was hiding something. He should have pestered the boy with more questions. He reined in by the cowbells, and Cody stopped beside him.

"Just tell me one thing, Cody. Despite our talk last night, did you do anything dangerous today because of Miss Becky?"

Cody sat silent and still in the saddle. Mason waited for an answer. He was thinking his son had developed a decent poker face, but looking at him now, he knew which cards Cody held. No answer meant "yes." By and by, Cody confirmed Mason's reasoning.

"I swore an oath of silence, Pa. I can't tell ya what ya want to know."

At that moment, Tom caught up to them from behind, and Miss Elizabeth rode up in her buggy from the direction of Leaning Rock.

Son of a gun! What are the odds they'd both show up at once? Mason shook his head in disbelief. "I fold, son. You go on up to the house. I'm in a hand with higher stakes."

"Yes, sir!" Cody took the time to tip his hat and smile in Miss Elizabeth's direction before bolting Athena up the trail to home.

"Howdy, Betsy!" Mason greeted her by fully removing his hat and replacing it on his head. Elizabeth looked fresh: her dress starched, her bonnet colorful and gay. Nevertheless, he offered her a drink from his canteen, but she declined, pointing to one on the seat beside her.

"Hello Mason, Tom." She nodded toward each of them.

"Howdy, Miss Elizabeth! You're a pleasant sight." Tom tipped his hat to her. "If you'll excuse me, I'm on official business." He turned his gelding to follow Cody.

"Hold up, Tom. There's something I want to say to you and Miss Elizabeth."

Tom rode over closer to the buggy so Mason could address them both from the same direction.

"Betsy, you and I have been friends for years. You're the prettiest and best-schooled and most caring woman in town. You can bake a prize-winning pie and stitch an open wound as solid and straight as a hem. You can drive and ride, and I wouldn't be surprised to learn you could shoot like Annie Oakley."

She flashed a smile at that last compliment.

"I've relied on you to help me with Cody; I've relied on you for companionship; I've relied on your kindness to keep me looking toward the future. I love you, Betsy, but I haven't asked you to marry me because I was fearful you'd answer no, and I was fearful if you answered no, it would tarnish our relationship."

"Um, Mason, that's the worst pro—"

"Let me finish, Betsy."

"All right. You go ahead."

"The fact is, I'd be happier to marry you than you would be to marry me. You've lived in town your whole life. You love working at Sam Hill's. You love the people and ordering and selling and making a profit. I can't see you as my ranch wife—as anyone's ranch wife."

"Well, don't you think that decision is up to—"

"Betsy, I know you and Tom shared a kiss."

Elizabeth turned her face toward Tom and raised her left eyebrow, but she remained quiet.

"Looking backward, it comes as no surprise that the two of you are interested in courting. You've spent plenty of time talking together on your rides to visit me—enough time to share hopes and dreams. I can see you as Tom's wife, Betsy. He would be faithful and honest and attentive, and he lives in town. You could continue working at Sam Hill's if you married him, even if you bore children. And I hope you do become a parent, because I know you love children and would make a first-rate mother. Tom, Betsy, it's not for me to do, but I give the two of you my blessing, and I hope we can all remain friends."

For an uncomfortable few seconds, no one spoke. Then Mason broke the silence, pushing for an answer. He looked first to the woman he loved. "Betsy?" When she didn't immediately reply, he turned to his best friend. "Tom?" He hoped desperately that neither of them would throw in their cards and walk away. "Somebody, say something!"

"Well, um . . ." It was unlike Elizabeth to be at a loss for words. "Well! Um. Yes! Yes, of course, I can remain friends with you. I just drove out here to check on Cody, but since you're back at the ranch, I'll be turning around, and I'll see you later in town."

"That's fine! And you, Tom?"

"Holy cow, Mace! I'll always be your friend." He prodded his horse forward and stretched out his arm for a handshake. "Thanks for forgiving me."

Mason met him halfway with a firm grip. "Shall we go up to the house, then?"

"I'll be up shortly to question Miss Becky. I'd just like a quick word with Miss Elizabeth."

"Fine." Mason tipped his hat, thanked Miss Elizabeth for coming to check on Cody, and left his friends to complete their business.

Once Raven was a few strides up the road, Tom dismounted and climbed into the buggy. He moved the canteen out of the way and sat beside Miss Elizabeth.

"My stars, Tom! Look what I've done." Tears began to trickle from her eyes.

He had never seen her cry. He wanted to wrap her in a hug, but he didn't dare. Instead, he spoke matter-of-factly. "You wanted to know where you stood, and now you do. He loves you, but he doesn't want to marry you. He's given you permission to move on."

"I only wanted to nudge him along, not spur him out to pasture! We never should have staged that kiss for Cody to see! Mason's so maddeningly chivalrous. 'Here, you can have my best friend instead.' " She pounded a fist into the palm of her hand. "Who is he to decide I wouldn't take to being a rancher's wife? And now what? Must you and I go through the motions of courting to continue the charade?"

Tom shrugged. "I'm willing if you are." He smiled at her and winked.

She couldn't help but giggle. That encouraged Tom. He lifted her chin toward his face and moved in for a kiss.

She pulled back and produced a hanky from up her sleeve. "It's too soon, Tom. Too soon."

As she blotted her face, he scooted away from her, feeling conflicted: shameful for being tactless, and elated that she hadn't outright rejected him. "I'm sorry, Elizabeth. Of course, it's too soon. So long, then. I'll see you back in town."

He climbed down and stood aside as she turned her buggy in the opposite direction. Then he remounted and rode up to the barn, where Cody was perched on the pasture gate with Shep lying at his feet. On the way in, Tom had noticed Miss Becky's red plaid shirt and some trousers hanging on the line to dry. No pantalettes today. He remembered his prior interview with Miss Becky and told himself he would do better at asking the right questions this time.

He tied his horse near the trough and opened the barn door to go in. Cody hopped down from the gate and began following Tom inside, but the sheriff stopped him.

"Whoa there, boy. Miss Becky doesn't need your help answering the questions, and I don't need your help asking 'em. Since you weren't there, I have no need to interview you. Don't you have some chores to do?" He thought Cody would turn tail, but he thought wrong.

"I know you're angry with me, Sheriff Claiborne, 'cause I told Pa about you and Miss Elizabeth kissin', but Pa said you're all still friends. Can't we be friends, too?"

"I'm not angry about that, Cody. I'm disappointed that you lack respect for the law. A lawman places his life in danger every day, just by pinning on a tin star. We can't abide folks who hamper our work with falsehoods or 'oaths of silence.' In my mind, there's a good chance you didn't do anything unlawful, you just went against your pa's rules or wishes. Making your own choices is part of becoming a man. When you're man enough to take responsibility for your choices, we can be friends. Taking responsibility means owning up to your involvement with the Apaches this morning. If you didn't break the law, I'm not obliged to inform your pa of your deeds, so I'll keep your confidences, but my advice to you is to fess up. Next time, and I'm certain there will be one, remember that it's often easier to ask forgiveness later than to get permission beforehand."

Cody nodded that he understood, and he retreated to the house to fess up, while Tom continued into the barn. The horses, even Bella Dama and her foal, were out to pasture, but Miss Becky was lying, awake, on the cot.

"Howdy, Miss Becky." He removed his hat and sat down at the foot of the cot.

Becky sat up and settled cross-legged, giving Tom more space, but she didn't look at him. She scratched her scalp with all ten fingers, then fluffed her wild hair outward, away from her face. She was wearing a red emancipation suit, topped by the bright pink shawl that Miss Hannah had given to her last night. "Mornin', Sheriff." She yawned widely, then slapped a hand over her mouth and muttered "faux pas."

Tom felt awkward seeing Miss Becky in her underclothes, but she was fully covered and didn't seem uneasy. "Mr. Campbell and I were out searching for you this morning. I'm pleased to see you're fine. You *are* fine, aren't you? Has any harm befallen you?"

Becky stared ahead, her eyes apparently focused on a stall's gate. Tom considered that maybe she was physically fine, but her ordeal had traumatized her, and she was unable to speak about it. "Miss Becky, I know your brother brought you here. I don't think he would have done that if you needed to see Doc Ritter."

When that didn't get her talking, he tried a different tack. "Miss Becky, if the Apaches kidnapped you and stole El Diablo, they need to be caught and brought to justice. It's the soldiers at Fort Bowie's job to capture the renegades. They need to know the number of braves and the types and amounts of weapons they're carrying. Can you help me with that?" When she failed to answer, he switched to yesterday's lesson. "What can you tell me about their ponies?"

When she still didn't answer, Tom looked down, exasperated, and for the first time noticed Miss Becky's carpetbag. It was cracked open, and on top of it sat her pink cowboy hat. He saw the hat was now decorated with a golden eagle feather rather than the pair of ostrich feathers. "What service did you provide the Apaches to receive such a fine gift, Miss Becky? Did you heal a horse?"

At this point, Cody entered the barn and approached the cot. "Beggin' yer pardon." Miss Becky eyed him, and he tipped his coveted hat to her. "We can go to the swimmin' hole as soon as we're done here, Miss Becky."

That news astonished Tom. He had figured Cody wouldn't be allowed off the ranch for a month, excepting for church. Cody's evident power of persuasion over his pa was impressive.

Cody interrupted Tom's thoughts. "I can tell ya my part now, Sheriff. Let me know when you're through questionin' Miss Becky."

"I didn't tell 'im anything, jus' like I spit an' shook I wouldn't."

"That was a fool thing to ask of ya." He took a load off, sitting down between her and Tom, and taking Becky's hand in his before he continued speaking. "The others knew it, and I knew it, and I shouldn't have gone along. Sheriff Claiborne is a lawman, Miss Becky. He needs to know the truth, but he won't share it unless he's legally bound to. Isn't that right, Sheriff?"

"Right!"

"I hafta tell 'im ever'thing? I'm not wantin' the soldiers to find my friends."

"Yes, the whole of it." Cody gave Miss Becky's hand a gentle squeeze. "Sheriff, if ya don't mind us bein' interviewed together, I'll start with what I know."

Tom thought better of his previous demand. He knew even then that Cody's presence would be useful, but he had wanted to teach the boy a lesson. Convinced that Cody had learned the lesson, he decided to utilize his help. "All right. You go first, Cody, and you can stay while I hear Miss Becky's adventure."

Cody explained how John and he had arrived at the base of the Dos Cabezas Mountains to discover Mr. Pruitt and Mr. Starley engaged in a skirmish with four Apaches. He and John joined in the fray, but the situation became grim when they realized they were trapped. Just when the hope of survival seemed lost, Miss Becky had stopped the fighting by pulling her gun on the youngest brave and requesting a parlay. The four white males and four Apache braves had gathered in a camp, where they laid down their weapons and smoked herbal tobacco wrapped in corn husk paper.

Miss Becky finally turned to look at the sheriff. "I smoked it, too."

Tom held his composure. He wasn't sure if she was trying to shock him or impress him, or if she was just speaking matter-of-factly, but he didn't react. "Go on, Cody."

"We all sat cross-legged in a circle and puffed little clouds of smoke. Me and Miss Becky choked on it some, but at least I've had a bit of experience smokin' cigars and corn cob pipes."

This information caused Tom to raise his eyebrows. He was learning a lot about Cody today. He wondered if Mason knew what his son had been up to, but he wouldn't be the one to tell him. He would keep Cody's doings to himself.

Cody continued, saying how the biggest obstacle to overcome was the ownership of El Diablo. With Hank Starley interpreting, they learned that the Apaches' quarrel was with Buck Pruitt. The Apaches maintained that Buck and his men had rustled the stallion and his mares from their lands. They were willing to concede the mares, but they wanted the great black stallion back, and they wanted Buck punished by white-man laws; that is, horse thieves hang. They were also for killing Hank, since he had, once again, trespassed, even with a bounty on his head.

The sheriff then learned from Cody that Buck claimed he had rounded up the wild horses from open range. He believed they were free for the taking by anyone who could catch them, including Apaches. If the Apaches had wanted El Diablo, they could have captured him themselves. The Apaches, in fact, were the thieves, having stolen El Diablo in the night, and the kidnapped Miss Becky was a witness who could attest to that.

Miss Becky broke in again. "Exceptin' I *wasn't* kidnapped. I told 'em El Diablo could hear the Apaches outside the barn an' was anxious. I got dressed so's I could be ready to ride. El Diablo wanted me to go with 'im, ya see, an' that's what I did. An' then in the smokin' circle I told 'em all they should let El Diablo decide where he wanted to live—jus' like the eagle feather got to decide. It weren't a gift like ya thought, Sheriff."

Tom was following the story until she mentioned the feather part, but he decided to let that pass.

"Anyways, El Diablo has spent time in town an' in the mountains with the Apaches, so's he knows what they're both like. Little Hawk fetched El Diablo, whose name in actual fact is Free Spirit. He helped me excape from bindings, but that was earlier.

Each person wantin' Free Spirit got a chance to caress 'im, an' he was angry fer Mr. Pruitt an' balky with Hawk an' unhappy with all, 'ceptin' me. He told me he was a free spirit an' jus' wanted to go home to where he was foaled. Hawk an' the other Apaches understood 'cause they feel the same way—they jus' wanna live where they were born.

"So's we agreed nobody owns Free Spirit. The Apaches will take 'im home, an' Mr. Pruitt swore to never go after 'im again. The Apaches understood that Mr. Starley wasn't tryin' to kill 'em—he was just tryin' to rescue me, so's they gave 'im a reprieve. Mr. Starley had given the Apaches my sorrel gelding, Snip, an' I got 'im back an' gifted 'im to Mr. Pruitt for his loss o' Free Spirit. Then I recollected the whiskey in my carpetbag, an' we passed the bottle 'round, which Mr. Starley finished off an' said was the perfect endin', an' it tasted better'n the tobacc-y, fer shore. John rode me double here, an' then he rode to town to make party plans. Mr. Pruitt an' Mr. Starley rode in also. My Apache friends are on the way to Free Spirit's birthin' place."

"Is that all ya need?"

Sheriff Claiborne summarized in his mind: Miss Becky had not been abducted; there were four braves; they had not harmed her or anyone else; they were heading toward New Mexico Territory. "Just one last item, Cody. What weapons did the Apaches carry?"

Miss Becky answered. "One Springfield carbine an' some bows an' arrows."

Cody nodded his agreement, and the sheriff thanked and dismissed them both. He would wire the information to the commander at Fort Bowie.

"Friends?"

"Friends!" For the first time ever, Sheriff Claiborne and Cody shook hands.

Chapter 8

The morning coolness had long since evaporated into late-morning warmth. It was the perfect time to swim. A buggy would be ideal, Cody thought, but the Campbells didn't own one. Therefore, he and Miss Becky hitched the team of sorrels to the buckboard. He considered it to be a man's job, but he wasn't about to refuse Miss Becky's help.

As he worked, Cody was thinking of his good fortune. He was exuberant to be taking Miss Becky to the swimmin' hole. Before he approached his father to confess that he'd disobeyed him and put himself in danger, Cody had decided that if given the choice of being homebound for a month or enduring a whipping, he would choose the whipping. He didn't remember ever having been whipped, but he thought his offense was whip-worthy. A quick punishment would be better than a monthlong one, and it would allow him to spend time with Miss Becky at the swimmin' hole and her party.

As it turned out, his father seemed out of sorts. Cody suspected he was tired from a fitful night and the early morning ride, plus he was probably pondering his decision regarding Miss Elizabeth. Mason apparently didn't have the energy to deal with a disobedient son. He had listened to Cody's story and apology and, surprisingly, he had said he understood that when someone you love needs help, it's difficult, if not impossible, to control yourself: instinct makes you act to try to save them. Then he said he didn't believe Cody was truly in love, but he could tell there was a strong attraction between him and Miss Becky. He wasn't sure if Becky reciprocated Cody's feelings, but that was for Cody to determine.

Cody had suggested that his father ride to town and participate in the bronc-bustin' contest like he had originally planned. It might improve his mood, and if not the contest, maybe playing poker and downing a couple of beers would cheer him. The cloud on Mason's face had visibly lifted at that prospect, and he had ridden out on Raven before Tom had even left. A discussion about the swimming hole hadn't arisen, and Cody had decided to follow Tom's advice. He was going, and if that was the wrong thing to do, he would ask forgiveness later.

Cody placed the picnic hamper with the burnt bacon and other foods into the bed of the wagon, along with Becky's carpetbag, his own valise containing a change of clothes and two towels, and his guitar, cushioned in a blanket. Miss Becky spent some time whispering to the team and caressing their ears before she climbed onto the seat and picked up the reins. Cody didn't bother to ask to drive.

The swimming hole was a natural land feature, large enough to accommodate at least fifty people at a time, but Cody and Becky were the only comers that noon. The other children were in town at the bronco-busting contest. The pool was deep enough in the center to jump or dive into, and someone had hung a knotted, thick hemp rope from a tree branch that could be used to swing out above the water for a fun plunge into the cool wetness. Walking into the pool was slippery, due to a slimy layer of algae on the rocks that edged the water, but once in, the footing was more stable. Miss Becky took one look at the swimming hole and shook her head no.

"Already took my chances with water today. This looks considerable worse. No sense temptin' fate twice."

Cody didn't try to change her mind. "Let's eat."

She was agreeable to that, so Cody set the blanket in a shady spot and motioned for Miss Becky to sit on it. He had burnt a full pound of bacon for her, and after she recited a prayer of thanks, he was happy to see her eat three strips. She also ate a carrot, an apple, and a biscuit. He figured that was the most he had ever seen her eat in one sitting. He ate a couple hard-cooked eggs and some leftover roast from two nights ago, plus some biscuits. For dessert, he offered up day-old churros that he had purchased in town the previous afternoon from Gordo's mother, who was selling them outside Sam Hill's when he purchased the carpetbag.

Miss Becky's eyes lit up at the taste of the sugar and cinnamon, which she licked off the doughy treat before taking a bite. "Yum! This is like Free Spirit an' leather."

"Sorry? I don't follow, Miss Becky."

"Never ya mind. I was jus' talkin' to myself." She turned her focus to the water. Damselflies flitted here and there. Closer by, small, black butterflies fluttered around fragrant wildflowers, and a mourning dove called sorrowfully. Up in the sky, a lone vulture was soaring on an air current. "It's real peaceful here. Kinda reminds me of the place I thought up 'Serenity.' I'd like to try another song. Would ya write it down fer me if'n I think one up? I have writin' paper an' a pencil in my bag."

"I'd take pleasure in that. And after ya come up with the words, I can help ya with a tune." He fetched the writing materials, and Becky lay quietly with her eyes closed, apparently thinking hard. Cody quickly became bored. "I'm goin' for a dip. Let me know when ya need me to write." There was the sound of a splash as he plunged from the rope into the deepest water.

When Becky opened her eyes after a spell, she saw Cody floating on his back in the water with his arms outstretched and eyes closed. Now and then, he would start to sink and would kick his feet to bring his legs back to the surface.

"Master Cody?"

He immediately righted and began treading water. "Are ya ready?"

"What's that ya were doin'?"

"Just floatin'." He swam toward her with sure strokes.

"Yer real good in the water."

"Thanks! Miss Elizabeth taught me how to float and swim."

"Think I could float?"

Cody was amazed by her interest. "Yes, ma'am, Miss Becky! I can teach ya. It'll be fun. I would keep ya safe in the shallows and would hold ya up 'til ya could float on yer own. Want to try? I'll help ya in so ya don't slip."

She began to undress, and Cody, taken aback, hastily turned away. John would throw a fit if he knew of her social faux pas, but he would never know. Before long, Miss Becky was down to her emancipation suit, which was all she owned that could pass for swimwear. Cody didn't own any either and was wearing the bottoms of a set of long johns.

Everything went well, and Cody felt Becky relax under the pressure of his fingers supporting her torso. She closed her eyes, just as she'd seen him do. Her body swayed in sync with the slow movement of the water, lulling her into a tranquil state, like the effects of a hammock gently swinging in a breeze.

Cody thought she had fallen asleep until she spoke to him in a low voice, as though she were trying to preserve the tranquility.

"Last time a body tried to teach me to swim, I was seven. He threw me in an' said, 'Sink 'r swim.' "

"John."

"Fer shore."

"That was cruel of him, but ya must not have sunk." He chuckled, trying to make light of her ordeal, but she didn't respond in kind.

"Did so. But I talked a horse onshore into comin' in an' rescuin' me. I hung onto 'im tight as a noose 'round a horse thief's neck."

"That was quick thinkin'. I'm glad it worked."

"I think John was testin' me. He likely would o' thrown me a line afore I drowned."

"I'm goin' to let go of ya now. You're doin' fine, but if ya start to sink, arch yer back more and use yer arms or legs to find yer balance. Don't fret. If ya start to flounder, I'll help ya."

Her legs started to sink almost immediately, but she was able to bring them up to the surface again.

"Folks with more fat on 'em float better, but you're still doin' fine."

"Floatin' would be best with eyes open on a moonless night. It would feel like driftin' in a river o' stars. I could make a song 'bout it."

"A song! I forgot yer song. What did ya think up?"

Becky frowned. "It was no good. I couldn't find rhymes. My idea was to tell 'bout how folks an' horses all come in diff'rent colors, an' ya can't always understand their words, but ya can learn to understand 'em, if'n ya understand they're the same on the inside."

Cody wasn't sure what she was trying to say, but he could see how she'd have trouble expressing it as a song. "Ya worked on it a long while."

"I made a poem fer John instead, but it's not all right."

"I'd like to hear yer poem, anyhow. Do ya remember it?"

"Shorely." She continued to float peacefully as she recited the words:

> Sittin' on a log,
> Tied, in a sacred place,
> By my own doin',
> I hear talk I don't understand,
> Like in a barn some ten years past.
>
> Are they speakin' to me or speakin' 'bout me?
> My innards swirl, 'bout to hurl.
> Shy, I try to say, "I's pukey."
> But this time, I close my eyes an' hold it in.
> An' still, I can tell they think I'm spooky.
> Then my feather burns.
>
> Ponies rest at a spring, hearin' my words,
> Not understandin' any better'n Hawk understands English.
> But at the end, Hawk frees me an' the stallion.
> He knows I speak with horses, 'cause the ponies told 'im so.
> I musta been real tired to pick up on 'em so slow.

When she had finished, Cody stood dumbly, stunned by what the poem had divulged.

Apparently, Becky was vexed by his silence. "I told ya it's not right. I shouldn't o' recited it to ya." Her eyes were open, and she looked angry. "I'm done floatin'. Lemme up."

He helped her stand and guided her over to the edge of the pool. "It's good Miss Becky. It's better than good! Thanks for sharin' it with me. I was just tryin' to commit it to memory, 'cause I got surprised by the endin'. You're sayin' that Hawk talks to ponies like you talk to horses? You're sayin' John calls ya Spooky 'cause yer first words were that you were goin' to puke and ya mispronounced it?"

"Yer sayin' that, not me. Poems mean diff'rent things to diff'rent people."

"Please don't be angry. I think it's a fine poem, and I'm sorry yer feather burned up."

"I'm not angry with ya. I'm riled up with myself fer sharin' what I meant to be only fer John."

Cody stepped out of the pool first, and then he offered Miss Becky a hand. "Let's dry off and eat some more churros, plus I told ya I'd have another gift for ya today."

She couldn't resist his offer. After eating more of the doughy sweets, Cody fetched his guitar. Around the neck was a friendship bracelet he'd woven from colorful ribbons he'd purchased at Sam Hill's. He presented it to her, and she allowed him to tie it around her wrist. He explained it was something to remember him by and a symbol of their friendship.

"I used purple, pink, aqua, green, yellow, and orange, so it would match any outfit ya wear, and if ya get in a tight spot and need ribbon, it'll be handy." He hoped to hear that she'd wear it every day and would never pick it apart, but she only said her standard line.

"Thank ya, Master Cody. It's the best gift I ever received!"

"It's only half a gift, 'cause I composed a song to go with it. It's called 'My Best Friend.' "

He picked up his instrument and sang confidently:

> My best friend was a horse
> 'til you came along
> Ya helped with some chores
> Ya sang me a song
>
> Ya spoke in a way
> That made me think;
> We shared some play
> We shared a drink
>
> I like who ya are
> Both soul and heart
> Please stay my friend
> Though we be apart

I'll believe in you
'til the very end
I'll always be yer friend
I will always be yer friend

Just as Miss Becky had waited in silence for Cody's response to her poem, Cody now waited. Miss Becky was clearly thinking about the song, but he couldn't tell from her expression if she liked it or not. Finally, she spoke.

"How did ya do that?"

"How do ya mean? I thought up the words first, and then I tried 'em out with some chords."

"How did ya know what I was thinkin' an' write from my view?"

"What?" He was confused, but he quickly played the lyrics through his head to see if he could suss out her meaning.

"How did ya know my best friend was a horse?"

"Aha!" Now he understood, and he felt elated. "Well, ya see, Miss Becky, I was meanin' *my* best friend was a horse, ya know, Star, before I spent time with ya doin' those things that made me like ya." He swelled inside. If she thought it was written from her perspective, then he was her best friend.

"Fer real? That's a comfort, a big one. I thought ya could read my thoughts."

"No, you're not easy for me to read, not like an open book. You're more like an interestin' cover with foreign words on the pages inside, but I'm learnin' the language."

"I'm deficient in showin' emotions. Sometimes my face doesn't match what I'm feelin'. John says I don't have any feelin's."

"John is jealous of ya, is all."

"Mayhap. No matter. Yer a real good song writer, Master Cody. Those words say the same as I feel, like I shoulda written 'em. Thank ya kindly fer the best gift I ever received in my life!"

"You're welcome!"

"I wanna gift somethin' to *you*." Miss Becky went to her carpetbag and returned with her peppermint stick wrapped like a mummy in the pink ribbon that Miss Elizabeth had given her. "Peppermint relaxes horses, so's ya know. I was gonna slip it to El Diablo, but I saved it fer ya instead."

Cody felt honored. She could have used it at the stables; she could have used it during the bronco-busting contest; she could even have used it at the Apache camp, but she had saved it for him.

"Thank ya kindly, Miss Becky. It's the best gift I ever received!" And Cody meant his words.

Becky looked happy. Heartened, Cody returned to making music. He strummed tunes, including "Serenity," and the two of them sang and talked for an hour, and when the time came, they were sorry to have to leave to meet the stagecoach.

*   *   *

Leaning Rock was booming from the demand for cattle and the railroad to transport them. Families had sprung up and were taking root like wildflowers in boardwalk cracks, but they were still outnumbered by cowpunchers. Wranglers rode into town on Saturday nights to spend their hard-earned wages on whiskey and poker and women. The saloon was bigger than the church, and truth be told, it was busier on Saturday nights than the church was on Sunday mornings. Those were the only two public buildings that contained pianos, but neither building was large enough to accommodate all the folks who were invited to Miss Becky's party. In the days of yore, a rancher's barn sufficed as a party venue. Folks would come from miles around to partake in the fun and food. The men would roast hogs and steers, and the women would bake their prize-winning breads and pies. Young folks danced and fell in love; old folks danced and reminisced. But John didn't have that luxury. No barn could hold fifty town and ranch families and fifty more cowhands. Thus, the shindig John planned would take place on Main Street.

John lay thinking, propped by pillows on the quilted bed in his boarding house room. He made a mental checklist. The stage transporting his family would arrive at 3:30 this afternoon, leaving just enough time for everyone to get settled in their rooms and ready for the party. He had contracted with the café for barbecued beef, beans, and bread, and he had procured cakes and pies from the bakery. The pastor enlisted the church members' wives to supply coffee and milk. Most of the church's pews would line the street, opening up space in the one-room building. After Becky entertained briefly on the piano, she would be free to interact with her guests, though knowing her, she would exit to interact with their horses. He had ridden to Benson on Thursday and hired a mariachi band to keep the party lively. After the formalities and entertainment, the guests would move outdoors to dance in the street to the mariachi music. The food would be set up in the church, but people would eat outside. He figured families with young children would arrive at 5 and leave by 7:30. Most of the cowhands would come for the food and then skitter over to the saloon, but those with eyes on pretty female folk might stay and dance. Both of those options appealed to him. The party would be over at 9, and the church would be back together, ready for Sunday's sermon, by 10.

John was a planner. His summer of gallivanting around with Becky was almost over, and his next two years would be spent in business school at Woodbury University. After graduating, he would help Papa manage the family business, eventually taking over all the administrative duties. But for now, he'd better rustle up

Becky. He had some information to tell her before they met the stage.

*   *   *

Main Street was beginning to bustle, with folks of all ages walking or riding into the center of town from the corrals on the outskirts. The bronco-busting contest had ended, and residents were ready to shop, take a siesta, or socialize in the saloon. After Cody and Becky had returned to town, he had left her with her brother at the boarding house so they could prepare for their family's arrival. Cody had then retreated to the bench in front of the doctor's office, where he waited until he saw John and Miss Becky making their way slowly down the street, stopping at every horse. John was tugging on his sister's elbow, urging her on, looking annoyed if she spent overly much time with any one horse. Cody moseyed over to them, and to John's relief, he offered to walk Miss Becky to the stagecoach station. John hurried off in that direction. He was well dressed in his signature black attire, with the addition of the same holster and pistol that he'd sported that morning.

Miss Becky was wearing clothes typical of a young lady, most likely chosen by Miss Elizabeth as appropriate for a Saturday in town, except that her outfit was topped with her pink hat and her brand-new eagle feather. Cody complimented her, saying how ladylike she looked, but to his disappointment, she reacted sourly, retorting that clothing isn't what makes a lady. She seemed to take an excessively long time with each horse, and he surmised that she was stalling.

"Itchy clothes?"

"Worse than skeeter bites."

"Excited about seein' yer kin?"

"Not 'specially. John told me somethin' fretful 'bout why my godmother's here."

"Can ya tell me?"

She shared some, but she became distracted and abruptly changed the subject. "I recited my poem to John afterward, fer spite. He won't ever have cause to re-tell his wrong account o' when folks learned I was a horse whisperer. No more 'I Spooky.' He thinks I meant 'I'm pukey,' but I told ya the poem wasn't all right. It was jus' part right, an' he doesn't know which part." She looked up at Cody and smiled a gloating smile. "I outsmarted 'im."

And me. Then it occurred to Cody that being called Spooky was a heap better than being called Pukey, but he said nothing.

After she had confided her trickery, Miss Becky picked up her pace, and she and Cody met up with John in front of the stage station, definitely after 3:30, but still before the stage arrived. Before long, four thundering horses drove up, drawing the coach and a cloud of dust behind them. Piles of trunks and bags swayed on top as the driver pulled the horses to a halt. He set the brake and dropped down to the ground to open the door. Miss Becky immediately walked over to greet the lead horses, and then she walked around behind them and greeted the wheelers. As the driver proffered his hand to an attractive lady with speckles of gray in her auburn hair, Miss Becky announced to the station keeper, who had come out to help with the luggage, that the lead horses were both ill with equine influenza and needed to be isolated from the other two lest they also become infected.

The man groaned. "Dang it all! They ain't the first ones, and it'll take 'em a good six weeks to recover." He shook his head in aggravation, and then he climbed aboard and proceeded up to the luggage.

The driver helped the lady down. She looked smart even after the long ride, clad in fancy clothes, wearing pretty paint on her cheeks and lips, and not a hair of her elaborate updo out of place. After she gracefully landed, he passed a forgotten parasol to her. Next, a man of medium stature and about forty-five years of age climbed down. His hair and beard were once bright red but were now showing signs of his age. His most distinguishing feature was a black patch covering his left eye.

"Papa!" John loped over to his father and shook his hand wildly, but before they could hug hello, Patrick McCoy turned to lift little Annabelle from the floor of the coach. Becky appeared just then, and Mr. McCoy handed the 3-year-old to her, greeting his older daughter with a nod of recognition and "Happy birthday, darlin'!" The little girl was even more vocal yelling "Spooky!" as loud as her voice allowed.

Becky held her sister out to look her over. "Looky at ya, Annabelle, all dressed up."

The tot was, indeed, all dressed up, looking very much like a child from France. Cody remembered Miss Becky saying that only one person was allowed to call her Spooky, and he concluded it was Annabelle.

Becky deposited the beautiful strawberry blonde with slanted sky-blue eyes on the ground, and the lady immediately snatched the child's hand protectively. Mr. McCoy began introducing John to the woman, Miss Reba Martin, while two red-headed ten-year-olds jumped one after the other to the ground.

"Master Cody, those there are my twin brothers Thomas an' Timothy."

Cody had never known any identical twins. He looked at them, fascinated. "How do ya tell 'em apart?"

"Timothy is meaner."

Cody wasn't sure that was a help, but maybe he could tell a difference when he was closer to them or knew them longer.

The stage driver busied himself catching bags being dropped or handed down by the station keeper, but there were so many that he enlisted Patrick and John to help him.

"Becky, darlin', while we're occupied, please introduce this young man to your brothers, and when I'm finished, I'll introduce you to your godmother."

"Yes, Papa."

As the introductions were taking place, a chipper and seventy-dollars-richer Mason Campbell was making his way back into town after the bronco-busting contest, walking with Tom Claiborne on one side and Miss Elizabeth on the other. The trio looked just as friendly as ever, as though their morning fuss had never taken place.

"Look! The stage arrived. Let's go meet the McCoy clan."

Mason wasn't as enthusiastic as Miss Elizabeth, but he could see Cody making the acquaintance of the passengers, so he went along with her wishes.

"Have you ever seen so many red-headed people?"

"Really, Tom. What an ill-mannered thing to say."

Mason stifled a laugh at Elizabeth's admonishment. He had been thinking the exact same thing as Tom and was pleased that Tom had spoken first and been the one to take Elizabeth's rebuke.

"I hold nothing against red heads. I was just saying I've never seen so many of 'em flocked together."

Miss Elizabeth started to respond, but Tom interrupted her. "Looks like duty calls." He took off running.

Mason looked for the trouble in the direction Tom was headed and cringed at the sight. Cody had just taken a wild swing at one of the McCoy boys. "Sorry, Elizabeth." He raced off toward the stagecoach, too, but he arrived too late—Cody's fist had found its mark in the boy's gut. The boy doubled over but didn't fall. A second boy appeared and threw himself at Cody, bringing him down. They rolled around in the dirt, each trying to get an advantage. Cody was bigger and stronger, but the McCoy boy was fast and fought dirty. He kicked, bit, and scratched.

Mr. McCoy pulled Cody off his downed son and held him captive while John heaved his brother to his feet.

"Are you cooled down enough I can let go of you?"

Cody answered with a curt "Yes, sir."

By now, the sheriff and Mason had arrived. They introduced themselves to Mr. McCoy, who asked them to call him Patch. Tom thanked Patch for breaking up the fight and asked if everyone was fine. All three boys answered that they were.

"You're too young to arrest for being disorderly, but I don't want any more trouble out of any of you. Do you agree to be civil?"

They did, so Tom left for his office to check on yesterday's prisoners, saying he'd see everyone at Becky's party.

"I was just getting to the bottom of this, Mr. Campbell." Patch turned to his daughter. "Becky, darlin', what's this about?"

She didn't have time to answer before John spoke up: "Well, Papa, you aspired for Beck and me to do some growing up this summer, and we have. As you can see, I'm man enough to carry a gun." He placed his hand on the weapon to point it out. Patch looked at him dubiously. His silence inspired John to finish his explanation. "Well, Beck's no longer a little girl. She's outgrown 'Spooky' and wants to be called 'Miss Becky.' She also made her first friend, this here Master Cody Campbell. When Timothy and Thomas started pestering and pinching her, it was only natural for Master Cody to stand up for her. If he hadn't, I would have."

"I see." But just to confirm, he checked with Cody. "Is that what happened?"

"Yes, sir. They were teasing her, calling her Spooky, and I lost my temper. I'm sorry, sir."

In the end, Patch and Mason settled on forgetting the matter if Timothy and Thomas would apologize to Becky and if Cody would apologize to the twins. Cody did his part with reluctance. He was truly sorry he had attacked a younger boy, but if he was tired of hearing Miss Becky's siblings torment her, he imagined how she felt about it. First it was John, and now it was these two. Nonetheless, there were apologies all around, and all was forgiven.

Meanwhile, Miss Elizabeth had befriended Miss Reba. They talked at length about fashion and a little about the incident. After the apologies had been made, Patch interrupted the ladies' conversation to introduce Miss Reba to Becky and to Mason. Becky stood frozen, until her father reminded her to be mannerly.

"What do you say to your godmother, Becky? Be sure to look her in the eyes."

"Thank ya fer the fancy pantalettes. They're the best gift I ever received."

"You're quite welcome. I'm delighted you like them. A young lady should have nice clothes to make a proper impression."

Becky backed away from the woman, and Mason stepped forward to meet her. He was immediately drawn to her feminine curves and mysterious eyes, and Miss Elizabeth didn't fail to notice. But Mason lost all interest when, as the family started its way down the street to the boarding house, he heard Miss Reba mutter under her breath, "Kate McCoy should have stopped breeding years ago."

*   *   *

With the bronco-busting contest over, the townspeople were primed for a celebratory event. They greeted Miss Becky at the door of the church and wished her felicitations and many happy returns. They were generous with their praise and compliments, but they didn't bring gifts, per John's request. One guest expressed her sadness about the gift ban. María Contreras, the young girl who had sewn the buttons on John's shirt, confided to Miss Becky that she thought every girl deserved at least one gift for her birthday.

"Don't fret over it. In actual fact, I've been gifted more presents than I could possibly use. My papa says the best gift is to give to others, so's I'd like to gift somethin' to *you*."

María's eyes opened wide in surprise. She could hardly believe her ears. "Really? To me?"

"I'm leavin' on the train tomorrow, an' I can't take my bicycle with me. I'd take pleasure if'n you'd accept it an' play with it every day an' sell rides to earn money."

"Your bicycle? You mean it?" She smiled big, showing her perfect teeth.

"I shorely do. An' if'n anything breaks, Mr. Starley," she pointed him out, "can fix it fer ya."

María squealed with delight. She thanked Miss Becky profusely for truly the best gift she had ever received, and then she ran off to tell family and friends about her good fortune.

After most people had arrived and paid their respects, Patch McCoy stood with Becky in the threshold of the church door so that his voice could be heard by those folks inside the building and those out in the street. He looked sharp, wearing a white shirt and skinny black bow tie with his slacks, but Becky looked ravishing, if not uncomfortable. She wore a royal-blue gown with three-quarter-length sleeves accented with lace and silver-colored, satin bows. A large rose-shaped flower was strategically placed where the V-neck ended at her bosom. She wore a corset to enhance her figure, and she wore a billowing petticoat beneath the gown's skirt. The skirt consisted of yards of shiny fabric and two more bows, both at her centerline: one at a point just above the knees, and the other just above her ankles. When she lifted the gown to walk, ruffle-y pantalettes could be seen covering her legs, and perfectly matched blue velvet, lace-up, heeled shoes adorned with a rose on their toes protected her feet. Her carrot-colored hair had been straightened and piled into a lump at the back of her head. Tendrils curled down past her ears, as though defying anyone to force the shape out of them. Her earlobes displayed a pair of pearls, a birthday gift from Miss Reba Martin, and her neck was bedecked with a strand of matching pearls, a gift from her parents.

The McCoy clan, the Campbells, Elizabeth Hill, and the sheriff were all inside the building, dressed in their finery. Many town families were milling around inside, their young'uns playing tag in and out between the older folk.

"Greetings, folks. Top of the evenin' to you. I'm Patch McCoy. Welcome to the celebration of my daughter Becky's fourteenth birthday."

Patch continued speaking, but his words were lost to Mason when Cody caught his attention and whispered that he thought she turned thirteen yesterday. Mason steered Cody away from the crowd and into a corner so as not to disturb those folks who were still listening to Patch.

"I suspect she was trying to avoid unwanted attention on her travels, son. A girl would attract less attention than a young lady."

Cody considered. "That seems like somethin' John would cook up, but I don't think Miss Becky would go along with it. She wants to be seen as a lady, Pa, even if she doesn't want to look like one."

"Huh? What are you saying, son?"

"She wants people to treat her like a lady whether she's wearin' a fancy outfit like tonight or boys' clothes, 'cause she's the same person inside."

"Then why do you think she fibbed about her age?"

"I think she's afraid, Pa."

"Afraid? You mean afraid of growing up?"

"Not exactly. More like she's afraid she'll lose her ability to talk to horses when she *is* grown up. That's what happened to Miss Reba."

"Miss Reba was a horse whisperer? Are you sure?"

"Sure, I'm sure. And John told Miss Becky that Miss Reba had come all this way to test her."

Mason was dumbfounded and didn't know what to believe. Miss Becky had been wrong about her godmother's age. Maybe she was wrong about her godmother having been a horse whisperer. John could be provoking her just to be mean. As he considered Cody's revelations, it occurred to him that Becky could have been named Rebecca after Miss Reba. What a coincidence that both Rebeccas supposedly possessed the same rare talent.

As though Cody were reading his father's thoughts, he added another thunderbolt. "There's more, Pa. Miss Becky says before she was called Becky, she was baptized 'Sarah.' "

Mason wasn't aware of anyone changing a child's name following a baptism. It was simply unheard of. He started to ask Cody another question, but the room had become more crowded, and an elderly woman standing nearby shushed the Campbells so she could hear better. Patch was issuing instructions.

"A buffet supper will be available to you shortly at the back of the room, and soon after, the music and dancing will commence. The mariachis we hired have not yet arrived, so's we'll begin our own merriment here in the church. Let's start with a rousing round of 'For She's a Jolly Good Fellow.' "

Cody wandered back into the crowd and joined in the singing, while Patch led the folks in the familiar tune and Becky stood stiffly nearby. When the song ended, Patch suggested a group activity called the calliope song. As the families began breaking into four groups: men, women, school-aged children, and small fries, he directed John to ride out to meet up with the tardy mariachis. Sheriff Tom Claiborne overheard the conversation and volunteered to ride with John. He thought he could help the young man if he ran into trouble, but it also gave him an excuse to avoid both Mason and Miss Elizabeth. He was feeling awkward around them, though he had put on a good show that afternoon, acting like everything was normal. In truth, their relationships would need time to mend.

Patch took charge of the men and taught them how to bend and straighten their knees to their part. The ladies formed a second group nearby. Miss Reba Martin gathered them around like a mother hen and helped them practice going up and down on their toes to their part. The McCoy twins, Thomas and Timothy, worked with the older children. Their part consisted of swaying side to side as they sang. Miss Becky enlisted Cody to help her with the youngest children, including Annabelle.

The song was a simple round, and within five minutes, everyone was ready to perform. The low voices of the men started: "Oompah-pah. Oompah-pah." Then the high pitches of the women joined in with their part: "Oom tweedle-dee. Oom tweedle-dee." Next, the twins' group merged into the song with their line: "Oom sss-sss. Oom sss-sss." And lastly, the tykes held their noses like they were jumping into the swimming hole and sang the syllable "nah" to the tune of "Did You Ever See a Lassie?" Thus, the youngest children sang a nasally melody: "Nah nah naaah nah nah nah naaah nah/ nah naaah nah/ nah naaah nah/ nah nah naaah nah nah nah naaah nah/ nah naaah nah/ nah naaah." As the song ended, the boys hissed an extra-long sssss, and the young'uns lowered their voices and stretched naaaaah as far as they could to indicate the machine's running out of steam. Then they fell to the floor in laughter, while some of the other participants bent over and patted their thighs or clapped their hands. But that rendition was only the beginning. In the next version, the macho men were assigned the sissy tweedle-dee part; the women were the hissers; the school children took the melody; and the tykes oompah-pahed. They switched parts twice again so that all the groups had a chance to try each voice, and each version created more laughter than the previous one.

With that activity completed and since the mariachis had still not arrived, those folks present were treated to entertainment à la Miss Becky. Cody knew from the supper at the Camp Bell Ranch that Miss Becky disliked "entertainin'," but he was unsure what that activity entailed.

Patch called for any young piano players who might be present. Elizabeth Hill was the most accomplished player in town. She accompanied the church choir, and she provided lessons to young'uns through old-timers to supplement her income, but mainly for the pleasure it brought her. She glanced around and pointed with an open palm to María Contreras. Patch motioned for her to take the piano seat and started clapping to encourage her. Then others joined in enthusiastically. María looked scared and unhappy, but she skulked up and took the seat. "I've just started learning. I can't play nada from memory. Let Miss Hill entertain you."

"Nae, nae, darlin'. You'll be perfect to start us off. What's your name?" He introduced her to the others, and then he directed her to play any eight notes of her choosing.

María set her hands on the keys and slowly played the C major scale with her right hand.

"That's grand! Now you, birthday girl."

Becky leaned over the girl and played the same notes in the same rhythm.

"Anybody could do that." It was María's brother, Gordo, speaking what everyone was thinking.

"Play again. Sixteen notes this time, and not a scale."

This time, María pecked at notes from all over the keyboard, from the deep basses to the tinkly trebles and everywhere in between. She randomly chose black keys and white keys and held some tones longer than others. The crowd counted aloud each time she touched a key, and when she had played sixteen, she stopped. Becky replaced her on the stool and perfectly duplicated her performance, note for note, holding each of the keys down for the same duration that María had.

The guests now understood the game. María was ready to go again, but an older child beat her to the stool and sat down. A woman's voice called out for him to play his recital song. "Do I hafta, Ma?" Apparently, he had wanted to play random notes. His mother, however, was proud of his learning and insisted he show off his memorized piece. It was an easy piece, and from her quick response, it was clear that Becky had no difficulty duplicating it.

From this point forward, Becky would close her eyes and listen as a song was played and then ask the person to point out the key where he or she had begun. A slight sixteen-year-old girl was nervous and made several mistakes, and Becky's rendition included them. The audience laughed the first time she duplicated a mistake, but some folks began to think Becky was purposely embarrassing the girl, and they were aggrieved by her insensitivity. To Elizabeth, and perhaps others who were musically inclined, it became obvious that Becky did not know how to play the piano. She was simply replicating what she heard.

The next player, a pretty girl of about Becky's age with braided hair, played a complicated song with chords and key changes. Like the girl before her, she too, struck some clinkers, but the song was long enough that they didn't spoil the overall effect. Not wanting the mood of the party to erode, Patch stepped in and announced that the classical piece was too difficult for Becky—she had reached her limit. The guests applauded loudly for the entertainment, and that would have been the end of it, except that Miss Reba Martin spoke up. "I can play it. Show me the note the song begins on."

Cody cut Becky out of the herd of spectators and away from the piano as Miss Reba took center stage. "That was fine, Miss Becky, real fine. How many notes can ya memorize?" But Becky appeared not to hear him. She was squinting at her godmother with head atilt. Then Cody saw her eyes pop open. "What is it?"

"Did ya hear? Did ya hear it, Master Cody? She made a mistake. She didn't play the song the same way that gal did, but nobody seemta notice. Nobody booed 'er."

Cody continued to listen, and he knew enough about music to realize that Miss Reba was correcting the sour notes from the first rendition and improving on the dynamics and rhythm. She, in fact, played the piece perfectly. Cody tried to explain that Miss Reba was being mannerly and that the audience was appreciative. For one, they didn't have to suffer through the errors a second time, but more important, she was helping the girl save face. Becky was silent for a long moment, clearly trying to puzzle out Cody's meaning.

"Ya mean that gal made mistakes, an' Miss Reba is fixin' 'em?"

"Yes'm, Miss Becky. That's precisely it."

"I can't do that."

"I reckon there's not another soul in the room that could."

"She was a horse whisperer. I'm a horse whisperer. If'n she can do that, I should be able to do that." She looked him directly in the eyes. "Don't ya reckon?"

Cody thought to say, "Maybe you'll learn," but he felt like a bit was holding his tongue down, and before he could slip the words out, she was speaking again.

"An' another thing, she musta known the letters weren't written by me, 'cause she must be a deficient speller, too. Don't ya reckon?"

Who knew what differences there were in the abilities of horse whisperers? Certainly not Cody. "Uh, Miss Becky, let's go outside for a while."

"Shore. It's too busy in here anyways, an' I wanna tell ya somethin'." She lifted her heavy skirts and turned toward the door, but she was accosted by a group of latecomers who wanted to meet her and chew over yesterday's bronc riding feat.

Cody made a hasty retreat to mingle among the guests, saying he would see her later. He found Gordo and other schoolmates, plus he spoke briefly to Miss Hill's parents, to Doc and Mrs. Ritter, and to other townspeople who sought him out.

Because the mariachis had still not shown up, after Miss Reba finished playing the piece, Miss Elizabeth graciously continued the entertainment by playing sing-along songs. The food had arrived, and Patch and the twins helped Miss Louisa and the café crew set up tables to place it on. Miss Reba supervised the arrangement of the food and stood by to help serve if she was needed.

"There's no sense in letting good food get cold." Patch called for the bowing of heads for the blessing. After the prayer, he announced what most everyone was waiting to hear: "Come and get it!"

According to family tradition, Thomas and Timothy, both being the next older sibling, had the standing duty of caring for Annabelle, just as John had been tasked as a youngster with watching over Becky. Annabelle was a sweet child: quiet, eager to please, and quick to smile, unlike Becky had been. The McCoy children lined up for the foodstuffs with other hungry folks.

Most of the guests took their meals outdoors to eat. Some of them stood balancing their plates, while others chose to sit on the pews that lined the street. Still others chose to sit on the ground and use the pew seats as tables. The outdoor partiers could hear the singing and enjoy the weather. Big, dark, fluffy clouds typical of late summers were rising above the horizon. A breeze had kicked up, and the temperature had cooled slightly, providing a pleasant respite from the hot afternoon.

Mason hightailed it to the buffet, but Cody was still full of churros. He worked his way back over to Miss Becky, waving at Hank Starley as they passed. Cody wanted to tell Miss Becky that she looked beautiful, but he had learned his lesson. Instead, he greeted her with a tip of his hat and tried humor.

"Howdy, purty miss. Do ya happen to need rescuin'?"

"Truly." She nodded several times. "I'd rather be tied to a blazin' saguaro with tears runnin' down my face than standin' here smilin', smilin', smilin'."

"C'mon then, let's go pay a call on some horses."

Miss Becky marched through the crowd and out the door with Cody at her heels, but they discovered that there were no horses hitched nearby. Unbeknownst to them, John had asked Sheriff Claiborne to require folks to keep the party area clear of horses. His rationale had been that some horses might be skittish from the music, but the real reason behind his request had been to keep the horses far enough away from Becky that she could enjoy her party without being distracted by them. He hadn't considered that she'd much rather be around horses than at any party—or maybe he had.

Cody and Becky found an empty bench across the street in front of the feedstore and sat down. From there, they watched the activity around them: Many folks were eating. Timothy and Thomas were soon to be among them. They were helping Annabelle get settled in the center of a pew. They set her plate in her lap and her tin cup of milk to her left on the pew's seat, and then each of them sat on opposite sides of her with their food and drink similarly positioned.

Cody prompted Miss Becky to speak. "What was it ya wanted to tell me?"

She stared straight ahead when she answered. "Only that I *remember*."

"What do ya remember, Miss Becky?"

"Ya won't believe me."

He took her hand and clasped it between both of his. "Sure, I will. Just tell me."

"Fine. I remember when my name was *Sarah*."

"What! Ya said ya were just a baby!"

Becky sighed deeply. "I knew it." She pulled her hand out of its cocoon. "Ya don't believe me."

She began rocking her body, banging her shoulders against the bench's back, and then her lips began to move. She was whispering something into the air, and he wondered if she was speaking to him or herself or even to God, because horses seemed too far away to hear her. Becky's rocking soon slowed, and then she babbled what he thought was, "I spooky." Now totally calm, she turned to look at him. "My social graces tutor says I must look folks in the eyes an' smile."

"I like it when ya smile." Cody smiled at her as he said it, and either his words or action must have encouraged her because she continued with her remembrances.

"Like I told ya, I have two baptism certificates. When I was birthed, my mama named me Sarah, but the second one shows Rebecca, an' Miss Reba as godmother. When I think back real hard,

I can remember bein' called Sarah. Anyways, as I grew, I was confused 'cause I could hear voices from far off, an' I didn't know where they were comin' from. I listened though, an' I learnt the language, horse language. Mama never wanted me near horses 'cause she thought little girls should stay in the house, so's I wasn't 'lowed out much, an' that made me angry an' sad. I cried a lot. I still cry a lot, 'specially when I'm away from horses." As she said this last, a tear trickled down her face. Cody pulled the starched handkerchief from his jacket—he was dressed in his Sunday best— and placed it in her lap. She took no notice, just continued talking: "One day when I was three or four, the voices were 'specially anxious, an' I tried to go to 'em. They were callin' like cows missin' their calves, on an' on, an' I ran from John, who was s'posed to be mindin' me, an' I followed the voices into the barn. It was then I fin'lly knew where the voices were from. An' I whispered softly in horse language at first, an' then louder, 'cause I couldn't hear myself over the crack o' Papa's whip, an' I yelled a word there's no translation fer. It sounds like 'I spooky.' It sorta means 'end o' the trail.' I meant I had found what had been callin' to me. Nobody knows 'ceptin' you."

Cody couldn't contain his excitement. "That's remarkable, Miss Becky! I didn't realize there was an actual horse language!"

"Sometimes I think I made it up. Sometimes I think the voices mean I'm certifiable mad. That's why I keep it to myself."

"And Miss Reba?"

"Well, John told me that Papa wrote to family overseas an' told 'em I was a horse whisperer. Miss Reba was the last known horse whisperer in our family, so's Mama made 'er my godmother an' she an' Papa changed my name from Sarah to Rebecca in 'er honor. I never gave this next any mind afore now, but now I've worked out that all those itchy clothes might o' been a signboard o' things to come, like 'ya better get use' to girly clothes 'cause yer gonna lose yer 'bilities an' hafta dress like a lady.' An' like I told ya afore, John says that Miss Reba lost 'er 'bilities with horses when she lost her girlhood. She came here to watch me an' test me an' see if'n I'm losin' my 'bilities the same way she did."

Cody couldn't imagine Miss Becky without horse whispering abilities. He felt sorry for her having to live with the knowledge that everything she'd known since she was a baby could dry up like a watering hole in the hot summer sun. But maybe she would be better off if she did lose her ability to talk to horses. Even if she could no longer talk with them, surely, she had enough knowledge and experience to always be a welcomed presence when horses needed doctoring or such. Maybe she would eat and sleep more. Maybe Miss Becky would even prefer an ordinary life like Miss Reba's. Her godmother looked and acted usual enough, though that piano trick was problematical. Cody could see why Mr. McCoy insisted that Becky play every day—she needed a break from the pressures placed upon her because of her abilities. Cody thought he understood why Mr. McCoy was throwing a big party for Becky. She had so much extra to deal with besides the typical troubles of growing up. Perhaps she needed to be a girl, a regular girl, before she became an adult.

"Uh, Miss Becky, do ya suppose Miss Reba could've just come to help ya through the transition, if there is one? If she shares her experiences with ya, maybe life will be easier for ya."

"I like my life the way it is. I wanna talk to horses forever." And now the dam broke, and a flood of tears streamed down her cheeks. She snatched the handkerchief from her lap and pressed it to her face.

Cody knew of only one way to make her feel better. She needed to be around horses. A barricade made from wagons had been set across the street to block it off so that only foot traffic could pass while folks danced. Two additional wagons would block the road farther down, leaving a large dancing area. One of those wagons was in position, and the final wagon was being driven down the street toward it, coming their way. The horses were mismatched in color, the one on the driver's right being black and the other white. As the driver reached the section of street near the feedstore, the horses began to whinny and fuss, so Cody called for the driver to hold up a minute. He encouraged Miss Becky to get up and greet the horses. Her tears dried instantly, and she ran into the street, holding her skirt way too high to be socially acceptable, but freeing her from tripping over the bulk. She whispered away to the driver's amusement, and when she was finished, she tickled the horses' ears, until finally, the driver said he needed to continue on his way.

"Strong horses, 'specially the dark one. They're nice, but they're nervous. The reg'lar pair are sick with the influenza. These are fill-ins. They use' to work 'round mines. The dark one's fearful o' loud booms."

Cody couldn't conceive how she had come to know all that information, but he believed her.

By now, many children had finished their meals and were running off their newfound energy by playing games in the street. Timothy McCoy wanted to join in, and Thomas consented to watch Annabelle so that he could. Their sister was almost done eating, and after she was, he could deliver her back to Papa or Miss Reba to mind, and he could join in the fun with his brother.

Annabelle reached for the cup of milk on her right, but Thomas pushed her hand away. "That's mine, Annabelle. Yers is over there." He pointed to her left.

She tried reaching across her body for her cup, but the immensity of the finery she was wearing and the plate on her lap made the task impossible. When she scooted forward for a better position, her leg knocked the handle. The cup tipped and tumbled, spilling milk all over the pew and dripping it onto the ground.

Thomas immediately pulled the napkin from under her chin and sopped up the worst of the mess, but that didn't solve the heartbroken look on Annabelle's face.

Thomas was the nicer twin. He didn't slap her hand or scold her, nor did he want her to cry. "It's fine, Annabelle. I'll fetch somethin' wet to wipe the spill, an' I'll bring ya some more milk."

The little girl's eyes brightened, and she smiled broadly at her champion.

"Just wait here fer me. I'll be back directly. Don't move!"

He positioned her squarely on the pew and repeated his instructions before leaving her.

*   *   *

The wind was picking up. It created a dust devil that swirled down the road beyond the barricade of wagons, causing some children to stop and point. Dark, heavy clouds hid the sun. Thunder rumbled in the distance, and banks of lightning flashed low in the sky. A curtain of virga hung to the east. A few heavy drops of rain fell and splatted on the sunbaked street, but the young'uns didn't mind. They continued to play happily, grateful for the coolness and the wetness. Some wished for more of a sprinkle than this spotty, thick spit from the skies, and their wishes were soon granted.

The final wagon, the one whose horses Miss Becky had greeted, was almost to its designated position in the barricade when another wagon sped through the remaining small opening to the street from the opposite direction. The clear sounds of spirited music and the shout of "olé" alerted the townsfolks that the mariachis had arrived! The children cheered and started to run toward the music, but just then a lightning bolt lit up the sky, followed by a big boom of thunder, and a cloud burst open, pouring rain down to the town below. The children screamed and ran for shelter in the church, stone deaf to the crunch of smashing wood and the sounds of animal and human moans and groans when the mariachis' wagon clipped a wagon in the barricade and spun into the one with the mismatched horses. That wagon driver had seen the danger and tried to move out of the way, urging his team to "haw, haw," or turn left, but his horses didn't obey, and then he saw why. Little Annabelle McCoy was standing in their path, arms outstretched as though she wanted a hug, and although the horses could easily have run her over, the white one stood still as stone, and the dark one turned right, pulling his teammate's dead weight, breaking the harness with his effort. The mariachis' wagon hit the empty wagon with such force as to overturn it, sending all four horses to the ground, and sending all the men flying, followed by a shower of violins, trumpets, Mexican vihuelas, and other instruments.

Sheriff Tom Claiborne and John McCoy were riding immediately behind the accident, having stopped to help the second wagonload of mariachis, which had become stuck in a fast-running wash from a flash flood following a downpour. Once they had gotten that group moving again, John and Tom had rushed to rejoin the party. Now Tom directed John to start assessing the injuries, while he scooped up Annabelle and galloped to the church for help.

Cody and Miss Becky were the next to arrive on the scene because they had sought shelter from the rain under the eaves of the feedstore. While John was evaluating the wounded men, Cody began unhitching horses, and Miss Becky started appraising their injuries. She knelt in the mud, concentrating on each horse and its needs.

Before long, Doc Ritter and his wife Margaret arrived and began working on the injured men. Doc Ritter recruited townsfolk to fetch his medical bag, put pressure here, and find something to use as a splint, as Doc Prescott, the veterinarian, was doing his own ordering. Six men and four horses needed doctoring. Miss Becky, Patch, and John McCoy each took charge of a horse, with Doc Prescott working on the fourth. Miss Reba had offered to help, but Patch put her in charge of minding his three youngest children. Mason and Tom helped with the injured men. Other men righted the wagon or stood by to do whatever they were asked. Cody made himself useful by collecting the remnants of the instruments. All the while, the rain kept falling.

*   *   *

John held his pistol cocked and ready to fire. "Spooky, move over. We can't save him. *You* can't save him. Let me put him down. Beck, *move!*

But Becky did not move, nor did she answer him. Her right fist held tight, deep in the dark horse's neck, connecting an artery and keeping at least some blood flowing. Her left hand gently held his left ear flat back against his head. The horse lay calm, and she placed her wet cheek to his and whispered and lightly blew her breath around his face and neck.

"Cripes. *Rebecca Ann McCoy, let him go!*" John holstered his weapon and moved toward Becky with arms outstretched, as though he planned to lift her up from beneath her arm pits.

A mix of teardrops and raindrops were streaming down her face, and she was whispering something to the horse, but she stopped for a moment, and in a barely audible tone she took a stand. "Touch me, John, an' so help me, I'll scream. Every horse in town will go wild. Ya want that?"

By now, the mangled men were on their way to Doc Ritter's office, and there were fewer tasks for the townsfolk to perform. A crowd of onlookers had gathered around Miss Becky. They protected themselves from the rain as best they could, and one kind cowboy, Isaac Williams, produced an umbrella, which he used to shield the girl, letting himself get sopped.

John backed off. "I need some help here. Mr. Campbell, this horse is suffering. See if you can talk some sense into my sister, so he can be put down."

Mason was applying pressure to a deep cut on another horse's foreleg, waiting for Doc Prescott to come stitch up the injury. It was the horse that John had initially worked on, but John had left the horse in good hands to check if he could be of greater assistance to his sister or his father. Mason looked up and evaluated the situation. "John, take this one back, and I'll, uh, see what I can do over there with Miss Becky." When John had taken his place, Mason stepped gingerly around the wounded animal's hind legs and was halfway to Becky when he felt a tap on his shoulder.

"I've got this."

Mason felt relieved when Patch McCoy passed him and approached his daughter and the dying horse. Meanwhile, his own son had wormed his way through the crowd and was standing beside him.

"What's happenin', Pa?"

They watched as Patch greeted Becky with a slight squeeze to her shoulders from behind. When she turned her face toward him, he wiped her tears away with his thumbs, and they heard them converse, though they could not discern the words.

"Becky, darlin', let me see the wound."

"No need. We can't fix 'im, Papa."

"Then tell me what you need me to do, so's we can give him peace."

"I'm givin' 'im peace, Papa. Believe me." She tossed her head sideways at a rag that lay on the horse's rump, and he handed it to her. Then she kissed the horse on his forehead. Afterward, with her left hand, she covered the deep wound with the rag as she released her fist and allowed the blood to flow. In a moment, her papa placed a second rag over the horse's head.

Becky stood and wiped her bloody hand on her ruined party dress. "Fer all ya folks standin' 'round, I jus' wanna say, this here horse was the one that saved my sister's life. He saw 'er an' veered away, causin' the crash, an' he was hurt the worse, an' I jus' want ya to know that he was a selfless horse with a lotta courage, but he was also a fearful horse—afraid o' gunshots, an' I jus' couldn't let 'im die from what he was most afraid o', so's I jus' whispered to 'im 'til he was calm, an' he didn't suffer, an' I'm real sorry I couldn't save 'im, an' now I'm goin' fer a walk." She rose, declined the umbrella, and began moving slowly down the middle of the street.

Cody followed her for several steps, until Patch ordered him to leave her be. Cody looked to his pa. It wasn't like Mason to interfere with someone else's parenting, but he couldn't help himself. He nudged Cody forward. "Go after her, son."

"What should I say?"

"You'll know."

Cody advanced on Miss Becky, and when he was even with her, he fell into step on her left. They walked, facing forward, all the way to the end of town, where its granite namesake stood towering above them, leaning, like a dead tree ready to fall to the ground. Cody thought she was so addled that Becky might walk straight into the rock, but she twirled before colliding, her soaked skirt catching a gust of wind and flaring momentarily, as if she were dancing, before flattening again as she leaned against the rock with her hands behind her, supporting her hips. Cody mirrored her turn and leaned against the rock beside her. By and by, Becky slid to the muddy ground, and again Cody followed suit. They both sat, facing the town, staring into the night. Finally, he spoke, choosing not to look her in the eyes, in case they were too sad to bear.

"Ya okay?"

"I reckon so. It's jus' not the way I wanted the evenin' to end."

He assumed she meant about the whole ruinous affair: the mariachis' tardiness, the accident, the injured horses, the horse she couldn't save, and even the rain, but he didn't want to mention those things. "Me neither. I was gonna ask if I could kiss ya."

She responded immediately. "I would o' said no."

Now he rotated his head to face her, his forehead scrunched questioningly. "I thought ya liked me as much as I like you."

"Mayhap. I jus' figure if'n ya hafta ask, yer not ready."

"That so?" He turned her face toward him, leaned in, and gently pressed his lips to hers. "Happy birthday, Miss Becky."

"Best gift I ever received." And her smile convinced him she meant it. But it faded quickly, and Becky now sat looking at and playing with her friendship bracelet, which Cody hadn't noticed she was wearing because it had been hidden beneath her sleeve, up past her elbow.

Cody was heartened to see it, happy that she had worn it with all her finery. "Sorry about yer party dress."

"Truth be told, I won't be missin' it. Sorry 'bout yer birthday hat."

He removed it from his head, shook some water off, and molded the crown into shape. "Truth be told, it needed some breakin' in."

The rain had slowed to a sprinkle and stopped just as quickly as it had started. The cloudburst was over for the evening.

After more time had passed, Cody spoke again. "Think we ought to go back?"

"Mayhap. Think they've cleared the road?"

"Could be. Think yer papa will come lookin' for ya?"

"Could be. Think yer pa will?"

They had their answers shortly because when they looked up, they could see their fathers riding side by side toward them. The horses whinnied their greetings to Becky, and she whinnied back in a perfect echo. Patch laughed at Mason's astonished look. "That's my girl!"

When the men dismounted by the leaning rock, Mason strode over to Cody and asked if everything was all right. He was relieved to hear Cody answer "fine." Simultaneously, Patch leaned over and whispered to his daughter. "Becky, darlin', you did a rare and beautiful thing for that horse tonight. I'm proud of you." She didn't say anything, so he continued. "Are you finished with your grieving?"

"Yes, Papa."

"Do you want a hug?"

"No, Papa."

Respecting her answer, Patch kissed her gently on the forehead instead.

"I guess we ought to be goin', Pa."

Before Mason could answer, Mr. McCoy broke in. "Hold up, if you please, there's something I want you all to hear." Patch sat down cross-legged in front of Becky. His knee made a popping sound on the way down. "I'm getting a might old for this, darlin'." Cody admired the man for sitting at Becky's level, but Mason was aghast that Patch would unnecessarily dirty up his clothes. He chose to remain standing. Once Patch was settled, he addressed his daughter, but his words were meant for all present. "Becky, darlin', Mr. Campbell has told me about some notions that need to be put to rights. I've already set John straight. First most, your name has always been Rebecca Ann McCoy from the day you were born. You were never named Sarah."

Becky recollected her manners and looked her father in the eye. "Truly? But I remember bein' called Sarah."

"Nae, darlin', you remember your twin sister, Sarah." He gave Becky a moment to chew on his words before he continued. "The two of you were as tight as though you were tied together in the womb. Look-alike red-haired girls, excepting she had a stork bite birthmark. You were smart as a genius from an early age, babbling away to each other in some made-up language that no one else understood, but it was clear that you both understood it. She called you Sassy, and you called her Spooky."

"Sassy." Becky tried out the name again. "*Sassy.* I don't know that name, Papa."

"She might've meant 'Sissy.' Anyways, you were a wee girl when an angel flew Sarah to heaven. One morning, she just wouldn't awaken. Your mama and I missed her terribly, but you missed her worse. You stopped babbling. You stopped playing. I've never seen such grief in a child, but with time you forgot. Then one day, you wandered into the barn and started babbling again, beginning with 'Hi, Spooky.' I about tumbled over from the shock of hearing her pet name. I thought you were make-believing your sister was there, but it was the horses that understood you. It was like you were talking to your sister's spirit through the horses. It gave you comfort. It gave Mama and me comfort. So's we cultivated it. And you became a horse whisperer. We allowed you to be called Spooky because it kept Sarah close to our hearts. We didn't know it troubled you, but I'll put an end to it today.

"Second most, John was correct about Miss Reba. She was a horse whisperer as a child, and she did lose many of her abilities when she grew up. She traveled here to help Mama with the bairns and with anything else that needs doing. I hope you can become close companions. You'll be needing company with John at school.

"I don't know what your future holds, but you are my daughter and a special person, and those things will never change. Becky, above all, I want you to be happy. I want you to play and smile and laugh. I sent you on this trip so's you could be a little girl again, full of curiosity, full of the spirit of adventure, and I'm content to know that you've made good use of the time and have also made a good friend, Cody here."

Becky didn't say a word about her papa's revelations. She simply arose and announced that she was ready to leave. She rubbed the horses on their faces as Mason and Patch mounted up. The men were ready for their children to climb up behind them, but Cody stopped Miss Becky as she was about to place her muddy blue velvet shoe in the stirrup. "Miss Becky, you are the most amazin' person I've ever met, and I've had a hay load of fun with ya, and I've learned more than any school-learnin' could teach, and I believe in ya, and I sure wish ya weren't leavin' tomorrow. Do ya think I'll ever see ya again?"

"Shorely, Master Cody. I shorely do."

Cody smiled broadly with the hope of it, while Patch offered Becky his hand. "Becky, darlin', owing to the slippery ground and that umbrella skirt, I'd be obliged if you would take my hand."

She did, and as she swung her leg over the horse and her mouth passed her father's ear, she whispered, "Papa, ya know 'bout Annabelle, right?"

Author Bio

Sherrie J. Lyons grew up in Prescott, Arizona, and is a graduate of Arizona State University. She enjoys wordplay, the outdoors, and spending time with family and friends, especially her husband of more than forty years.

Sherrie has written works in a variety of genres. Her first novel, *Luke's Legacy*, was a sci-fi/fantasy story written in the *Star Wars* universe. It was published on a fan-fiction website. She next penned *The Macava,* another sci-fi/fantasy novel. It won third place in an Arizona Authors Association writing contest but has not been published. She then switched gears and wrote a play, *The Tragedy at Cambria*. It was originally published in an online journal, the *Oregon Literary Review,* and it is now available in print. After a long hiatus, Sherrie wrote *The Adventures of Miss Becky McCoy*, her first Western. In addition, Sherrie has played with poetry. Some of her poems have been printed in journals and books. For more information, visit Sherrie's website at **sherriejlyons.com.**